SKOOK

SKOOK

A Thriller by
William R. Burkett, Jr.

ABSOLUTELY AMA/ING eBOOKS

ABSOLUTELY AMAZING eBOOKS

Published by Whiz Bang LLC, 926 Truman Avenue, Key West, Florida 33040, USA.

For information contact:
Publisher@AbsolutelyAmazingEbooks.com
ISBN-13: 978-1496110169
ISBN-10: 1496110161

A dedication of sorts

Richard Brautigan called the Pacific Northwest a haunted land where nature dances a minuet with people. Bill Simp said there is more wild land between towns on the east and west side of the Cascade Range than between towns in Texas. There really is a Carbon River Gorge on the western edge of that high lonesome, where coal was king in the vanished mining towns, and there remains a king's ransom in coal reserves beneath the rugged terrain.

This story is dedicated to the miners of all nations who labored in the dangerous mines to provide fuel to coal-burning ships and locomotives before oil. Many were buried in the small cemeteries, prime of life cut short by mining accidents, and others lived to a ripe old age to spin tall tales about the Gorge to a credulous outsider. And to the Goulash Mafia, who taught my son the ways of the mountains.

You won't find my Carbon Gorge on any map or GPS, or any of the residents with whom I populated the place. My oldest granddaughter, daughter of my mountain-man son, once asked me, about another tall tale of mine, "Granpa, how much of that is *true?*" To which I replied, "How much of it do you *want* to be true?" She was very young to have perfected that feminine eye-roll of exasperation: "Oh, *Granpa!*"

I expect a replay of that conversation when she reads this.

SKOOK

Chapter One

The old-time farmers up on the Enumclaw Plateau used to say you should never cut hay before the Fourth of July, because the summer pause in Western Washington's constant rains was never a good bet before then. Before you could get the hay bundled and under cover, the rains would come back and ruin it. Sometimes even July wasn't safe.

This particular year, though, I sold the hay off our five acres to some neighbors who raised Morgan horses, and they had it cut and field-dried and bundled and gone within a week of the Fourth. The sunshine held, and because of the acidity of the poorly drained soil, I now could look out over five acres of almost solid dandelions. Beyond the yellow blanket was a wide unused pasture that for some reason didn't grow dandelions like my land did.

By political subdivision, we lived in a small town. By geography, the town sprawled wide and nearly as empty as a rural county, aside from a short main street a mile from my place: old brick buildings that looked like a movie set for a Thirties story about Tommy-gun wielding bank robbers. The town border encompassed the riverside cemetery behind the brick downtown and ran upstream along the White River. The riverbed was about a quarter-mile from my driveway. The city line carried upstream another mile or so before it broke at right angles from riparian habitat to enclose the last town street, past the deer-proof fences at the agricultural extension farm and the grim brick barracks of the old state school for retarded children.

The school resembled a cross between a penitentiary and a Second World War prisoner-of-war camp. At one time the number of inmates had doubled the town's population. My wife, who had volunteered at the school as a teenager, said new wards of the state were being housed closer to civilization these days. There had been talk for years of closing the place. There were a lot of local rumors about that school, some of them ugly, none of which my wife was willing to hear, but living only two or three pastures from its back fence gave me the creeps.

Past the school's front entry, the city-line took another right angle to parallel the first Douglas-fir-clad foothills back to close the loop at the state highway. En route it crossed defunct railroad tracks that led to vanished coal mining towns up Carbon River Gorge.

Every time I turned off the state highway and bumped across those rusting rails, the pulse of the world seemed to slow, as if the last fifty years of history stopped on the highway side. I once drove right past Main Street after coming onto the plateau from Tacoma. Much to the merriment of bucolic in-laws to whom the town seemed perfectly ordinary, I had to find a phone booth in Enumclaw to call home for directions. I grumbled the town had Brigadoon-like tendencies to vanish; my superstitious Southern soul could feel the strangeness because I was raised by a grandmother with the second sight. My wife reminded me that same grandmother called me the Absent-Minded Professor.

The whole town plot sat squarely on a massive prehistoric mudflow from an eruption of Mount Rainier. They called it the Osceola Mudflow for reasons unknown, which played mental tricks on me since the only Osceola I knew about was a Seminole chief in Florida. The data said over five thousand years ago a 460-foot-deep lahar surged down White River Canyon and covered 130 square miles before it stopped.

Lahar from the word for god in Sumerian; it had become an Indonesian word, and then the world's, for the terrifyingly unstoppable and therefore godlike pyroclastic regurgitations of a volcano. I was living on top of one of the most famous lahars on the planet. As a boy, going to a Georgia drive-in movie with my aunt and uncle to see a movie called *Stromboli* that featured death and destruction by volcano, I was smart enough to ask what kind of fool choses to live in the shadow of a volcano.

Now I was one of those fools. Sometimes, looking from my office window across the forested foothills to the white loom of Mount Rainier gave me a hollow feeling in the pit of my stomach. This particular July, I had been living for four years in what seemed at first blush a kind of earthly paradise after other places I had been. The Tacoma-born author, Richard Brautigan, called the Pacific Northwest a haunted land, where nature dances a minuet with people. That always seemed a winsome description until I came to live in the town behind the tracks on the famous lahar, with the mountain that was god looming behind the forested hills.

That was before the haunted land invited me to my own dance.

Beyond the town line, forested foothills rose in serried rows toward the volcano, an illusory barrier to its potential violence. The White River took its name from silt coming off Rainier's melting glaciers, following the same path of least resistance the enormous ancient mudflow had followed. Between my office window and the foothills were small scattered independent berry farms, a couple of small horse-breeding concerns, and newer homes with a few acres like mine. In and around those properties were large tracts of unused pasturage from failed dairy farms, dense islands of mature Doug fir, overgrown apple orchards from vanished homesteads, and huge surreal wild-blackberry tangles. The rich humus that supported and nourished it all had been laid down over fifty centuries. But you didn't have to dig more than a couple of feet to be into the cement-like gray of volcanic effluvia.

Elk raided my pear orchard in the autumn. Coyotes team-hunted field mice on the frozen pasture in winter, with an occasional side dish of the neighbor's bantam chickens. Crisscrossing deer trails were cut permanently into my field. It wasn't unusual to find black-bear scat around the blackberry tangles that swallowed the back fence. It was as close to living in the country, and still be connected to central water, gas and sewage, as you could get.

I thought my dandelions were just as pretty as the daffodils that occasioned parades and princesses in sea-level valleys eight hundred feet below our haunted plateau. My closest neighbors didn't share my view. They didn't like it when the dandelions sent snowdrifts of seed spores to pollute their carefully tended lawns. My wife fretted about their disapproval.

This particular July I had other things to worry about.

With the dandelions in full bloom, I was seated at my old Olympia office-model typewriter, trying to write my way into an urban tale about the mean streets of Los Angeles. The story involved blackmail, corruption, and payoffs to city councilmen in the vein of Raymond Chandler, with a dash of Joseph Wambaugh for leavening. Before I moved to the Northwest, all that had seemed urgent and edgy and real. It seemed like children's games to me now. The writing was heavy going.

In the angled peak of my roof, near the living-room chimney, the brass elephant bell that I had placed so carefully chimed once.

I caught my breath to listen.

My Labrador retriever, Harry, who had been sprawled asleep beside my desk, raised his head and cocked his ears.

The bell chimed again.

I purchased the elephant bell as whimsy from a candle shop in Morro Bay, California in what now seemed another, safer lifetime. I was charmed by the tale the shopkeeper told: that old-time Indian mahouts bedecked their tiger-hunting elephants with the bells. Tigers learned to associate the bells with big-bore double rifles and danger, and avoid the sound. Unarmed native villagers, traveling in tiger territory, began to carry and shake the bells to try to ward off man-eaters. May this house be safe from tigers was their mantra when they hung the bells to catch prevailing breezes at home in their fragile shacks.

It was just a charming story at the time.

When I found it necessary to calibrate angles of

prevailing plateau winds to place my whimsical bell just so, the charm had long since worn thin. The villagers' mantra had become my personal prayer.

The elephant bell began a steady, melodious tolling that told me a breeze was freshening off the White River bottoms behind me, blowing toward the forested slopes beyond town. I had placed the bell to catch just such a breeze, protected and mute when the wind came off the mountains. Harry got up and went to the screen door. He whined, scratching at the screen, staring hard toward the rear of our property. Then he growled; a deep rumbling sound full of suppressed fury.

I called to my wife, who was in the kitchen at the front of the house. "Where's the boy?"

"Having a nap in his room," she called back. "Why?"

I called Harry away from the screen door and heeled him down the hall to the boy's room as my uneasiness mounted. The boy *wasn't* in his bedroom, which looked out over the pasture. The screen from his window had been pushed outside onto the flowerbed. I had one of those vivid, sickening flashbacks with which combat veterans are all too familiar.

Before I could react, Harry jumped onto the bed—he never got on a bed without permission—and launched through the window. I didn't wait to see him go. I turned and ran for my office.

It was happening again.

I yanked open the deep desk drawer, pulled out my big pistol, and pushed through the screen door. The elephant bell continued its tolling. By the time I got across the deck, Harry was ramming through dandelions a hundred yards away, scattering seed stuff as he went. I wrapped my hand around the cylinder of the big revolver in a reverse grip, barrel down, to hide its profile as much as possible from nosy neighbors, and started jogging.

Irrelevant thoughts bounced through my mind, my breath already coming hard. That I was very glad now I had gone ahead and spent an enormous amount of money for the big revolver. Glad I had hands big enough to engulf the cylinder, so only the stainless barrel showed below my fist, the less noticeable wooden grips above. That no, those recent Dirty Harry movies were not correct, the .44 Magnum was not the most powerful handgun in the world. Dick Casull's Wyoming-built .454, heavy in my hand, made Elmer Keith's favorite toy seem anemic.

The uneven pasture made hard going. I couldn't see Harry anymore; he was in among the head-high blackberry tangles that lined the rear fence. I couldn't afford to slow down. I couldn't afford to fall. As I approached the edge of my property, a town dog off across the flood plain opened up; outraged barks of protest. Whatever had come down from the foothills, following scent borne on the river-bottom breeze, had finally moved upwind of outlying homes. A second dog answered; the deep bay of a hound. I knew a couple of guys over there kept packs of bear hounds, Plotts and Redbones, brave as lions. The hound sounded like he wanted to get into it right now with something he hated.

Finally I approached the fence, sweat pouring in my eyes.

The boy was there, sturdy four-year-old legs trying to propel him beneath the lowest strand of rusted wire. Harry

7

had him by the seat of his corduroy britches and wouldn't let go, though the boy's feet pummeled him. Harry rolled his eyes back at me like it's about time you got here. I went to my knees, grabbed the overalls, and bodily hauled the boy back through the fence. He let out a blood-curdling yell of protest.

Something screeched in answer from an old apple orchard across the neighbor's field.

The town dogs shut up as if a switch had been thrown.

Harry, mildest of dogs, bowed his neck and let go that terrifying growl again; he remembered that particular screech. I tucked the boy under my left arm, kicking and fussing, and got the .454 reversed into firing position in my right, thumb on the hammer.

"Stay, Harry!" I said sharply.

I could feel him getting ready to go through the fence with an old score to settle. But I couldn't go with him, not this time; and he would be overmatched alone.

"Stay!" I said again. He lay down, reluctance in every line of his body. But his training prevailed.

"Good dog!" I told him. "Good Harry! You caught him before he could go through the fence. Good dog!"

Then all the distant bear hounds opened up at once, ready to go to war. The town dogs got their courage up and joined in. Cutting through their racket came one final fading inhuman screech, retreating beyond the old orchard. It sounded frustrated. I waited there in the blackberries, unwilling to turn my back, unwilling to try to walk backwards toward the house. When Harry finally relaxed and reached up and licked the boy's face, I felt the tension flow out of me. When we got back to the house, my wife was waiting on the deck.

"What were those dogs going on about?" she said. "Coyotes? Or a bear in those apples back there?"

"I don't think so," I said.

She looked at the boy. He had quieted and was now happily riding my shoulders, hands twisted in my hair. "I thought he was in his room," she said.

"He went out the window. He was all the way to the back fence when Harry caught up with him."

She had the Northwesterner's typical blasé attitude. "Boys will do that. Go exploring."

"That's too far to go exploring on his own!"

I was angry at her with no real justification. She had no way to know why I was upset. If she remembered the night it all began, she certainly didn't remember it like I did. Because I never told her everything that happened.

"You're just being paranoid," she said. "Didn't you ever go exploring when you were that age?"

"I lived in a city when I was that age."

"Poor you."

She tightened her lips when she noticed the pistol I had shoved down in my pants behind my hip to carry the boy. "I hope the neighbors didn't see you carrying that cannon around out there."

I had nothing to say to that. I put the boy down on the deck. The front of his overalls was covered with mud and grass stains from trying to crawl through the fence. The elephant bell continued to toll and the wind still carried our scent to the foothills. But the danger was past. For now.

Chapter Two

Moving to the Pacific Northwest seemed like a good idea at the time. My wife was pregnant with our son and I was spending far too much time on airplanes, crisscrossing the country from crisis to crisis for my employer of the moment. Miami, Tampa, Atlanta, St. Louis, Los Angeles, San Francisco—the roll call sounded like a country-western road song.

My employer wanted to transfer me to Washington, D.C., headquarters as my base of operations. That was when the District was vying with the dangerous rust-belt cities for title of murder capital of the nation. It was no place to bring a child into the world. For once we had plenty of mad money laid by, so I turned in my resignation and we packed up and headed west. My mother-in-law had died the previous spring, her house stood vacant, and the family didn't want to sell it outside the family.

I figured with the cocksure arrogance of an East Coast reporter that West Coast newspapers would salivate for a chance to get me on the payroll to show too-laid-back Northwesterners how to kick some official butt. My visits to the Northwest and a cursory look at the way its governments handled things convinced me that breaking killer stories would be like hunting in a game preserve. And I of course shared this sentiment with Seattle and Tacoma editors in interviews.

I reckoned without the perverse provincialism of the

Pacific Northwest. They couldn't conceive of an outsider being able to hit the ground running. Why, I didn't even know how to pronounce Puyallup or Sequim! Didn't matter the number of cities in which I had practiced my craft or the clippings I could show to prove I could drag down the powerful. I was completely flummoxed.

Meanwhile, our son was born in Tacoma General, a healthy happy baby. After a brisk battle with my previous employer's insurance carrier, we got the birth covered. My wife of course had no trouble finding a job after the boy was weaned. Hell, she was a Northwest native! So she drove to Tacoma from what I was beginning to think of as our personal Brigadoon, and worked as a secretary for a company importing inboard-jet motors from New Zealand for salmon and steelhead fishermen who ran their boats up shallow, prop-killing Northwest rivers.

I settled into a period of house-husbandry before I ever heard the term, and got to see the boy take his first steps with his chubby fingers securely anchored in Harry's thick neck fur. He quickly learned to use patient Harry as a mobile walking aid, and covered the whole house that way before he could navigate on his own. I was duly impressed. Paka, Harry's mate, was less patient, but clearly doted on the boy like a littermate. I thought it was cute when the three of them curled up together in front of the fireplace, like puppies in a pile, for a good long snooze.

In the meantime, I happened onto what looked like the makings of a good story I could sell to the *Seattle Times* Sunday Magazine to demonstrate my wares. It was a return to my roots, because my first published stories as a youth were features for a southern Sunday magazine.

I was going to tell the story of the vanished coalmine towns in Carbon River Gorge.

From all the research I had been able to do, it didn't look like the story had been touched for years, if at all. My wife was friends with the wife of one of the two men who still mined a little coal. Like all die-hards, Bob Petosky had a vaulting vision of a return to greatness of the Wingate Seam on the heels of the Arab oil embargo. The first time I sat down with him, he showed me chunks of his Wingate Seam coal. He said it was of the highest quality, much finer and capable of far more BTUs than the stuff they were strip-mining back east in Montana or gallery mining in West Virginia. I took some home and burned it in my fireplace. The smell of burning coal catapulted me back to my earliest childhood, when we heated the Georgia house where I was born with coal.

The story just grew and grew. I discovered when the old coal companies that mined the Wingate and Butler fields went out of business, driven into receivership by the advent of cheap oil, all their records had been donated to the University of Washington. On a day when my wife could take off to watch the boy, I drove into Seattle and immersed myself in boxes and boxes of files with the willing assistance of an archivist who had a particular fondness for the coal files. No one had ever organized or indexed them and he told me excitedly there was a master's thesis lurking in those boxes for the right researcher.

He was probably right, but what I wanted was the story.

Eventually I winkled out an amazing tale of coal men

with their back to the economic wall, proving over and over again that coal was far more efficient for a number of purposes—heating state facilities, powering the old donkey engines of loggers—than that upstart, oil. They had the facts on their side, but not the public relations and deep pockets of Big Oil. One by one, they lost their most lucrative contracts; the minutes of their final meetings recorded their bewilderment that local companies working a local natural resource and employing local men had been outmaneuvered at every turn by the interlopers.

The handwriting was on the wall, even though coal was going for only $4.06 a ton while oil cost $1.19 a barrel. At those prices, coal saved $4 a day over oil in the same type of application, when a dollar *was* a dollar. It didn't matter. In one of the last reports to stockholders in 1936— after one big coal company suspended operations—a coal executive complained that oil was already up *another twenty-one cents* to $1.40 a barrel "and bound to increase...with the thousands of mechanical contrivances that are being manufactured..." But, he concluded sadly, no one was interested in his dark prophecy.

It was good stuff, enough to fill a couple of notebooks, far more than I really needed to set the tone for my story, but it's always better to have too much than too little. Now I was ready to deal with the human element up there in the Gorge.

It was Petosky who arranged for me to use a little vacation cabin on the Carbon River down a narrow dirt road from the two-lane county blacktop. The county road ran through the three barely-surviving coal towns and dead-ended against the Carbon Glacier entrance to Rainier

National Park. I could use the cabin while I interviewed the few surviving old-timers who lived up there, and walked the cemeteries full of mid-European surnames of miners killed in constant cave-ins. The Cascade Mountain coalfields were treacherous going, and a lot of immigrant miners sacrificed their lives on the altar of King Coal.

My wife and I talked the idea over. She could handle getting to work on her own for a few days if I could take the boy and the dogs with me to the cabin. It wouldn't really be roughing it; a power line came down from the county road to supply lights and refrigeration; there was pure well water for drinking and bathing, and a big fireplace with free coal if it got chilly. It would be a bit of an adventure, I thought.

A bit more than a bit, as it turned out.

But things started out smoothly. I packed the truck with some groceries and dog food, loaded my motley crew, and added a couple of rifles and a case of hand loads I had been working on, with the idea of selling a story to one of the new firearms magazines that came out in the seventies.

Of all the old timers that my host brought down to the cabin, one of them was quite a talker, with a treasure trove of anecdotes that rounded out the spotty recollections of some who had grown absent-minded. Mr. Tuchi was a native of Northern Italy who had come to the New World to make his fortune and send for his fiancée. We got the coffee perking and settled in for a long talk.

"Dose were de days," he said with a sigh.

He admitted the first time he had seen the gloomy guts of a coalmine it scared hell out of him. But veteran miners—who had worked coal in Silesia and South Wales and Finland and Pottsville, Pennsylvania—took him in hand and taught him his trade. They talked him into putting fifty cents down on the betting pool about when the next "creep" or "set", their jargon for an often-fatal earth slippage, would occur; they were fearless men who laughed at fate, those burrowers in the dark places.

He was a good storyteller. Under his still-accented English, the vanished towns and the mines they served lived again in all their vitality. The miners were hard-working, hard-drinking, hard-playing men. Some of the best times were when he'd come out of the hole blackened from head to foot, had a good wash and a heavy boarding-house meal, and strolled in freshly laundered duds down to socialize at the coke ovens.

The brick ovens were beehive-shaped and built to last—he said they were still there, but I hadn't seen them yet—a long row of them as close to the mine shafts as feasible. The high-quality raw coal they dug was shoveled into the ovens and burned free of all impurities, transformed into first-rate foundry coke. The rail cars took it away to the coal wharfs in Tacoma.

"De coke, it took a long time to cool," he said.

When all the ovens were busy, they filled even the mountain winters with warmth and a pervasive red glow. Work schedules had to wait on the cooling coke, so there was time for young miners and the daughters of older miners to do a little sparking along the hardstand between the ovens and the railroad siding.

We had a little difficulty in translation when he tried to tell me about miners who owned a kind of bicycle and liked to perform stunts before an admiring audience who brought out folding chairs to watch the show. Finally Petoskey helped me get it straight: Tuchi was describing those old-fashioned velocipedes with the huge front wheel. Sometimes there was music. In the early 1900s, they still talked about the fiddler whose airs had never been matched in the seven towns, but succumbed to the lure of easy money in the Alaska gold fields and died out there, a reminder that life was short and dangerous.

Not that the coalminers needed reminding as they placed their bets on the next cave-in. Mr. Tuchi once put in twenty-five straight hours digging frantically through a cave-in to reach his best buddy and other men. The rescuers found them too late to do anything but see that they were buried again with a little more formality in the little Roman Catholic or Eastern Orthodox cemeteries. My host stayed on for each interview and drove the old timers back up the hill to Wilkeson or Carbonado, the last two coal towns with any population at all. He said he was learning things about the old days, too.

"It's good you're getting this stuff down," Petosky said during the interview with Tuchi. "You've seen it: a lot of the old guys left don't have his kind of memory about how it was, back in the day."

The old Italian's eyes were turned far inward, focused on the past that he spun so vividly to life for us. He waved a hand vaguely. "Dis was where the biggest hotel was. Right out dere."

I looked out on a wide vacant meadow shaded by big Doug firs and maples that climbed the steep slope to the county road. A pair of crows lifted lazily above alders along the Carbon River, the only movement besides the quiet slide of the water.

"Here?" I said. "Right here?"

"You betcha. An' houses and shops and a livery stable and Chinese laundries. Musta been a t'ousand people living down here den, when I was a boy."

"How old were you when you came over?"

"I was nineteen. Born in the last century, I was. Dey started me at $3.60 for eight-hour shift. It got to be $8.25 after I was at it for fifteen year, along about 1920. I was here t'ree year before my girl come over an' we marry. She was a good wife, made do on what I got in the mines."

"And the venison you took out of these hills," Petosky said. To me, "Mr. Tuchi was quite a hunter back then. He got a 210-pound blacktail buck that was the biggest one taken for years. He was the first man in these parts to use a scope sight on a .30-30 Winchester."

"Had to mount it onna side of de gun," the old miner said, demonstrating with his hands. "So de shell can eject outta de top. You know?"

"I do know," I said.

"Paid for itself, dat scope, 'cause I could see horns inna de black timber and shoot quick, before anybody else could see horns." He smiled widely.

"There was salmon to eat, too, all the way up Carbon Creek and Gale Creek," Petosky said. "So thick you could pitchfork 'em, so I'm told. Before my time, though."

Something dark passed behind the old-timer's eyes and he stopped smiling.

"I doan mess wida dose salmons backa den. Nobody better mess wida what's left of 'em coming uppa de creeks now. De wild men don't like it, an' dey got to eat too."

"The wild men?" I looked at Petosky.

18

"Now don't get started on that old wives' tale," Petosky said, chuckling. "We're trying to do a serious story here, Mr. T. Not make city slickers laugh at us."

The old Italian's lips tightened. "I know what I know. Why you t'ink so many sets and creeps you canta 'splain."

Petosky shook his head slightly at me. "It's a different kind of mining up here," he said. "The coal will just be sticking up out of the ground at one place—and then the seam goes straight down two hundred feet. Break through a fault and suddenly you've lost the seam. It's moved off a hundred feet at right angles. It's like a damn jigsaw puzzle and the overburden is unstable. Dangerous as hell all by itself, without any old wives' tales to scare you."

"I ain'ta no old wife," the old Italian said sullenly. "I dugga good men out who wouldn't leave-a dem salmons alone. And den went to deir funerals. I'm ready to go home now."

Just then my son woke up from his nap in the little bedroom off the kitchen and let out a wail that signaled fouled britches. Old Tuchi stood up stiffly. "Time I get home."

"I'll drop back by to explain," Petosky said quietly.

The old man paused in the doorway. "You keepa dat child safe, up here in dese here mountain. You hear? Doan let him cry too much. Not good for babies to do dat, up in here."

And then he was gone.

Chapter Three

I got my son cleaned up and dry and powdered his butt with Johnson's baby powder, just like my mother and grandmother did for me. Then I warmed his bottle and slipped in a teaspoon of Hershey's chocolate syrup, without my wife around to monitor. That was the way I liked it when I was his age, and my son seemed to like it just as much.

I read over my notes while he worked on the bottle, and the two dogs curled up at my feet. I could hear the wind pick up outside, coming up the Gorge, and the light shifted; clouds must be rolling in from the coast. It was late autumn and the temperature was probably dropping, but my son made a warm bundle in my lap. It was one of those moments of contentment that come along once in a while to make life worth getting up for in the morning. I wasn't far behind my son in drifting off to happy dreamland, untroubled by the strange end to my interview with old Mr. Tuchi.

The dogs woke me with ferocious deep-throated barking; Labradors are nothing if not protective. The barking didn't bother my son. He was sound out. I gently eased him down on the old couch and got to the door in time to see Petosky climbing out of his old pickup. I told the dogs to hush and they instantly obeyed, their job done. When Petosky came in, they swarmed around his knees wagging happily. They already knew he was a dog person.

He gave them both a good ear rub and butt scratch, and asked if there was more coffee.

"Not only coffee, but some wild blackberry pie my wife baked," I told him. "Right off the bushes behind my house."

His smile was a happy one. "Your wife's mom was the best baker in these hills. I wonder if it rubbed off."

"If it didn't, it's still plenty good enough for me. Dig in."

We settled at the little kitchen table and for a few minutes just addressed the pie. I was still in my stranger-in-paradise mode back then, thinking life just couldn't get much better even if I did live in a strange little town on top of a prehistoric cataclysm.

He pushed his pie plate back with a sigh. "I have to say she's a chip off the old block. Tell her that for me, will you?"

I said I would. "Now, tell me about the wild men."

He shook his head. "So many of those immigrants came straight out of superstitious little villages in the Old Country, you know. Vampires and demons and ghosts—all of that was just kind of the accepted thing."

"Tell me about it," I said. "I grew up in the Deep South with a grandmother everybody believed was a real witch."

He laughed. "No lie? Then you probably understand how these old timers get some of their notions. Mr. Tuchi used to claim that when he was out hunting, he saw these wild men of his catching salmon, down in the water just like those bears in Alaska."

"I wonder if the local black bears do that?"

"Dunno, but if you squinted just right you could turn a

bear into a wild hairy man, scooping fish with his hands. Ever field-dress a bear?"

"I'm more of a duck hunter."

"Should have figured that, with your Labs." He smiled when Paka came and leaned against his knee, staring up at him soulfully. "Okay to let her lick my pie plate?"

"She knows a sucker when she sees one. Go ahead."

I called Harry over and put my plate down for him so he wouldn't feel slighted. We sipped our coffee and the dogs slurped happily.

"What about a field-dressed bear?" I said.

"With the fur off, the body looks almost too much like a human's," he said. "A bear with a bad case of the mange—it happens—could maybe look like a primitive man wearing furs."

"Mr. Tuchi seems to have built up a whole thing around them: salmon eaters who don't like poachers," I said. "Like stories mothers tell to scare their children into behaving."

He nodded. "The lowland Scots once had a lullaby to the effect that if the children didn't behave the Black Douglas would get them."

"Petosky doesn't sound like a Scots name," I said.

He smiled. "I read a lot, winters when it's too wet to work my mine."

"Speaking of which," I said, "it looks like a storm blowing in out there."

"Getting to be that time, all right. You want to take a walk through the town here? I can show you some stuff."

"What town?" I said.

"This is what's left of Lower Fairfax. Back in the day it

was a real rip-snorter, like Mr. T. said. Hotel and all."

"It's hard to imagine," I said. "Let's go."

I loaded the boy into his nylon and aluminum papoose rig and put him on my back. We walked out through a swirl of falling maple leaves across the glade, the dogs romping ahead, noses down. Halfway to the river's edge, Petosky paused and went to one knee, feeling among the low brushy growth.

"Ah. Here it is." He stood and lifted, and a wide heavy metal trap door groaned up out of the ground on rusty hinges.

"I would never have guessed that was there," I said.

"The cellar of the old hotel," he said. "The first ones who got into it after they tore the hotel down, and carted off all the wood and the stone, found some neat old bottles and stuff in the cellar. It's been picked clean long since."

"How big was the hotel?"

"At least two stories, with the whole front made out of Wilkeson sandstone, and a bar with a dance floor off to the side."

That uniquely figured sandstone was Wilkeson's one remaining claim to fame; there was Wilkeson sandstone in the state capital buildings. A small quarry, back off a spur of the county road, still milled small amounts of it for architects and builders. The old machinery that did the heavy milling work was powered by coal; they were Petoskey's biggest customer. My mother-in-law had fronted her retirement dream house, which I now called home, with slabs of the stuff. Now, as hard as I stared at this uneven ground, I couldn't visualize a two-story stone-fronted hotel on a busy street. I shook my head as he lowered the trap door back into place.

"The Northwest doesn't take long to cover up any trace of civilization, does it?" I said.

"You think that's something? Come on over here to the river."

Paka splashed happily in the shallows, trying to tempt Harry in to play with her. No dice; Harry was the most water-averse Labrador I ever saw. He would go to work if he had to, when there were ducks on the water, but beyond that, uh-uh. Petosky pointed to a jagged outcrop of rock, festooned with creepers and moss.

"What do you suppose you're looking at?" Petosky said.

"I have no idea."

"It was a buttress for the railroad bridge that came through here and crossed the river to Lower Melmont. Melmont was the end of the line. They had a roundtable there to turn the locomotives around. But you won't find a trace of it anymore. They tore up the steel for scrap in the Second World War. Same for the tracks through here, and on the bridge itself. I don't know how they missed that trap door. The river took care of the rest of the bridge one spring flood season."

"My god, it's like looking for traces of a lost civilization," I said.

"Well basically, that's what we're doing," he said. "The lost civilization of the seven coal towns. Did you know that Tacoma owes its existence to these towns?"

I'd seen the blackened snags and sagging piers along the Tacoma waterfront, all that was left of the sprawling coal docks from the age of coal-burning ships, but I thought his statement sounded a touch grandiose. I told him it sounded like a case of the tail wagging the dog as we followed my dogs back toward the cabin.

"Oh, no," he assured me. "These coal reserves up here, especially Wilkeson's, is what made Northern Pacific push a railhead into Tacoma. Tacoma was just a wide spot on the mud flats then, but it was the closest salt-water access to the Wilkeson coal reserves."

A gust of wind kicked across the meadow. The temperature was definitely dropping. "You need to let me show you how to get to Upper Melmont next," he said.

"Where the turntable was."

"Nope, that's Lower Melmont, like this is lower Fairfax. Upper Fairfax was up there on the county road where those folks built that Swiss-looking house a few years back. Mildred told me she was coming up to her Melmont cabin with one of her special cases tonight, so she can show you where the turntable was, and where the coking ovens still are."

"Mildred?"

"Mildred is the granddaughter of one of the real old-timers who ran the biggest mercantile in Wilkeson, back when it was quite the boomtown. The population was put at five thousand in 1903 when he opened his doors. Kids from Carbonado would sneak down to buy penny candy from him to avoid paying company-store prices."

"Five thousand!"

The Wilkeson I was getting to know was a narrow string of old homes, weathered house trailers and maybe half a dozen businesses strung along either side of the rusting rail spur and the county road. The two largest buildings were an Eagle's Lodge and the Wilkeson-sandstone school, where my wife went to grammar school before they shut it down. I was learning how tight and clannish the surviving townsfolk were; my wife's having attended grammar school up here made her an honorary member of the clan and gave me entrée by dint of marriage.

"Five thousand," I said again. I wondered if he was pulling my leg.

Petosky jingled his truck keys and looked up at the racing clouds. "Definitely a storm brewing. Yep, five thousand. Last census? There were 284 of us, not counting dogs, cats and chickens." He grinned. "Most people in Tacoma have no idea they have a town to live in because of us. How does that Roman saying go? Sic transit Gloria Mundi?"

Petosky was a surprising man. I liked him quite a bit. I got him to take half the pie to his wife and kids, and he seemed pleased at the homey gesture. He said he had to go "outside" tomorrow, as if leaving the Gorge was a major voyage. We agreed to meet up on the county road at nine, so he could show me how to get to Mildred's isolated Upper Melmont cabin, in her family since the glory days. She now worked "outside" herself, at the Soldier's Home in Orting. He told me her special charges were very old, shell-shocked veterans that she brought up with her on a rotating basis to escape the regimentation for a while. I thought it seemed a fine thing for her to do.

He hesitated, already in his truck with the engine running. "If you're curious, Mildred has some of her own ideas about Mr. Tuchi's salmon-eating wild men. I suppose there could be another whole story in that. Like a fairy tale, you know? If that kind of thing interests you. See you in the morning."

Chapter Four

The storm broke that night. I built a hot fire in the fireplace with some of Petosky's Wingate Seam coal, spread a blanket in front of it and played with my son. He had a string of those multi-colored egg-size pull-apart beads and some old-fashioned wooden alphabet blocks. He loved popping those beads apart and scattering them from hell to breakfast. He already had figured out that if he slung them away from him, Paka would pick them up and bring them back. She'd drop them right by him and stand there wagging like crazy waiting for him to do it again. He was learning to stack four or five blocks one on top of the other, and then kick hell out of them to see how far they'd tumble before she was on them, trying to bring back two at once while he chortled. Harry could not shut off his tracking radar. He knew where every bead and every block flew. But it was beneath his dignity to involve himself in puppy shenanigans. He lay with his muzzle between his paws, eyebrows twitching to follow the arc of every missile. Occasionally he would utter an almost human sigh.

Sticks and twigs pattered on the flat tin roof. The wind shrilled like a lost ghost around the corners of the cabin. The lights flickered a time or two and I thought about that drooping power line descending through the trees from the county road. Let one good-size branch break loose and we'd be in the dark. I primed and pumped my Coleman camp lantern and laid a flashlight by just in case, but the power held.

When the rain cut loose, it came in monsoon torrents as if to make up for dry September days just past. It roared on the tin roof as loudly as I imagined one of those old coal-fired locomotives sounded from under the vanished bridge to Lower Melmont. I fed the boy his bottle when he had played himself out, put down food for the dogs, and built myself a chili omelet with salsa, an acquired taste from my sojourns in Southern California. The dogs scooted outside for a nightly constitutional during a slight lessening in the downpour, got their business done and came back in and sprayed the whole cabin down shaking out their wet fur. Then they sprawled a safe distance from the blazing coal to dry out. That feeling of smug contentment crept over me again.

I uncased my old Royal portable typewriter and noodled along, converting some of my notebook entries and expanding them with remembered details I hadn't written down. My story of the vanished towns was beginning to take form and substance. I decided to let Mr. Tuchi's contribution mulch and went back to fill out the section on Burnett. Blink twice on the way to Wilkeson, I typed, and you will miss Burnett. If Wilkeson now could muster 284 souls exclusive of livestock, I doubted that Burnett could boast 20, perched beside the road on a wooded slope above the locally notorious Chinaman's Slope.

But Burnett's coal, and the men they hired to mine it in the latter part of the nineteenth century, stood at one of those crossroads in the affairs of men where local and international politics clashed dangerously. It was about a quarter of a century after a certain Van Ogle, around the time of the Battle of Bull Run, walked up to a cliff face in the Carbon Gorge and broke off a chunk of what proved to be some of the best coking coal on earth.

Poor Van Ogle got excited as John Sutter in that mill in California. Gold was precious metal, but coal was the engine of nineteenth-century commerce. The story goes that the more he looked, the more coal he found, and the more suspicious he became of his good fortune. He just kept stumbling over the stuff until he finally decided that if there was that much of it, and no one else was dancing a jig about it, it must be worthless. He didn't even stake a claim.

Others did, and when they needed cheap labor to mine the black lode, they turned to Chinese coolies. The Burnett coal that filled Tacoma waterfront bunkers, and made it a major port of call between the days of sail and diesel, was picked and shoveled out of the ground by Chinese miners. Far across the Pacific, times were tough in Imperial China. The only real export the Emperor had to offer the world was the indefatigable coolie.

By 1886, six hundred Chinese lived in a close-packed tent city on Chinaman Slope below Burnett, their backbreaking labor powering the coal-fueled ships of the world that called at Tacoma. They took their pay in gold double eagles and, so the story went, buried it beneath their tents until they could send it home to their families. By 1886, the Tacoma Knights of Labor had had enough of immigrant labor taking their jobs, and formed an angry mob to march on Chinaman Slope. They drove the Chinese out of their tent town and put it to the torch. It was a miracle there wasn't a slaughter.

I paused in my typing as the wind picked up, flinging debris against the roof. Particularly loud bangs would rouse the dogs with lips curled back over their teeth, suspecting an intrusion. Then they would settle back down. I had found nothing about running Mr. Tuchi's Chinese laundries out of the coalfields, so apparently the Knights of Labor considered washing clothes beneath them.

It was amazing to me, given the slowness of communications back then, how fast the Imperial Court in Peking got word of the attack on Chinaman Slope, and how fast the mandarins in turn grabbed the attention of the White House in no uncertain terms. The Washington Territorial Governor got his marching orders in a matter of days, and railroad flatcars were commandeered and sent up Carbon Gorge to rescue the coolies from the angry union men. They were hustled aboard quickly and shipped off to Portland to avoid a worse international incident.

They were hardly down the tracks when rumors raced through the Gorge that they were packed off so quickly they hadn't had time to sort through their burned-out tents to retrieve their buried gold stashes. Petosky told me treasure seekers still combed the now heavily forested slope looking for gold coins. If anyone had ever hit the bonanza, they weren't talking.

Poor old Van Ogle—certainly one of history's biggest losers. For 99 years, Chinese and then European miners sent enough coal pouring out of those seven towns—four vanished and three on life-support—to power all the locomotives of the Central, Southern and Northern Pacific; Northern Pacific's ocean steamers; and the steel mills in Seattle, Portland and Tacoma. The beehives turned out so much coking coal that by 1880 the dockside San Francisco price of coke was halved. A total of almost 22 million tons moved out of the Gorge by the time the coal companies went belly-up. The Bureau of Mines estimated there remained *362 million tons* buried under 54 square miles of rugged terrain.

I closed up my typewriter for the night on that thought. By the time I was writing this, the first Earth Day had come and gone, and environmentalism was the new craze for those who would soon be without a Vietnam War to kick around anymore. Anybody tapping natural resources in the seventies was now viewed as the new LBJ baby killers. Meanwhile, up in Carbon Gorge, nature had obliterated almost every trace of a 22-million-ton mining operation as if it had never existed.

Three towns where all that was left was the memory of their names: Fairfax, Melmont and Spiketon, which had also been called Morristown. One town so utterly gone that local memory was dim even as to its name. Two more towns hanging on grimly and one fading like the Cheshire Cat—but I had a hunch the last sight of Burnett would not be its smile.

The dogs trooped into the bedroom with me and found spots at the foot of the bed. The warmth of the coal fire didn't quite reach in here and it was chilly and damp. I snuggled my son in extra baby blankets and wrapped my Eddie Bauer down vest around him for a snug cocoon, then kicked my boots off and crawled under my zipped-open sleeping bag fully clothed—another of the simple pleasures of camping out without wifely supervision. The fire made dancing shadows on the ceiling through the open door. I tucked my son in the curve of my arm and let my mind wander as the storm renewed its overhead assault. Salmon-eating wild men, who stalked and entombed miners who poached their fish, drifted around in the corners of my mind.

I had been out on Carbon Creek once with members of a hairy, inbred-looking family, some with strange fleshy protuberances growing on their faces. They made me think of *Tobacco Road,* Erskine Caldwell's book that infuriated my Georgia kin before I made grade school. They poached deer with .22s. They wired knife blades to broom handles and knelt, silent as blue herons, above eddies on the creek where returning salmon and steelhead—supposedly protected on that creek from all fishing—rested in their upstream battle to the spawning gravels. They had been doing it so long their knees wore moss away in their favored spots, leaving muddy indentations. Their lodgings were so well hidden it would take a seasoned woodman to find them unaided.

A former outlaw biker, working in an auto-wrecking yard on the county road near Burnett, led me to the strange tribe and told them I could be trusted. The biker had resurrected the old Pontiac Bonneville my wife drove to work. He sold it to us for forty dollars rather than stripping it and sending it to the automobile-graveyard recycle plant on the Tacoma tide flats, and showed me how to keep it running.

I had asked him where they got the fresh salmon that

seemed to keep their big smoker at the wrecking yard going round the clock. If the yard crew liked you, you were invited to lunch. Even if they didn't particularly like you, but knew you to be worthy of trust, they'd sell you smoked salmon out the back door for a good price. I was lucky enough to be on both lists, so he took me to their source.

The strange family that supplied the wrecking yard lived in the depths below the Burnett Bridge, and traded salmon for parts off wrecked vehicles to keep their old junker on the road, or cash for staples. Their albino patriarch, Aaron, shunned all daylight. He lurked in their concealed ramshackle tarpaper shack well back from the creek tinkering with his augmented Citizen Band radio set, eavesdropping on CB chatter to keep tabs on game wardens and the fisheries patrol. If he spotted a Game or Fisheries vehicle on the high bridge, he keyed his microphone through a loudspeaker buried on the moss-covered roof: two long bursts of static for Game Department, three short for Fisheries Patrol. His brood would melt into invisibility. He managed their small commerce in poached salmon and venison.

The Cascades were full of such hidden pockets of outlaws or ex-hippies or survivalists living off the land. Aaron's brood evinced no fear of skulking wild men who might resent their poaching; I thought maybe they *were* Signor Tuchi's wild men. I was wondering what Mildred, the Soldier's Home nurse, would have to tell me about that when the storm lulled me to sleep.

Chapter Five

Mildred Fenton thought my son was cute as the dickens in his little yellow rain boots, and hunkered right down on the wet ground outside her cabin to tell him so. He was just past two that year and still navigated with the rolling walk of a sailor just on shore. The doctor said he was physically precocious, which usually meant he would lag behind in words, but he was coming along. And shy he was not.

"Hi!" he said with a blazing grin, flung out his arms and marched right into her, almost setting her back on her trim rump in the mud. He chortled and she laughed out loud and enfolded him in a close embrace, whereupon he reached up and planted a resounded wet kiss on her chin.

"Oh, my!" She picked him up and stood in one movement, with the grace of a dancer, and smooched him right back. "This one is a lover." She smiled at me. "I bet he'll be giving the girls fits before too many years go by."

Mildred Fenton was what they used to call a woman of a certain age. She could have been anywhere between thirty and fifty, moderately tall, slim, but with appropriate curves here and there, modestly on display in snug wool slacks and a light roll neck sweater. She had those rubber L.L. Bean pac shoes on her feet. Her dark hair, with veins of silver sparkling in it, was pulled back into a kind of chignon. She had regular features, a nice smile, and that pale, fresh complexion that I had come to associate with women of the Northwest. Her best feature was a pair of vivid violet-hued eyes. A trained reporter notices these things in less time than it takes to tell them.

Her family cabin was three times as large as the vacation cabins in Lower Fairfax, walls and roof sheathed entirely in well-weathered cedar shakes. A gravel-dinged old white International Travel-All stood in the dooryard; people of the Gorge didn't go in much for automobiles.

"Bob Petosky told me you'd like to see the coking ovens," she said. "You're writing a story about the old days for the Seattle papers?"

I said I was.

"You talked to Mr. Tuchi? Isn't he an old dear? And boy, can he spin the yarns."

"I liked him a lot," I said. "I'm thinking this story is turning into a darn good yarn itself. It's hard to believe there's so little in the newspaper files about it."

She jiggled my son on her hip and absently chucked him under the chin. He grabbed her fingers and laughed. "Hi!!"

"Hi yourself," she told him. "You already said that. Can you say Mildred?"

He studied her. "Mil-dwed?"

"Close enough. Yes, Mildred."

"Mil-dwed? Hi!"

She was having a good time with him. "It's a bit of a walk to the ovens. Not sure his little legs can carry him."

"I've got one of those modern papoose packs. He likes to ride."

"Facing forward or back?" she said quickly.

"Forward. He likes to see where we're going. Why?"

"Did you know that the papooses in tribes that were faced forward instead of backward developed their reflexes much faster?

"I didn't know that. He seems pretty well-coordinated to me, but what else would a dad say, right?"

"Right. But you're on the right track. Where's mom?"

"At work in Tacoma."

"Wow, pretty modern arrangement, for the seventies. I can't get over what a good-looking boy he is."

She had those lovely violet eyes, wide and candid. I suppressed the urge to tell her something I said to cute gals who kept on about how handsome he was: *I can make you one just like him.* Didn't seem the time or place.

"Let me just throw some feed out for my chickens and we can go," she said.

I got my papoose pack frame out of the truck while she headed around the corner of the cabin. I left the dogs in their kennels in the truck camper shell, and their ears drooped unhappily. Mildred Fenton came back out the front door of the cabin. I was surprised to see that she had a rifle on a sling over the shoulder of a canvas farm coat. She saw my glance.

"Fresh coyote tracks around the chicken house," she said. "They didn't get in—I built it pretty stout—but if I spot one, I'm going to discourage the hell out of him."

I nodded, and she led out across another of those empty meadows that I was beginning to realize marked the former sites of the coal towns.

"So this was Upper Melmont," I said.

"Yes. My dad rebuilt this cabin after the Second World War, when they tore the rest of the buildings down and carted them away. They had some temporary structures here then—mining picked up a little during the war years. All gone now."

At the edge of the meadow, an eroded dirt track zigzagged toward the river. As we picked our footing on the slippery mud, rain began to patter in the trees. She pulled a Vietnam boonie cap out of a capacious pocket and fitted it somehow over her hairdo.

"We're going to get a little wet," she said.

"We're ready for that," I said. I had on my leather bomber jacket and a leather baseball cap. I handed her a miniature version of a rubber Sou'Wester hat. "Would you mind putting this on him? I can't quite reach."

"Oh, how cute! It matches his boots and jacket."

While she stood close helping my son with his headgear, I got a good look at her rifle: a very-well-kept Winchester lever-action Model 71. Awfully heavy ordnance for coyotes; the 71 only came in .348. It was a favorite of brown-bear guides in Alaska, worth almost a thousand 1970-value dollars. Maybe it was her only gun; I wondered how such a slim woman handled its considerable recoil.

"This road was graveled back in the day," she said over her shoulder as we headed down. "It all just washed away."

The rain steadied into a typical Northwest drizzle out of a leaden sky; the storm had gone on over to tangle up with the higher mountains. The temperature seemed to be falling instead of rising as the morning went along.

"De-uh!" my son suddenly shouted in my ear, startling me. "Da! De-uh!"

And there they were, two blacktail does drinking in a spring at the base of an embankment a few feet off the road. They raised their heads to watch us pass and froze into immobility.

"He's got eyes like a hawk," Mildred said softly. "He saw them before I did. That pool where they're drinking? It's where the ground slumped after they dynamited a coal shaft in the face of that little hill."

"De-uh!" my son repeated loudly. For some reason they didn't spook at his voice.

"Yes, son, deer," I said.

He said it maybe a dozen more times, in a kind of happy little chant, as we reached the bottom of the grade. Another meadow, but here the alders were taking it over.

"Lower Melmont," Mildred said. "See the ovens?"

All I saw was brush and trees and the slant of the rain. "No."

"See that little ridge running along there with all the little alders growing out of it? There they are."

She led me around the corner of the ridge, and now I could see the regular line of curving brickwork here and there among the forest litter and the tangle of small alder limbs and skunk cabbage and ferns. When she pushed aside a screen of ferns, there was a dark opening behind it.

"Door to one of the ovens," she said. "Here." She reached down and came up with a loose brick, charred at one end and covered with lichen. "A souvenir."

We spent maybe an hour wandering around down there under the enclosing trees with the rain tapping down. A spread of forty-foot-tall alders stood where the Melmont roundtable had been. The forest had completely reclaimed any evidence of the hardstand Mr. Tuchi recalled with such fondness from his socializing nights while the coke cooled.

At the edge of the alder copse above the vanished roundtable, we startled a ruffed grouse into thunderous flight. My pulse rate jumped, and my son shrieked with glee. When I looked at Mildred, her rifle was in her hands, her face expressionless.

She reslung the rifle, looking embarrassed. "Sorry. It startled me."

"Grouse do that," I said. "You must have been a forward-looking papoose when you were little."

"What?"

"Excellent reflexes. If that had been a shotgun, you'd have roast grouse for dinner."

She laughed, and looked at her wristwatch. "Have you seen what you came to see? I need to be thinking about getting back. Ralph will be waking up from his nap and I don't like to leave him alone."

"Ralph is one of your veterans?"

"I only brought Ralph this time. He's a kind of loner, doesn't play well with others. He was a Montana cowboy in the real cowboy days before he went to war. I think he developed the habit of solitude over there on the other side of the Continental Divide."

I picked up my souvenir brick from where I'd stashed it, and we started back up. I could see she was holding back for me, and told her to go on ahead. I needed to walk slowly to avoid a fall with my son on that slippery mud. She hesitated, but shook her head.

"I wouldn't be a good tour guide if I left a greenhorn alone in these woods." She said it lightly, but her eyes shunted around and I wondered why she was nervous. We took our time getting back to the top. She seemed to relax once we were in sight of her cabin.

A big burly bear of a man with an old-fashioned skinned-sidewall haircut—all the visible hair iron-gray—was rocking in a chair on the front porch. I smelled burning tobacco. When we got closer, I could see the telltale tag of a bag of Bull Durham hanging from the pocket of his flannel shirt.

"He still rolls his own," Mildred said. "Says the only places he could ever smoke indoors was the Army and bunkhouse, so not being able to smoke in the Home doesn't bother him."

He stood up slowly. "Mildred. I was asleep."

"Yes, Ralph. How are you feeling?"

He considered this carefully as if it might be a trick question. We stood on the porch and waited. He ground his smoke under his boot heel and carefully fieldstripped the butt, tossing the remains into the rain. He had a hard time bending over.

"Hungry," he said finally. "I feel hungry."

"I'm fixing us some hamburgers with all the trimmings for lunch," she said.

"I'm hungry," he repeated. "I'll go wash up." He lumbered slowly inside.

"Shellshock from the First War," she whispered to me. "He has his good days and his bad days. He always does better out here."

I told her I thought it was fine that she brought the veterans out to her cabin during her time off. She shrugged it off and called them her "boys." Then she asked me if my son could eat a hamburger.

"He'll gum it pretty hard," I said.

"How about French fries?"

"A bad habit I've taught him, according to his mother. He loves French fries."

"Well kick the mud off your boots and come on inside. I've got plenty." She unslung her Model 71 and went inside. I noticed she didn't clear the chamber or unload it and wondered about the safety of a loaded bear rifle around a shell-shocked vet, but I didn't say anything.

I still hadn't asked her about Mr. Tuchi's wild men. I thought lunch might give me a chance to bring it up.

Chapter Six

Lunch with Mildred Fenton and Big Ralph was pretty interesting. She must have had four pounds of hamburger to mold into patties, and an enormous cast-iron skillet to grill them in, plus a deep-fry basket arrangement for French fries made from fresh potatoes, which it turned out Ralph had already peeled. He sat patiently slicing them into strips with his big paws, deeply focused on the job at hand. Mildred marshaled the meal with the quick, unwasted motions of a skilled short-order cook. With my approval, she filled one of my son's bottles with cold Coke to hold him until the fries were ready.

"I was weaned on Coke," I said. "I grew up in the South."

"I wondered. There's an accent still. Some parents are pretty uptight about things like a Coke for their children."

"That would be the parent in Tacoma," I said. "Ralph, you're pretty handy with that Chef's knife."

"French fries," he said. "Love 'em!" He didn't look up from his work.

"Fwenfi?" My son said. "Fwenfi, Da?"

Ralph looked up then, with a grin on his weathered old features. "You betchum, Red Ryder. French fries! Love 'em."

"Love 'em," my son imitated, like a parrot.

Once we were settled in to eat, my son marched around the small kitchen table and crawled up on Ralph's lap without so much as a by-your-leave. One of those big mitts came up and petted his hair gently. My son took one of Ralph's fries and began to gnaw it. Ralph beamed.

"Thank you for letting him do that," Mildred Fenton said. "Ralph is just a big kid himself. I know he misses having kids around."

"Did he have a family?"

"Nobody knows, and he can't really answer. He's been in soldier's homes since Armistice Day."

More than sixty years. "Good god," I said.

"There are a lot of sad stories at the Home," she said. "We do what we can for them. Your son is really good for him."

When we had eaten all the hamburgers and fries we could hold, Mildred brought out the ice cream, Neapolitan, to the mutual joy of Ralph and my boy. Years seemed to drop away from the old man's face as they tucked into their bowls side-by-side, my son still perched on his lap.

When I mentioned that I should let the dogs out for a constitutional, Mildred said, "Go ahead, your son is perfectly safe there," and I believed her. Then she produced four leftover patties. "For your pooches. I love dogs."

"I'm surprised you don't have one up here, it's so isolated."

Her face lost expression. "I did." Then she seemed to shake herself. "In fact I've got a Husky pup at home now. But I don't bring him up here. Don't let your dogs wander too far."

I thought about that while Paka and Harry made short work of the hamburger, nuzzled my hands to make sure that's all there was and then trotted off to do their business, sniffing the news off the underbrush. Harry was about fifty yards away when he almost buried his nose in the mud and growled. I went over there quickly and spotted paw prints in the mud. If she had no dogs here, it had to be those coyotes she was worried about. Harry didn't like coyotes.

I kenneled the dogs and went back inside. Ralph and my son had moved to the snug front parlor, crowded with old wicker vacation furniture, and Ralph was trying to show my son how to play checkers. My son thought they made fine wheels, and rolled a couple of pieces across the table. Ralph caught them out of the air as they fell. He looked at them like he'd never seen them before. Then his brow lightened and he rolled them back. My son caught one and missed the other, and clapped his hands in glee.

"Looks like Ralph's the one getting the lesson," Mildred said softly. "Look at him! This is so good for him."

They rolled checkers back and forth until half of them were on the floor on my son's side of the table. Then he yawned broadly, crawled down from his chair and went to Ralph and held his arms up. Ralph picked him up and cradled him tenderly. He was asleep in minutes, head on Ralph's broad flannel shoulder.

"You think it's all right to go out on the porch and leave them there?" I said. "I'm kind of craving my pipe after that good meal."

"They'll be perfectly fine," she said. "I'll bring us out some coffee and join you."

I was firing up my pipe when the monsoon came back, drawing a cloud like falling smoke across the meadow. The sound on the shake roof was far quieter than the tin roof of my vacation cabin.

"I love the smell of a pipe," Mildred said. "My dad smoked a pipe. Not too many younger men do anymore. It's a shame."

I thought that if I wasn't married, I might consider proposing on the spot. These Carbon Gorge people were really appealing to me—including poor Ralph. I puffed for a while and we drank coffee and watched the rain.

"I have a couple of questions," I said finally. "If you don't mind my asking."

"About the coal towns?"

"Actually—no. Bob Petosky said you might be able to tell me something about Mr. Tuchi's salmon-eating wild men that he used to see out in the brush."

"Oh." She regarded me levelly over the brim of her cup. "Is this for your story about the Gorge?"

"I don't think so. It wouldn't fit, and I've already got a ton of stuff that's really interesting. I guess I'm mostly curious."

"I'm curious why Bob told you to ask me." I had the impression that she was not pleased.

I shrugged. "Fairy tales from the Old World transplanted to the New."

"Is that what Bob said?"

"More or less."

She said nothing for a discernible time, gazing off across the rain. When she spoke again, she surprised me.

"Are you one of these anti-gun nuts like so many in the media are these days?"

"Absolutely not. I know what you mean. I never

mentioned that I'm a hunter on some of the newspapers I worked for. Just to avoid the hassle."

She nodded. "I couldn't help notice you were surprised I brought a rifle along today, and that you kept looking at it. That's why I told you about the coyotes."

My turn to nod; I puffed my pipe in silence. She was leading up to something, and I wanted her to find her own way to it. The rain beat down and my stomach was uncomfortably full—I had eaten too much.

"Do you know much about firearms?"

"A little," I said. "In fact I'm working on a freelance story for one of the gun magazines about custom hand-loads."

"My coyote rifle is actually a Remington bolt-action .222."

"Not the .348," I said.

"You do know guns."

"Marauding bears up here too?"

She gave me a look, and sighed. "There's one word you will never hear cross the lips of anyone who lives in the Gorge. The folks up here absolutely hate being laughed at."

I waited.

"That word is Sasquatch," she said, watching for my reaction.

"Okay," I said neutrally. "Also known as Bigfoot, right?"

"We call 'em *skooks* up here in the Gorge. Know anything about 'em?"

"Big and hairy and run through the woods," I said. "Plus the big feet of course. I wear a size 14 boot. I had a boss once who listened to that description of a Bigfoot and said hell, I *hired* one."

She gave a short laugh. "You see? It's always a joke. We don't like getting laughed at and nobody from outside knows what we're talking about if we say skook." She stood and put her coffee cup down. "I want to show you something. Grab you cap."

She went back inside and came out with a dark-green hooded rain slicker—and the .348.

"Are they okay in there?"

"Both sound asleep," she said. "Ralph is snoring. We won't be long."

She led me around the cabin in the downpour. Rain ran down my neck under my jacket and drained off my cap brim. Her hooded form blended with the foliage as she moved ahead of me past the chicken coop and onto a path into the woods. We didn't go far before I could hear the river above the sound of rain. It sounded like a rapids. She stopped, turned and leaned close, holding her hood off her face.

"Right here is where they came onto the trail last winter when it snowed," she said. "I was out looking for coyotes."

"What came onto the trail?"

"Naked footprints. In the snow! But not huge footprints—they were so small I thought for a minute some poor child was running barefoot in the woods. But they were actually about my size foot. They went this way."

She led down the path until we came to the lip of the cliff. I had been right, the rock formations down there narrowed into a white-water chute. She turned back to me.

"You can't see it now—but the ground and the snow

were ripped up right here on the edge, where it went over. It landed on the rocks down there. Something must have frightened it—maybe a pack of wild dogs."

"Coyotes, now wild dogs. There are wild-dog packs up here?"

"Oh, yeah. Pets left to run loose that form up and breed. They sound like jackals on a kill—not like coyotes at all. They're not afraid of people—they're not afraid of anything."

"They chased a child over the ledge?"

"Not a child. An immature skook. That's why the footprints in the snow were so small. It died on the rocks down there." She pointed.

"Why didn't this make the news? All I've read says they've never seen a young Bigfoot, which adds to the idea that it's all a hoax."

"I saw a young one. A young one with its head broken open on those rocks, dead. It was one of the saddest things I've ever seen. I could see it clear as day. I've got good eyes."

"What did you do?"

"I went back to the cabin for my camera. And of course I'd left it at home that day. By the time I could get there and back, with all the snow and ice on the roads..."

"It wasn't there anymore," I guessed.

"Right. I stayed down here that night, I don't really know why, and that was when I heard the most god-awful screeching—like something in terrible pain. No, like grief. Like something in awful grief."

She was speaking so matter-of-factly that I had to give myself an internal shake. Was this the story Bob Petosky wanted her to tell me? I asked her that.

"Let's start back," she said. The rain hadn't let up a bit and it was damn chilly. "Bob of course thought I imagined the whole thing. Maybe I did see a child without many clothes down there—kids from that state school are escaping all the time, some of those teenagers are pretty big, and more than one of them has come to harm."

"Barefooted in the snow?"

"A lot of those poor kids are as damaged mentally as Ralph. They might not feel the cold like we do."

"So if that's what you saw, where did the body go?"

"That's the thing, see—none of the rescue squads were called out. And it would have taken a major effort to get down there, lots of manpower."

"But something took it away." We were almost back to the cabin.

"The skooks came and got their child. I'm sure of that. I'm pretty sure wild dogs chased it to its death. I know *they* blamed dogs."

I felt a creeping little chill that had nothing to do with the temperature. "Who blamed dogs?"

"*They* did. Mr. Tuchi's wild men, skooks, take your pick. After all that screeching, when I let King out to do his business that night, I heard this horrendous slam against the side of the house. King never came back. When it was daylight I found fur and blood frozen on the wall. But King was gone."

"King?"

"My first Husky. I named him for that old TV series." Her face was grim as death.

"Never saw him again?"

"Oh, yeah. What was left of him." Her voice could have cut glass. "They dumped him down there where the baby was found. Like they were sending a message about dogs."

"God in Heaven," I said.

"His body was down there until scavengers dragged off the bits."

Chapter Seven

The rain continued all afternoon and it got colder. My wife and I had agreed I'd come home tomorrow, so if I didn't test my hand loads this afternoon I might not have time in the morning. My son was tired out after his big day with Mildred and big Ralph, so I fed him his afternoon bottle and put him down for a real nap this time. I left the dogs in the bedroom with him, to protect their ears from rifle fire, and got out my rain gear and rifles and hand loads.

I dug a couple of home-made target frames out of the back of the truck, paced off about a hundred yards across the meadow to the embankment that climbed to the county road, and nailed them against some alder stumps. Then I crawled up in the camper shell to get out of the rain and laid a folded blanket across the top of the dogs' fiberglass kennels for a shooting bench. My seat was an old milking stool I picked up at an estate sale in Enumclaw.

I kept mulling over Mildred's Sasquatch story as I got set up. She didn't seem noticeably crazy; like Signor Tuchi, she saw what she saw. Just another unexplained tale to weave into the rich tapestry of Northwest folklore, this one told by what I'd have to say was a credible witness. Then I put speculation aside to concentrate on the work at hand.

The hook for the story I hoped to sell to one of the guns and ammo magazines was reloading heavier-than-conventional bullets for the 7mm Remington Magnum.

The 175-grain was the largest then commercially loaded, considered good medicine for elk; an honest five-hundred-yard elk cartridge according to Pete Brown, one of the good old gun writers of my youth.

Some pundits—they were coming out of the woodwork with all the new gun magazines in the seventies—thought the 175-grain was too light for the big bears, or even moose. I couldn't say from personal experience. As I'd told Petosky, I'm mostly a duck hunter. But I wondered if the heavier, partitioned bullets I loaded in new brass would show the same inherent accuracy every other load did in my 700 Remington. The rifle was my birthday present from my father when I graduated from high school and for over ten years the only rifle I owned.

The company that built the heavy 7mm bullets said they would provide better penetration into the vitals of heavily muscled bears, moose, and African plains game. That was the theory anyway. I didn't own a chronograph, but a cranky old gunsmith who lived on the state highway toward Bonney Lake did. He had kind of taken me under his wing. He even gave me little carefully-marked paper cups full of different powders to try so I wouldn't have to buy a whole pound just to load a dozen cartridges. We could check velocities at his shop range, where I usually did my sighting-in. Accuracy plus velocity plus bullet construction should give enough for a brief article to add to the debate.

My other rifle was a trim Ruger bolt-action in 7mm Mauser, a gift I gave myself to celebrate my decision not to take the transfer to Washington, D.C. The famous African hunter Karamojo Bell reportedly harvested tons of elephants with the 7mm, not recommended practice for any but iron-nerved professionals. Jim Corbett, the celebrated hunter of man-eating tigers in India, once used a 7mm when he had nothing heavier to drop a big Bengal that had recently feasted on a hapless villager; Corbett called it a .275, but it was the same cartridge. The Spanish used 7mm military Mausers to give the Rough Riders hell in Cuba, and Boers armed with 7mms ran rings around the British in South Africa. I had always wanted a rifle chambered for the round for sentimental reasons, from reading all those adventures when I was young.

I warmed up with a few shots from the Ruger, and walked down to check the group. The Ruger had mild recoil, about like a twenty-gauge, and its sharp crack was completely muffled by my shooter's earmuffs. The new Redfield scope was off; I was throwing them low and left about five inches. The group was okay but nothing to write home about. I dialed the scope in and shot another group. This time the holes in the target puddled over the bulls-eye, a little larger than an inch. I adjusted the scope again, to throw about three inches high, and trudged back through the steady rain. The third group was satisfactory; I was sighted in if I decided to take the Ruger deer hunting.

The big Remington kicked quite a bit more. I once ran 56 rounds through it one long day at the range, wearing a light flannel shirt, and felt a little punchy afterward. This time I draped its soft case over my rain jacket to soak up recoil and fired for group with my usual hunting loads, to check the zero. The Weaver four-power, old as the rifle, hadn't moved over the summer and the group was under an inch, with two of the three holes touching; the same accuracy the big rifle had right out of the box that first Christmas.

So I broke out my new hand loads. Equal and opposite reaction being what they are, the heavier bullets made the gun buck noticeably more than 150-grain deer loads. When I walked through the rain to check, the point of impact had moved. That was to be expected, but the group had opened up to two full inches. I didn't like that. Maybe my hand-weighed powder charges were inconsistent. Maybe I had flinched a little after the first heavier recoil. I went back and tried again, this time concentrating hard, letting the break of the trigger take me by surprise. That tightened the group to just at an inch and a half. Maybe I was demanding too much. Anybody using the heavier loads on heavy game would not be firing at long enough ranges for slightly larger than one-inch groups to matter.

Daylight was beginning to fade under the trees. I adjusted the zero to move the new heavy slugs onto the bull and fired another group, trying not to hurry. Muzzle flash lit the interior of the camper shell. To the unaided eye, the targets were just a pale blur now. I went up to check. The group was still over an inch, but right above the bull. I decided to call that good for my first effort with the heavy bullets. Trying to race the falling light would just open the groups, and prove nothing about the load.

I was carefully peeling the wet targets off the frames when somebody spoke behind me, a deep gravelly voice. I felt like I jumped a foot; I guess all this talk about wild men and Bigfoot had slipped into my subconscious.

"Reasonable shooting," the voice said.

He stood maybe a dozen feet away from me in the glade, a literal giant of a man, almost a head taller than my six-feet plus. Grinning, showing snaggle teeth. His fuzzy old green wool mackinaw looked as if it was soaked clear through with rain, and water ran unchecked down his big bald dome to soak his wild beard and drip from his bushy eyebrows.

He was between me and the rifles in the truck.

This all flashed through my mind in an instant. Then I noticed his feet. They were big. They were big and hairy. They were big and hairy—and bare. He was standing in a puddle and didn't even seem to notice.

"I *said*," the deep voice raised and boomed, "pretty good shooting."

"I thought you said 'reasonable.' "

"Huh! Heard me the first time huh? I thought you might be deef from blastin' all them rounds inside that truck shell."

"I've got earmuffs. I left them in the truck."

"Smart man," he said. "I usta be a huntin' guide. Shot too much with no *kwolan kloshe nanitch*. No ear pertection. So I'm getting' on for *ikpooie kwolan*. Deef as a stump. 'Course I'm pret-near old as these hills, so you gotta expect some deficiencies."

He seemed friendly enough, but he had come on me like a ghost, and some of his words sounded like gibberish to me. That, and his big bare feet, spooked me. I wondered how the dogs had not heard or scented him, even inside. Ghosts don't have a scent, my grandmother would have said.

"You all sighted in now, for deer season?" the stranger

asked.

"Close enough." I took a couple of tentative steps to the side, thinking to walk around him back to the truck. "If you don't mind my asking," I said, "where the devil did you come from?"

He laughed, a big booming haw-haw, and seemed to notice the rain puddling in his thick eyebrows and dripping in his eyes. A big paw went up and swept the water away, then squeegeed his scalp. The ends of his eyebrows stood up like horns when he put his hand down. While his elbow was raised, I saw a big sheath knife on a rope belt around the sodden jacket. It looked bigger than a Bowie; hell it looked as big as a Roman soldier's gladius.

"I wuz walkin' by up on the road," he said. "Heard the shootin', and came down to see what was up. I kinda *kloshe nanitch* up here in the Gorge."

"You what?"

"*Kloshe nanitch.*"

"I would have sworn you said 'closely manage.'"

The big laugh boomed again. "Close enough. Means keep watch, in Chinook Jargon. You gonna stand there and let them targets soak to pieces?"

I had forgotten I was holding them. I used his reminder as an excuse to move toward the truck, kind of crabwise. Chinook Jargon; that must have been the other gibberish too. But he didn't look like an Indian; this was getting weirder and weirder. I didn't want to put my back to him and that big knife. He turned and drifted with me, big feet planting so softly in the puddles there was no splash.

"You walk soft for such a big man," I said when I

reached the truck.

"There's a trick to it. No shoes help quite a bit."

"Aren't your feet cold?" Talk about your inane conversation with a giant weird stranger in the dusk in a vanished coal town.

"Naw, there's a trick to it," he said. "Friends a' mine in the Himalayas taught me. Some a' them Nepal holy fellers, yuh know?"

For crying out loud; I half-expected gibberish he would describe as Nepalese for "there's a trick to it." I knew there were strange people in these hills, but this apparition was taking the cake. Some kind of religious hermit? Or a lunatic escaped from a horror film? I was close enough to grab one of my rifles now. But of course both of them were unloaded. I wondered if my old infantry training in butt strokes would come back to me if I needed it. I was half afraid the walnut stocks of my sporters would just shatter on that man-mountain if it came to that.

"Didn't mean to make y' nervous," he said. "Onliest reason I injin'ed in here was cause it's dangerous to spook somebody with a loaded *calipeen*."

"Rifle?" I guessed.

"*Kloshe!*" he said with a big grin. "Means *right*," he added.

"I'm not going to ask whether that's Chinook or Nepalese," I said.

He had a rumbling chuckle. I couldn't make out his features in the gathering dark. He was just a huge man-shaped shadow with voice like an out-of-tune pipe organ. He didn't respond to my crack, but kept on talking.

"Nearly spent time in a hoosegow in Nepal after the

colonel's lady-wife got nervous with her *calipeen* in camp that time."

I was under the tipped-up gate to my camper cap, out of the worst of the rain. Other than that one move to clear his eyebrows, he didn't even seem to notice the rainfall. I leaned into the truck bed and put down the targets and came out with my Remington, the bolt still open where I had left it to cool after the last shots. He didn't seem to notice that either.

"It's not loaded," I said, tipping the action toward him.

"Good safe gun handlin'," he said in an approving rumble. "Too bad the colonel's lady-wife didn't. Course they was some said she did it a'purpose."

"What did she do?"

"Huh. Blew the back of his head off with a .30-06, that's what."

"Jesus Christ!"

"Huh. *Saghalie Tyee*—Jesus—shore warn't in Nepal *that* night. Had to pack that poor soul all the way down the mountain from huntin' camp on them little horses they got. About like a Shetland pony to me. My feet dragged." He chuckled hoarsely. "And then the local con-stabb-u-lary, bless their little Oriental hearts, almost tossed me in the jug. Good thing I was on good terms with them holy fellers."

Of course my son took that exact moment to wake up and raise a howl about the state of his britches and being in the dark.

"That young'un do have a set of lungs, don't he?" the big man said. "Guess that makes you the feller up here to write about the coalmines an' all. Figured so."

"You know about that?"

"Huh. Everybody in the Gorge knows about that. We talk to each other, you know."

At the door of the cabin, Harry let out a loud woof. He sounded confused.

"Heard us talkin'," the big man rumbled. "But he can't wind me. All I smell like is the wind and the *snass*. Rain," he added before I could ask. "He a good dog?"

"The best," I said.

"Better keep him close, up in here. These woods is dangerous for good dogs."

"Yeah," I said. "Mildred Fenton told me about her King today."

"You know Mildred? A good woman. Now that with King was a crying shame an' a tragedy. But it goes to show what I mean about it bein' dangerous up here for good dogs. You better go tend to your young'un."

"Soon as I get my rifles put up."

He chuckled. "And soon as I go back in whatever hole I crawled outta, huh? Time I was headed home anyway. I'm goin'."

He dematerialized. I never heard him go. My son continued to wail. Harry woofed again, and you could almost see the question mark at the end of it. I slipped a round in the Remington's chamber and closed the bolt quietly. The rain beat down. I slung the Ruger on my shoulder and closed and locked the truck and made my way cautiously to the door.

Harry wanted to come out. His hackles were up and he had that focused look he got when he locked on a wounded honker. But I wouldn't let him out. Not until I had a fully loaded rifle and a flashlight. I locked the cabin door behind me and went to tend to my son.

Chapter Eight

The dogs needed to get out and do their business, and paced back and forth at the front door, their eyes following me for any sign I was about to head that way. It was pitch dark now, and I had every light on in the cabin. I got my son cleaned up and dry, and damned if he wasn't hungry again.

My nerves were twitching as I went through the domestic motions of fixing him a bottle. The dogs knew something was different; they could read my tension like an open book. That added to their nervous pacing. I felt like yelling at them to down and stay, but I wasn't upset with them and managed to control myself.

When I had the boy settled with his bottle on the old couch, I dug into my big old wooden box where I stored my camping stuff and came out with my duck-hunting lantern. I hadn't even thought about it when the lights flickered from the storm, but now I wanted its candlepower. It had a big spotlight mounted on top of a six-volt battery and Eveready claimed its beam could reach a quarter-mile. It certainly had lighted up many a pre-dawn duck marsh.

The dogs just about stampeded past my legs, when I opened the door. I had the Remington slung upside down behind my left shoulder, European style, for a fast draw if necessary. The beam from my lantern lit up the meadow like a stage, throwing long shadows behind the dogs as they sniffed and urinated; stabbing long bright corridors down the cathedral aisles between immense fir trunks beyond the clearing. As soon as he relieved his bladder the first time, Harry made straight for where my barefoot visitor had stood, put his nose down, and started toward the woods. Maybe the stranger did only smell of wind and rain, but it was a wind and rain that Harry could trail.

I called him back. I didn't want him going out of my sight. Paka did her business with a lady-like squat and then did her own search of the meadow, but stayed close. I stood in the doorway with the lantern so I could keep an eye on my son on the couch. I had added a couple of pieces of coal to the fire in the grate, and didn't want him wandering over there while my back was turned. I had locked him in the bedroom with the dogs while I worked with the rifles to keep him out of trouble, trusting either him or Harry to let out a howl if they needed me. I was still learning what a twenty-four hour job it was, looking after a kid.

I gave the dogs ten minutes. Not really enough to stretch out the kinks, but I couldn't control my nervousness beyond that. The cabin that had seemed so cozy in the storm now felt like a trap. I had been enjoying the isolation of not having a phone after so many years when a phone ruled my life. Now I badly wanted to reach out and talk to someone in the real world, reassure myself it still existed out there.

It was a measure of my unease that I now thought of my odd little Brigadoon on the lahar as part of the ordinary outside world. The Gorge had altered my perspective of "strange." The closest pay phone was in

Wilkeson; I used it each night to check in with my wife. She was lonesome, but supportive of my effort on the story because of her own connection to this weird Gorge. She was glad the boy and the dogs were having an adventure. Thinking about the phone, I got the dogs back inside and put food down for them, then banked the fire and dressed my son in his coveralls and puffy fake-down jacket and a cute little watch cap.

He clapped his hands. "Goin' ridin?"

"Yes we are," I said.

"See Raff?"

It took me a minute to decode. "No, not tonight, son."

He was disappointed but not for long and was all ready to go when I got into my leather bomber jacket with some rifle cartridges in the pockets.

"Can you walk with me to the truck?" I said.

He stuck a hand up to hold. I had both rifles, one slung over each shoulder, unwilling to leave one in the cabin with the big hermit or whatever he was wandering loose. The dogs scampered out. My son happily stomped his yellow boots through each puddle we passed. The rain was slacking off. A chill breeze that promised real cold created movement everywhere. The big lantern's beam stabbed deep between shadowy trees and chased every boogeyman. But the sodden woods seemed alien and strange to my newly jaundiced view.

The dogs kenneled themselves promptly—they liked going for a ride as well as my boy did. I slipped my Remington into its leather saddle scabbard along the bottom of the truck seat, butt toward the driver's door, and put the Ruger behind the seat before I lifted my son up.

The Ford's bright headlights swept the gently thrashing foliage as I turned up the muddy track to the county road. Under that blast of light the place was just a meadow; the encroaching forest was just a tangle of big trees, improbable fans of ferns, and skunk cabbage.

The ruts were full of runoff and the truck's rear end danced a little. We made it up to the road without too much slipping and sliding. In less than ten minutes we were passing the boarded-up sandstone fortress that was really a grammar school, and bumped across the rusty rail spur into beautiful downtown Wilkeson. Muddy vehicles lined the narrow road in front of the handful of establishments.

It was only seven o'clock but seemed far later; the dense Gorge night seemed to squeeze brightness out of few lights. They were still pumping at Boots Rubery's gas station. Lights were on in the tavern, the little general store, and at the Pick n' Shovel. The little restaurant and bar was the closest thing to a tourist attraction in town. Hikers and day-trippers on their way to the national park stopped there for the local color—wood floors, log walls, old mining equipment mounted on the walls—and stayed for good burgers and the Tillamook ice cream. It was the only local hangout besides the Eagles Club, and I wasn't an Eagle.

When I got my son out on the cracked sidewalk, I could hear a low buzz of conversation from the Pick 'n Shovel. I decided to put off calling home until I settled down some, and we went through the cowboy-movie batwing doors. The first person I noticed was Bob Petoskey, hunched over a table in back and expostulating to several men and women, waving his hands. He wasn't loud, but he didn't look happy. He glanced up when I came in and immediately beckoned me over. The waitress arrived at the table the same time I did, a slim young blonde in Levis and a down vest.

"I bet that young man wants some Tillamook ice cream," she said.

My son clapped his hands and tried to say Neapolitan. I won't even try to duplicate the sounds. I translated. She went away to get him a bowl of ice cream—one scoop of each flavor, since they didn't have Neapolitan—and me some coffee. Petosky pulled up a chair for me and introduced me to his audience, the men all gyppo loggers and some of their wives.

"You got here just in time to hear my rant," he said. "That's good. It belongs in your story."

"Okay," I said. "What's up?"

"The goddamned mine inspectors have closed me down," he said grimly. "I met with them today. No dice on an exemption. They're gonna make me dynamite the shaft closed!"

Chapter Nine

Petosky's announcement gave me a warm rush of something like gratitude, because it chased Gorge phantasms out of my mind with a real by-God news story about destruction of the last coalmine. I helped my son spoon some strawberry off his dish of three flavors before I reacted to Petoskey's anger.

"So," I said neutrally. "The end of an era."

He blinked. "Yeah, I suppose it is. I was so God-damned mad I wanted to cut their heads off and shit down their necks."

"Bob," one of the women said. "There's a child present."

"Shit!" he said—and then almost comically covered his mouth. "Sorry. Joan's right. Sorry. But that's the last operating mine on the Wingate Seam," he said, voice rising. "I'm out of business. Dammit, that hurts! Coal is in my blood."

"Why exactly are they closing you down?"

He had alluded to problems his little two-man operation was having with the mine inspectors when I first met him. He now explained the issue, punctuated with profanity—immediately apologized for—and sweeping gestures. I bounced my son on my knee between each bite—one chocolate, one vanilla, one strawberry—and listened.

"Federal regulations!" The twist he gave it made it

sound like profanity. "The government passed a bunch of safety regulations aimed at those big East Coast mines that keep blowing up and killing people. I asked for an exception."

"No grandfather clause for small operations like yours?"

"Nope. We were never on Congress's radar—they probably didn't even know we existed out here. A few of the shoestring outfits asked our Congressmen to get an exemption clause tacked on, so the inspectors held off. But the amendment never got out of committee. They told me today." He rubbed his face with both hands.

"So it's curtains for King Coal up here."

"I guess it is. God *damn,* I hate this."

"Bob..." Joan was a plump, peaches-and-cream redhead who didn't like him ignoring her self-appointed role as protector of my son's ears. But my son had other things on his mind.

"Raff!" he said loudly. "Da! Raff!"

Mildred Fenton and the big shambling veteran stood in the door. She gave me a little wave as they moved to a table. My son was squirming like crazy.

"Raff, Da!"

"I'll be right back," I said. "My son wants to see Ralph."

Petoskey laughed. "They're about the same age mentally. Poor Ralph."

"Sorry to intrude," I said. "My boy just had to see Ralph."

The old veteran's face lit up. "Hey, little dude. Roll any checkers lately?"

"Raff!" my son said. "Down, Da!"

I put him on his feet and he marched around the table and raised his arms. Ralph scooped him up and sat him astride a big knee and began to bounce.

"Horsey!" my son said. "Da, Raff do Horsey!"

"Ralph has made a fast friend here," Mildred said, smiling. "I bring him here for the ice cream. From your son's face, I see he's already had some." She picked a paper napkin off the table and reached over to dab his mouth. He scrunched up his face and pushed her hands away.

"Horsey, Raff. Do horsey!"

"I can't do horsey and eat ice cream too, little dude."

My son thought this over. "'Kay! Ice cweam!"

"Can he eat ice cream with Ralph like they did today?" Mildred asked. "Ralph talked about your son all afternoon."

"Sure," I said. "I did want to ask you something."

She gave me a look. "About Mr. Tuchi's wild men?"

Ralph looked up. "Wild men? Norgus porgus, carry yorkus!"

My son looked up at him with fascination. "Norga porga, Raff?"

Once more, an ordinary Gorge conversation had veered straight into the Twilight Zone. I knew that phrase, from a book I'd read long ago. I was so surprised I forgot I wanted to ask Mildred the name of the barefoot giant who said he knew her.

"Where did Ralph pick that phrase up?" I said.

"Ralph may be...damaged," she said slowly. "But he remembers things. He knew some of those—those *wild men* that Mr. Tuchi talks about, back when he was a young cowhand. Before he went to war."

"Norgus porgus carry-yorkus," Ralph said triumphantly.

"He *knew* some of them? Here?"

"No, no," she said. "Montana, the summer range in the Rockies. He said skooks came out of the high timber and scared the cattle with their stink." She paused. "He said they never harmed any livestock. They tried to talk to him. That's the best he can describe how they sounded."

The waitress was standing patiently by. "The usual for Ralph, Mildred?"

"Ice cream!" Ralph said. His little echo repeated it happily.

"I'll go get my son's bowl," I said.

"Thank you," Mildred said. "Your son has made Ralph's day. It warms my heart. Your son is such a good boy."

I smiled, but my mind was whirling; I would have bet ten dollars Ralph had never even heard of the book in which I read the phrase he popped out with. I decided to file that away and check my library when I got home, and went back to interview Petosky while he was still wound up. But Petoskey had another wrench to throw in my spinning brain before he got back to his laments.

"I hear you met Joe Consonants today," he said.

"Joe—Consonants?"

He smiled. "Not his real name of course. He's middle European stock, his daddy was a miner. One of those strange names with so many consonants you can't get your tongue around it. Hence, Joe Consonants."

"The only person I met today was a giant who runs

around barefoot with a short sword on a rope belt and mumbles in Chinook Jargon."

Petoskey laughed. "That'd be Joe. The jargon is part of his tourist act. He stopped by here for coffee. Said you're pretty good with a rifle. High praise, from Joe. He's a legend in the Gorge. The tourists love his tales."

"He started to tell me one. About a hunting accident in Nepal? It seemed a tad far-fetched."

"No, it actually happened. Well, at least the colonel died of a gunshot wound over there. His wife came back and lived in Carbonado for a while. I think she had a thing for big Joe, but he lives in a cave up toward Mowitch. She couldn't corral him indoors."

I tried to imagine the huge man as the object of a lethal Army widow's affection; I couldn't quite bring that into focus. It was a lot easier to imagine him living in a cave. If "skooks" wore wool mackinaws and carried giant knives, Joe would *be* one. He had big enough—bare!—feet to make somebody wonder at his tracks.

"Somebody really hired him to guide them in Asia?"

"The colonel did. Got all his paperwork taken care of, paid all his expenses. Said Joe had the most experience with what he was hunting."

"In the Himalayas? I don't get it."

"The colonel hired Joe to hunt him up a Yeti."

Chapter Ten

When I got her on the pay phone outside the Pick 'N Shovel, and after I filled her in on our son's new buddy Ralph, my wife was sad to hear about the Petoskey mine being shut down. "I'll call his wife tomorrow to commiserate. Poor Bob's going to be miserable."

"He liked your pie," I remembered to tell her. "Said you were a chip off the old block, the old block being your mother."

"They're really good people," she said. "I don't suppose there's any chance your story might affect that decision on the mine."

I sighed. She was remembering other places, other unreasonable or unjust things I had stopped or reversed as an investigative reporter.

"I doubt it," I said. "It's just a Sunday feature story. This development gives it an up-to-date hook, but I'm afraid that's all. Remember, I'm just free-lancing these days."

We thought about that. Finally she said, "Have they taken you to see the coke ovens yet?"

"A lady named Mildred Fenton did. She's the one who was hosting the Soldier's Home guy, Ralph. You know her too, I suppose."

"Of course I do." Her voice tightened, meaning she didn't like what she knew. "I knew her husband too. He wasn't from around here. He ran off with a blonde go-go dancer from one of those joints in Tacoma."

"He must have been an idiot."

"Now don't," she said drily, "go making eyes at Mildred. She's not your type."

"I didn't know I had a type."

"Well you do—and I'm it. Are you coming home tomorrow night?"

"That's still the plan, unless the skooks chase me out of the Gorge."

"Uh-oh, who have you been talking to? I'm surprised they mentioned that to an outsider, even one related by marriage."

"So you know all about Bigfoot," I said.

"You forget, dear," she said sweetly, "I *sleep* with Bigfoot. When he's not off chasing Veteran's Administration nurses anyway." She never let me forget my old boss's wisecrack. But adding that snarky comment about nurses meant I probably shouldn't mention that Mildred had eyes like Elizabeth Taylor's.

"You think there really are wild men up here in these mountains?" I said instead. "That's what old Mr. Tuchi calls them, wild men."

"You really have been doing your homework," she said. "How is Mr. Tuchi?"

"Spry, and sharp as a tack. When he got into remembering the old days you could almost see the coke ovens aglow on a winter evening."

"All gone to dust now," she said.

"Well, alders and moss and skunk cabbage, to be perfectly accurate," I said. "But gone, just the same."

"Bob said after the Second World War, those old-timers used to tell the younger miners to just hang on for a few more years," she said. "They were just sure the mines would come back, now the government knew the quality of the coal from those wartime operations."

"But it didn't happen."

"No. The younger men mostly do gyppo logging now. But a lot of them had to move away to find work. And now the last little mine is being trampled by the government. That's so sad."

"Bob told me tonight he has coal in his blood," I said. "I think they all do. Except maybe Joe Consonants. Joe told me he smells like wind and *snass*, which he assures me means rain in Chinook, so that's why Harry and Paka didn't smell him coming down to the cabin. He moves like a ghost, big Joe. A bare-footed ghost."

"It's not quite cold enough yet for his shoes," she said matter-of-factly. "When it's real winter time he'll dig out those old clod hoppers of his. So Joe came to see you?"

"And of course you know all about him, right? The legend that walks like a man—barefoot?"

She laughed. "Joe's perfectly harmless. You sound like he spooked you."

"A ghost that materializes out of nowhere, to comment on my target shooting? Yeah, he spooked me."

She was still laughing. "I'm glad you didn't shoot him. Did anybody tell you they had postcards made with his photograph to sell up there to the tourists?"

"That detail has escaped my attention."

"Joe told my mom he was very proud of that. When Mom drove that rural mail route from Burnett to the park boundary, she'd give him a ride in the bad weather. She was one of the few he'd take a ride from. He walks all the way up and down that Gorge road, and all over the hills besides. Says it keeps him young. But he liked talking to Mom."

"Everybody liked talking to your mom," I said.

We talked a little about her mother, a divorcee of South Dakota pioneer stock who came out to Tacoma to look for work and married into the Northwest when a rugged Norwegian logger latched onto her. I had married into the Northwest when I latched onto their youngest daughter. They were both gone now, her mother just two years ago. We talked about some of her mother's adventures until Mildred and Ralph came out, my son toddling happily between them with a hand stretched up to each. The ice-cream social was over.

"Wants to talk to his momma," the old vet said, and told the "little dude" he'd see him later. They walked off while my son yelled "Bye Raff, bye!" I held him up to the phone. "Mo! Mo!" he hadn't quite got the second M for Mom yet. "Raff do horsey! Blay cheggers, Mo!"

We were all laughing by the time he finished his recital. I snuggled him against my shoulder to say goodnight. Her knowledge about big Joe, coming on top of Petoskey's strange tale of an Army colonel obsessed with bagging a yeti, had stilled my qualms about going back to the cabin. Joe was, in fact, just the local character. Every neighborhood in America has one, but—being the Gorge—Joe had to really be weird to be noticed. I didn't say that. My wife was very protective of the sensibilities up here.

"Have you heard a weather report?" she asked when we got ready to say good night.

"I don't even have a radio up here, remember?"

"Well keep your eye out. There's a big storm rolling in from north. That front that just came through was holding it off. Temperatures are supposed to really drop tonight."

"Joe might have to get out his clodhoppers."

She laughed. "You just be careful up there. Snow predicted for the higher elevations. Those roads can be really bad when it snows."

"If your mom could make it in that old mail truck, the Ford will be fine."

"Knock on wood!" She said.

"You spent too much time around my grandmother and her Southern superstitions," I said.

"Do it anyway, Smarty. I don't want those to be your famous last words."

So I pulled out my pipe and tapped on the bowl against the phone so she could hear it. Couples do silly things like that.

I got the dogs inside the cabin and the boy settled and the fire stoked up, then went back outside to feel the weather. The temperature definitely was dropping. There was that suspended sense of a storm pending. So I backed the truck around to aim straight at the muddy road, and pulled my bag of tire chains and bottle jack close to the tailgate between the kennels. Those chains had carried us through serious snows during Pennsylvania winters, and I didn't think the Gorge could offer anything worse.

At least in terms of a snowstorm, I was right.

Chapter Eleven

The boy was sound asleep when I got back inside. He'd had a big day and lots of fresh air, and I was betting he'd sleep right through even though it wasn't quite nine p.m. It felt later. I was yawning myself. I bundled him up in the down vest and sleeping bag and came back out to put on a fresh pot of coffee and transcribe a few notes about the closing of the last coalmine. The dogs were asleep in front of the fire.

I didn't make it a half hour on the typewriter. I just left a page halfway completed and moved to the couch to gaze at the coal flames and think about everything I'd seen and heard today. I was asleep before I knew it. The dogs woke me, cold wet noses shoved insistently into my palms. The wind had picked up, and there was an insistent whispering rattle on the tin roof. The dogs went to the door and waited. When I opened the door and beamed my big lantern across the meadow, it was snowing. Small hard kernels of snow slanted through the beam, first this way and then that way. The truck already had a thin coating.

I stood in the doorway out of the wind and watched the dogs track up the dusting of snow around the truck. Normally first snow got them all frisky and prancing, but this time they acted differently. Both of them had their noses down, crisscrossing like they were hunting. I was getting chilled without a coat, waiting for them to settle and do their business. They kept putting their noses up into the shifting wind and then back on the ground. Several times they sneezed violently, like something the wind told them was not of their liking.

"Hurry it up, guys," I said impatiently.

They looked at me, and went right back to their sniffing.

"If you didn't need to go, why did you wake me up? Do your business!"

Harry lifted his leg on a low patch of snow-sprinkled brush. Then he trotted stiff-legged to the edge of the cabin and urinated again on the corner. Paka watched him and finally squatted. Before she was finished, Harry had moved to the edge of the porch steps and doled out another teacup of yellow urine. Just for a moment, I thought his urine smelled awfully strong. Then I realized it was something else, a threading of stink on the wind, gone almost as I realized it.

Paka faced the dark and growled.

It felt like my neck hairs stood up. I had never heard her growl like that. Harry turned to look that way, and bowed his neck.

"Paka, come!" I said loudly. She glanced back, but that was all. I repeated it, even louder. "Get in here, dammit!" Her ears drooped and she came, glancing over her shoulder. Her tail was tucked tight between her legs. I motioned her inside and she went. Harry looked at me.

"Inside," I said. "Now!"

He went. I stayed at the door another long moment, pushing the lantern beam here and there. The snowfall was thickening and the beam bounced, not carrying deep into the woods like before. I closed the door and went to warm myself at the fire. Harry was slurping up water from his bowl, as if trying to replace all the liquid he'd spread around. He'd been marking his turf, I realized. Paka was backed up to the fire, tail still tucked, muzzle still wrinkled as if she was getting ready to growl again. She looked so half-wild and strange that I almost felt afraid of her.

"Paka," I said. "Down and stay!"

She didn't want to, but her muzzle smoothed out.

"Don't make me repeat myself, young lady," I said sternly.

She lay down, her eyes walled toward the door. Harry flopped down beside her, shoulder to shoulder, but did not relax. His gaze burned a hole in the door.

"I don't want you tangling with coyotes up here," I said to them. "Settle down now!"

I had both rifles back in the cabin. Now I loaded both of them. Either one was too much for a coyote, but it's what I had. Since I had re-zeroed the big Magnum for the heavier loads, that's what I charged it with. They would punch through a coyote without any expansion at all, but I wasn't sure what my scope tinkering would cause in terms of point-of-impact for my deer loads. It never occurred to me—then—to pivot the scope on its Weaver swing-away mount to use the iron sights.

I leaned the rifles on the couch and got another cup of coffee. The dogs' antics had driven sleep right out of my head. I wondered if Mildred's chickens were in for a raid tonight. I hoped her chicken coop was stout as it looked. The wind settled into a steady moaning around the corners of the cabin and I charged the fire with fresh coal. Gradually the heat began to permeate the whole room. The chuckling of the coal in the grate overpowered the soft hiss of snow on the roof. It was almost midnight.

I snapped awake to a loud crash on the tin roof. The dogs went crazy, howling like wolves, teeth bared.

"God damn it, hush!" I yelled. "It's just a branch that snapped off."

Crash. I flinched, and the dogs ignored me, raving like demented things. Was a whole damn tree coming down on us? I jumped up, stood over the dogs and yelled right in their faces. This time they shut up.

Something heavy was rolling down the slant of the tin above our heads. Its uneven progress sounded like an out-of-round bowling ball.

Tree limbs didn't make sounds like that. It reached the edge of the roof and I heard a heavy thud outside as whatever it was hit the ground. Before I could move, another missile landed on the roof with the same loud bang. Then a couple more, not quite as loud. The dogs started in again. This time I didn't try to hush them. I was too busy throwing on my Filson wool mackinaw and grabbing the Remington. I didn't have time to be afraid. I went straight to killing fury.

We were under siege.

Chapter Twelve

Chunks of rock were being rained down on the cabin's roof. That was what I heard rolling off, a rock. From the impact, they were big, heavy rocks. Which argued a lot of strength behind them. I had my Remington in my hands, facing the door. The dogs were there, scratching furiously, trying to get out. Their full-throated baying was deafening. But I still heard every missile that smashed onto the tin above our heads.

In the bedroom, my son woke up and added his squall of fright to the uproar.

His presence was what sent me straight to killing fury without time to be afraid. Endanger blood of my blood, and my Rebel genes know only one response: all-out war. I gripped the rifle tightly.

Out in the blowing night, something screeched in response to my son's wail.

It was the most blood-curdling thing I ever heard.

Something smashed against the front door like a sledgehammer. The dogs backed off, still raving.

I almost fired through the door. It was a near thing. Only a lifetime's rituals of safe gun-handling stopped me. My son was screaming in terror; the dogs were going crazy; the rocks kept raining down. Another one whacked into the door, hard. It shuddered under the impact. I had to see what I was confronted with before I fired.

But I knew.

All the joking and winking were over now; all the cynical disbelief about mythical cryptids dreamed up by tall-tale tellers. It takes me far longer to write it here than it took me to remember the 1924 Siege of Ape Canyon, and know history was repeating itself.

Mount St. Helens is famous now for its eruption, but in the 1970s it was still just another in the string of dormant volcanoes that included Rainier. In 1924, in a canyon near the mountain, a cabin full of rugged miners had been deluged by big rocks flung by huge hairy bipeds. All night long they were besieged, firing back out the window at dimly seem shapes, unwilling to go out to confront their attackers. One of the miners swore he dropped one. But at daylight there were no carcasses. The whole thing had been reported breathlessly by the Portland *Oregonian* on July 16, 1924. Fifty years before I thought it might be an adventure to camp out in Lower Fairfax.

Later, cynics said prankish kids from a YMCA camp up on the canyon rim liked to pitch rocks into the depths. They theorized what the miners saw, distorted by moonlight, was those capering youths. None of the YMCA campers ever had reported coming under sustained rifle fire from below, but facts never interfered with a good theory.

Another rock crashed into the door. I knew I couldn't keep the dogs from charging out if I opened it. But this had to stop. I had to deal with whatever was out there, and go see about my son.

I opened the door.

The dogs surged out, damn near knocking me off my

feet. Then I stumbled over a rock the size of a half-deflated basketball. My lantern probed the snow. The flakes were fatter now, coming down thickly, blocking the lantern's beam. I held my rifle one-handed, braced against my hip.

The dogs slammed to a halt just on the edge of the light's reach, growling, daring whatever was in the dark to come and fight. If they'd kept going they would have been all on their own. Maybe generations of hunting close to the gun kicked in to keep them close; I don't know. I grasped the fore-end of my rifle with my lantern hand and looked through the scope: white glare. Belatedly I remembered the swivel mount and pivoted the scope aside. The iron sights stood up blackly against the glare-back of the lantern.

That God-awful screech came again, from down at the river. The dogs turned as one. They stood rooted, their noses questing. Then I smelled it too, that tracery of skunk-like stink on the wind. Another part of the legend coming true. I don't know how many seconds ticked by. It seemed like hours.

The next sound was a truly horrendous crash, accompanied by the brittle tinkle of falling glass.

On the backside of the cabin.

My son shrieked. The dogs broke, racing for the corner of the shack, barking furiously. I stumbled after them.

The image that confronted me is burned in my brain.

Light streamed over a huge hairy form bent over, half in the window right above my son's bed.

Paka launched. She fastened her teeth into the thing's haunch and clung like a limpet. The thing screamed and jerked back out through the window. Eyes glittered redly in the lantern beam. It swiped Paka loose with a thick hairy forearm and she flew brokenly across the snow. The thing straightened on its hind legs. Its head was lost in darkness above the broken window. It turned toward the woods and Harry made his lunge. The thing shrieked again and yanked its arms high above its head as Harry fastened on its lower stomach.

I shot it square in the chest. I never felt the recoil or heard the shot.

It staggered back against the wall, jolted by that heavy partitioned slug. But it didn't go down. And it didn't reach for Harry. It turned, arms still high, and started for the woods again.

I shot it in the center of the back, trying for the spine.

This time it went down on what served it for knees, jarring Harry loose. He rolled clear, slow to get up. Before I could get another round chambered, the thing struggled up with a horrid vitality and ran, vanishing into the snowfall in a split instant. Harry shook his head and started to follow. I yelled at him and he stopped. He came to heel as I ran back inside to my son. The bed was empty. The bedclothes straggled out toward the shattered window. The stench in here was awful. That was why the thing had reached its arms up as Harry charged.

The damn thing had my son.

Chapter Thirteen

You never know how fast you can move until you absolutely have to. You don't realize you can focus every atom of your being into a laser-tight beam on a single goal until the crisis erupts.

I could say events blurred after I found my son gone. That wouldn't be accurate. I could say time stood still. That's not right either. It was like I stepped outside of time.

In my altered state, seconds ticked by like hours. I reloaded my rifle with preternatural care. I crammed extra cartridges in the pockets of my Filson. I went straight to where I had left the leashes for the dogs, though in normal life I forget such things and have to wander around like an absent-minded professor. I leashed Harry and looped the end over my left wrist. I grabbed the big lantern.

Then we went to get my son back.

In the back of the cabin, the lantern showed a spray of dark blood and tissue against the wall where my first shot went through. Paka was a still lump, snow already collecting on her body. No time to mourn; I forgot her as if she had never existed and let Harry tug me to the disturbed snow where the thing fell. Blood fanned out on the snow where the second heavy round had gone through. It was still steaming in the cold, which gives some idea of how few seconds it had taken me to get on the trail.

Harry put his nose down and pulled me forward. I had

my rifle slung muzzle down behind my left shoulder, the leash in my right hand and the lantern in my left. I wouldn't release Harry until it was time to shoot. This processional of thoughts marched through my brain with perfect clarity.

The blood trail was easy to follow. With the lantern I could have followed it without Harry. But it never occurred to me to waste time trying to leave him behind. He tugged me along as fast as I wanted to go, damn near trotting. Somehow my boots found the right spots on the uneven terrain without conscious thought. My breath exploded in white puffs, and sweat ran down my face, even in the cold. I was ready—and able—to follow that thing across the whole damn mountain range if it came to that.

Every so many feet, a pink froth of blood to the side of the disturbed snow steamed quietly. Lung shot, I identified dispassionately. That will slow it down. The trail led down along the river, and I experienced a burst of dread: if it forded the river I might not be able to follow. Immediately suppressed—I damn well *would* follow.

But it turned upstream, and stayed on this side. The land rose where the invisible rock walls of the Gorge began to close in. Running up any kind of grade would normally wind me quickly; this night, over lumpy uneven ground, half blinded by the snowfall, I didn't even notice. Under the Filson wool, my body was a furnace. Sweat was running down my back, soaking my armpits. I sleeved sweat out of my eyes without breaking stride, the lantern's beam stabbing wildly.

Harry growled. Then I smelled it—that terrible stench.

The vagrant wind had shifted, pushing that smell

down on us. Harry turned away from the blood trail. I tugged him back, but he resisted. He wanted to strike at an angle into the brush, following the airborne scent. The wind shifted again, and the scent eddied away. But not before I caught the metallic tang of hot blood. We were close. Then I knew why Harry tried to turn.

The thing was trying to circle us.

I gave Harry his head. We left the river and crashed through thick low-lying skunk cabbage and salal. Harry just kept driving, growling steadily now. We clambered over a windfall, a dead tree whose girth was waist-high. Another blow-down loomed ahead, a forest giant felled a long time ago by the vicious Gorge winds. It lay aslant the rising ground, partly elevated from the humus by the shattered stubs of its branches.

The lantern picked up a patch of wild mushrooms, torn and ripped. Red drops glistening. The thing had come between these two deadfalls. Harry wanted to go under, but it was too high for me to climb. I dragged him uphill to go around the base of the tree. I could see the root system standing far higher than my head where it had been wrenched out of the soil when the tree fell. I could still smell that awful odor on the shifting wind.

Harry hit the end of the leash like a freight train, tearing it from my numbed fingers. He plunged into the hole left by the tree's root ball, barking furiously. The bark cut off suddenly, replaced by his rumbling growl. I switched hands with the lantern, twisted my rifle up with my left and against my right shoulder in one movement and pushed up to where Harry had vanished.

The thing had gone to ground in the stump hole.

Harry had hold of its hindquarters, shaking his head violently, tugging backwards.

A tremulous little voice said, "Hawwy?"

The thing moved. It raised a massive arm weakly, as if to shield itself from the lantern beam. A weak mewing sound issued from its snout. Blood pulsed from an exit wound where its sternum would be, making a wet bubbling sound that my weirdly acute hearing picked up under the sound of the wind in the trees. Sucking chest wound, my turbo-charged brain supplied, snapping back to retrieve the phrase from my Army training days.

Then the arm fell limply, and something like a heavy sigh racked the huge body. It seemed to subside into itself. A thick trickle of blood wormed out of its nostrils. The stench was awful. I sidled forward and pushed the muzzle of my rifle against the thing's half-open eye. The eye didn't react.

I kept the muzzle pressed there, thumb on the safety, finger on the trigger, while I freed my left hand to move the lantern beam over the body. My son, naked except for his Pampers diaper, was tucked protectively into its elbow, pressed close to its breast.

Its breast.

The thing was female. He was sucking on the nipple. Lactation leaked from the other nipple in a flaccid breast above his head, and matted in its bloody fur.

My son raised his arm in unconscious imitation of the last movement of the beast, reacting to the light. He rolled his eyes back at me with that drugged look I remembered from before he was weaned. The nipple popped free and milk bubbles drooled down his chin.

There was blood spray from the lung wound on his diaper.

I wasn't ready to remove my rifle from contact with the dead eye. Adrenaline was roaring through me and I was panting hard, now the chase was over. I carefully perched the lantern in the body fur and moved the big arm holding my son. It flopped away loosely and he slid down. One-handed, I managed to get my left forearm under his armpits and lift him against me. He was warm to the touch from the body heat of that thing. In moments though he began to shiver.

"Coallll, Da," he chattered. It sounded like coal.

"It's all right, son. You'll be warm soon." My voice sounded creaky.

The lantern hadn't moved or shivered where it sat on the body. Harry kept worrying at it like he planned to eat it, but there was no reaction. The thing was definitely dead. I had to put my rifle aside to open my Filson and button my son inside against my chest. I hunched a little so he wouldn't slip down, and grabbed the rifle again.

The thing was still dead.

I drew in a deep breath, trying to shift mental gears from the locked-in death march I had been on. It was over. We had to get back to the warmth of the cabin now. I re-slung my rifle and used one hand to hold my boy in place, the other for the lantern. I found the end of Harry's leash and grabbed it in my lantern hand.

"Drop it!" I said sharply.

He paused in his fierce gnawing to look at me.

"Drop it, Harry." I tugged the leash. "It's over. We have to see about Paka. Let's go."

He gave one last vicious bite and turned loose. Once he was moving, he came along quietly.

"Good dog," I said. "Good Harry. You found him for us. Good dog."

Burdened with my son, I had to maneuver around the deadfall I crawled over on the way in. Once that was past, Harry took the lead again, back-trailing us to the river. A lot of tension had gone out of his posture. I hoped that meant there were no more of those things lurking. I didn't know if I could fight back with my son under my coat. My focus now was to get to lights and warmth. Fear began to niggle at the edges of my mind.

It seemed a long time to get to the river; I couldn't believe we had covered that much ground. It was a long slow trudge back to the cabin. There must have been at least two inches of snow down by then, and the wind turned my sweat-wet face to ice.

The door was standing open. I hadn't even remembered to close it. My son was asleep inside my coat. I locked the door and put him down on the couch under the Filson before I took my rifle to the bedroom—just in case. Snow drifted in the window, building a little pyramid on a big rock lying among glass shards. I gathered the sleeping bag and down vest and bedcovers and took them into the other room, closing the bedroom door against the draft. The fire was nearly out, but came to snapping crackling life with some cedar kindling before I added coal.

I didn't want to confront the issue of poor Paka. But I was damned if I was going to leave her for those things to do with as they had done to the husky King. I bundled my son up on the couch, waited until the room was getting warm, told Harry to stay, shrugged into my leather jacket and took my rifle and lantern out into the storm. Paka was just a white lump when I found her. When I brushed the snow off, she was already stiffening up. But I felt shattered bones shift when I lifted her.

That was when it all finally came crashing in on me. I stood there holding the corpse of my brave loyal Lab and started screaming curses into the teeth of the wind. I screamed until I was hoarse, holding her broken body against my jacket.

When I finally wound down, the tears came, hot and bitter, spilling on her fur.

Chapter Fourteen

I unlocked the back of the truck and laid Paka in her kennel. I tried to arrange her in her usual sleeping curl and kept trying to get it just right until I realized what I was doing and stopped. I had to get hold of myself; anything could sneak up on me while I was fussing with that. I patted her head and closed the kennel door. I couldn't form words. Those would have to wait until I buried her.

The snow was still coming down, the wind swirling it in every direction, creating nerve-jumping movements in the lantern beam. I picked my rifle off the tailgate and walked a circle about twenty yards from the cabin, trying to look everywhere at once, but mostly looking for fresh sign.

There were no new tracks in the snow. As I circled the cabin, the wind pushed the chimney smoke down across me; that old coal-fire smell of safe childhood winters on the other side of the continent from this wild and savage place. The lights of the cabin looked unreasonably cozy and cheerful against the dangerous night.

All I saw now was vulnerability.

When I completed my circle I went to the truck and cranked it up. When the engine settled to idle, I turned on the bright headlights. They blasted through the flutter of the snowflakes. I could see the road out, a smooth white ramp now.

"Truck, don't fail me now," I said, suddenly remembering my brag to my wife in some other lifetime, when the world was sane.

Back in the cabin my son was still asleep and Harry was grooming himself like a cat in front of the fire, licking his paws and then rubbing his muzzle on the carpet. He was leaving wet red smears; he had definitely taken a chunk or two out of that thing. He paused when I came in and I thought he might be waiting for Paka to follow. Who ever really knows how much their canine companions know? He went back to grooming. Maybe he had been sniffing the cold air I brought in with me, and it bore nothing more to alarm him.

I would leave almost everything here, come back alone in the daytime to get it. But I made one quick trip out with my Ruger and my typewriter case. I closed up the back of the truck. Harry would ride up front with us. I couldn't bear the thought of kenneling him beside his dead mate. I banked the fire and put Harry's leash back on—I wasn't about to risk an errant smell on that wind luring him away. He hopped in the front seat. I closed him in and went back for my son. Each trip I had my Remington slung so I could get at it quick.

I left the sleeping bag behind and wrapped my son in my down vest for the trip across the yard. Harry vacated the seat for the floorboards. Just in that short moment of sliding my son across the seat, my back felt horribly exposed. I leaned my rifle, muzzle down, on the floorboards beside my leg. I couldn't use the scabbard without getting out of the truck; if I had to open that door again I wanted to come out with the Remington in my hands.

The truck heater was putting out a lot of warmth by now. I rested my numbed hands up on the dash near the heat vents and settled my thoughts. Now there was only one task left: to make it up to the county road without stalling or sliding off in the brush.

I turned on the windshield wipers to clear the snow.

My heart nearly stopped.

Pinned in the truck's brights, now obscured and now not by falling snow, a huge figure was lurching down the road right at us, throwing a huge black shadow behind it.

I gunned the engine. The old 460 roared.

Run it down? Or get out and shoot? I shoved the shift into first.

The damn thing had a furry arm raised now, a big black paw held up like a traffic cop. The wipers slashed snow back and forth, and the wind-driven snowflakes surged. I eased the clutch in to avoid spinning the wheels, and we started to roll. The thing in the headlights picked up its pace into a shambling run, still coming right for us. It started waving that big paw in a completely human gesture, its other arm pumping with its awkward sliding run down the slope. It almost lost its balance—I saw it slip—and threw its arms out to the sides.

Its left hand held a rifle.

For one tiny fraction of a second I thought I had utterly lost my mind. In another split fraction, I finally realized what I was seeing. The furry arms were mackinaw sleeves, the black paws were mittens.

It was Joe Consonants.

He put that big mitt up to his mouth and shouted

toward me, "Wait! Please wait." His voice was so strong it overpowered the heater-blower, the engine, the wind.

I put the truck in neutral as he hit the flat ground and shambled toward me. In some corner of my mind I noted that he was no longer bare-foot. His old colorless britches were jammed into shin-high buckle galoshes, the buckles unsnapped and flapping as he ran. Galoshes, for a snowstorm.

He brought up against the wide nose of the Ford with a thump, bracing on his hands. He dropped his head and sweat gleamed on his bald dome. His breath plumed above him like a steam engine. He was panting heavily. His left mitten was wrapped around the receiver of his rifle, barrel slanted up into the snow. I put my foot down on the emergency brake and stepped out into the snow, bringing the Remington with me. I dropped it into the crook of my arm and turned. The barrel was elevated, but all I had to do was shift my grip to drop the front sight onto him. Harry whined. I shut my door softly.

"What do you want, Joe?" I said. "I'm leaving. I damn near ran you down."

He nodded jerkily. "I saw. I heard." He pushed himself off the truck and noticed my rifle. He nodded once more, and dropped his own rifle into the crook of his left elbow, pointed off across the Carbon River. A wordless acknowledgement that I had the drop.

"You know who I am now, I see." His breathing was coming under control.

"Joe, I'm leaving this place. Right now. I really don't have time for a chat."

"There's death in your voice," he said.

"I've got a dead dog in my truck," I said bitterly. "She was a good dog. A fine dog. Brave as they come. You told me these woods were dangerous for good dogs. You were right."

"What happened down in here tonight?"

"Joe, I don't think that's any of your business."

"Did yuh shoot your own dog then? Accidental, like?"

"Big man," I said, and didn't recognize my own voice, "you are right on the edge this moment. Right on the edge. Step back."

He squinted at me through the snowflakes. "You are a changed man."

Maybe he was right. I was seriously considering just shooting him on the spot. "I am a man on my way home, Joe. Leave it at that."

"I'm awful sorry about your dog," he said. "Other'n that, nothing else appears amiss, I see. Onliest reason I asked about the dog, I heard rifle shots way back up on the county road. Two of 'em. Big gun, sounded like." He glanced at my rifle. "Then later, a lot of the most God-awful yellin' I ever heard. I never heard such rage an' pain. I didn't even know the human voice could sound like that."

"You're sure what you heard was human?"

He still was squinting at me, his big head canted slightly. "I know human, and I know other. It was human."

"A kind of human," I said.

"The kind of human that made Neanderthal extinct." He wiped his black mitten across his still-perspiring face. He was so overheated there was actually a tracery of steam emanating from him, whipped away on the wind.

"I had to hoof it from Wilkeson," he said. "A fer piece

to run for an old fart like me. Some fellers from Carbonado took me far as the Wilkeson Eagles, but that's far as they were goin'."

"You need to step from in front of my truck," I said. "I'm taking my son and my remaining dog out of here now."

"You still got yore son? Praise be! I'm sorry I got here too late." He lifted the elbow cradling his old lever-action fractionally and I finally registered the size of the action and thickness of the barrel. This was no .30-30, this was an 1886 Winchester. They only came in old-fashioned big-bore rounds like .45-70 and .45-90. Joe had come loaded for bear.

"Don't s'pose Bob would mind if I went inside to dry out before I chill down and catch p-moany, and get a drink of water," the big man said. "I'm awful het up an' parched from all that runnin' at my age."

"Here." I dug out the cabin key, threaded to a small well-polished chunk of coal. "I left some stuff in there, so lock it when you're done. I'll pick up the key from Petosky."

The big man took the key and headed for the cabin. I waited, unwilling to make my run at the snowy road before he went inside. He was looking at the roofline as he reached the porch. Then he diverted and squatted by something in the snow. He came back to me carrying a big rock under one arm with all the effort I might use for a loaf of bread. He flipped the rock into the snow and wiped his mitt on his jacket front.

"You didn't ask me what I got here too late for," he said. "So I 'spect you know."

"Another time, Joe."

I left him standing in the snowstorm and drove out of there. The truck took us all the way to the top without a bobble. The roads hadn't turned to ice yet, and I drove very slowly and carefully, so it was an uneventful drive out of the Gorge. The snow thinned to minor flurries by the time I dropped elevation to State Road 410. There was some traffic back and forth on the highway, as if this were just another night. To my Gorge-attuned sensibility, they all seemed to be driving way too fast. I waited a long time for a good break in the traffic to get up on the highway.

So of course some idiot came zooming up my tail and stuck there, bright lights flashing for a pass though we were in a 35-mph speed zone. The asshole sat on his horn. I immediately pulled onto the shoulder. Instead of blasting past—why not, if he was in such a hurry?—the truck slowed and crawled by me, two bearded men in logging shirts flipping me the finger, faces contorted. Probably drunks on the way home from the tavern. I met their angry eyes calmly, knowing they were dead men if they got out of their truck and bothered me, on this night of all nights.

Whether it was my expression—I have no idea what my face showed—or they just thought better of it, the truck accelerated away. I sat for a long count, perfectly calmly, waiting to see if their beer courage returned. The truck stayed gone. Finally I snapped out of my lethal trance and headed home. Joe Consonants was right. I was a changed man.

How the hell was I going to explain all this to my wife?

Chapter Fifteen

When I turned into our driveway, half the lights in the house were on. I could see my wife looking out the kitchen window, almost like she expected us. She normally would have been asleep long since. She was on the front stoop, wrapped in her old maroon bathrobe, by the time I parked. As soon as I had our son in my arms, Harry bounded out the door and ran prancing and wagging to my wife.

They'd always enjoyed a special bond. She was the one who spotted him in a city pound on the other side of the country, curled up shyly in a puppy pen while the others stood on the wire yapping and trying to attract attention. When she stooped down and spoke to him, he uncurled and came right to her as if recognizing his savior; he was eight weeks old. She spent a lot of time spoiling him the year I was flying all over the place, and complained when he automatically shifted attention to me when I got home. I represented hunting dummies to retrieve, scent drags in the woods, duck wings tied to a fishing rod for him to chase, but she felt slighted. She really loved that dog.

Now she barely gave him a quick pat on his head. He sat wagging, waiting for more. Then he followed her as she came to me along the walk, still wagging but a little subdued.

"Is my son okay?" was the first thing she said.

Storm flags flying that had nothing to do with the

weather. When the boy irritated her for some reason, he was *my* son. When I failed to measure up to some unspoken standard as a father, he became *hers*.

Her voice awakened him. He popped his sleepy head out of the down vest and said, "Mo?"

"Thank god!" She took him away from me. "This old down vest of yours?" she said as if she couldn't believe her eyes. "Where's his winter jacket?"

"I'll get it tomorrow."

"You *left* it up there?"

She peeled my vest off and just dropped it in the mud. Turned on her heel, hugging him close, and marched back inside. Over her shoulder I could see she had a fire going in the living-room fireplace.

Harry looked at me. I looked at Harry.

"Welcome home, Harry," I said. "Now you say it."

The poor dog looked like he thought he was in trouble. I squatted and pulled him into my arms. "You're not in trouble, Harry. You're the best dog there ever was. Bravest, toughest, best. You and..." My throat closed. I couldn't say Paka's name, or he would start looking around for her.

I tossed the vest on the seat and sheathed my rifle in its scabbard, still loaded, before I locked the truck door. Harry examined the yard for evidence of interlopers before we went in. I didn't discourage him; I was fresh out of patience with nighttime surprises. By the time he re-established all the urine-warnings his bladder was good for, my wife was back on the stoop.

"Where's the boy?" I said.

"Eating Neapolitan ice cream. I bought it for tomorrow, but since you're home early I figured why not?"

The corners of my eyelids stung for no accountable reason. Certainly not because the boy was doubling down on his ice cream rations.

"Are you coming in?" she said. "The heat is getting out and I need to talk to you."

Now what had I done? The Gorge seemed off somewhere in another lifetime. "We're coming."

"Where's Paka?"

Harry cocked his ears at the name, and immediately started looking around. Goddamn it.

"Don't say her name again," I said. "Harry will get upset."

"What? Why? Where is she?"

"She's in her kennel."

"Well, let her out!"

"She can't come out."

"Why won't you let her come out? Did she misbehave?"

"I didn't say I won't let her out. I said she *can't* come out. And no, she didn't misbehave. She was as brave as anything I ever saw in my life."

"Brave? Is she hurt? We can call the vet..."

"No vet on earth can help her now."

"Oh, God. Harry," she said. "Come here, you poor old thing."

The only part he really got, I feel sure, was that finally he was getting his accustomed loving from the woman who rescued him. She sat down on the steps and cradled him in her arms, crying into his neck fur. The heat was still blowing out of the house; I thought it pretty wise not to bring that up right then. The woman's tempers were mercuric in the best of times. She had gone from snappish to sentimental in the blink of an eye.

I laid a hand on her shoulder and one of hers came up to cover mine and squeeze. "Are *you* all right?"

"I've been better. But I'm all right." I squeezed her shoulder gently. "Let's go inside. You can tell me what you need to talk about."

"Oh!"

She disentangled from Harry and stood up. He leaned happily against her bathrobe, his world put right. Baby-stealing monsters he took in stride but a momentary failure to show affection from his humans bothered him. He was some dog, Harry.

We all trooped into the kitchen where the boy announced loudly that he was having Neapolitan, Da! Though only his mother and I could have figured out the word. I noticed the red eye of the percolator burning on the counter and went for coffee.

"I put it on as soon as I knew you were coming," she said. "The roads were pretty bad up there, huh?"

"I took it really slow. But how did you know I was coming home tonight?"

"I didn't until the phone woke me up. It was Bob Petoskey. He told me you were on the way home. He was surprised you weren't already here."

"The thing is," I said, "how did Bob know? Last time I saw him, I was staying."

"Joe Consonants told Bob you left just before Bob got down to Lower Fairfax."

"Wait. *Bob* went down there tonight too?" It was like the damn Gorge was trying to reach out of the night and rope me back in. "Why?"

"He was in the Eagles when a couple Carbonado guys mentioned they gave Joe a lift. He wanted them to take him all the way to Fairfax but they wanted a drink before the Eagles shut down. Joe *never* demands to be taken to a special spot."

"Joe's habits seem to be a major topic up there," I said. "It was snowing like hell, and all he had on his feet was galoshes. So he wanted a ride a few miles farther along. So what?"

"So Joe had his Yeti rifle with him," she said quietly. "Joe told those Carbonado boys he was afraid the skooks were going to attack you. A lot of people in the Gorge worry about Joe and his Bigfoot obsession. That's why Bob lit out of there for Fairfax."

Joe's Yeti rifle; of course she had to mean the big old 1886 Winchester in .45-70 or .45-90 or whatever big-bore round it turned out to be. What else would he call it, after guiding the ill-fated colonel and his lethal lady in the Himalayas?

"Is it unusual for Joe to run around in the snow with his Yeti rifle?" The echo of my question sounded slightly mad to me.

"Bob was worried you were okay. He said he thought at first there had been some kind of land slippage. Some pretty big rocks did hit the cabin," she said. "But now he thinks maybe some Gorge kids just wanted to scare you. He was afraid Joe got it all confused and might shoot some stupid kid by mistake."

I pulled out a kitchen chair. "If somebody was dropping boulders on my head and killed...you know who...I would have shot them myself," I said. "And not by mistake."

She ignored that, hovering over our son, which he didn't mind as long as it didn't interfere with the trajectory of his ice-cream spoon. He was smeared almost up to his eyes in three different flavors. Harry leaned against her knee and studied each flight of the ice-cream spoon as carefully as a flight of mallards.

"You can have what's left when he's done, Harry," I said.

My wife looked at Harry. "Ice cream is the only thing on his entire mind right now," she said. "Yet he's a widower. Right?"

"If you use that term for dogs."

"Suppose you'd forget me that fast, if you were a widower?"

Jesus Christ. Here went that mercury skittering up and down the barometer of her moods again.

"Honey, Harry is a *dog*," I said. He cut his eyes at me when I said his name. "Dogs live in the now. That was then and this is now: ice cream."

"Nice avoidance," she said.

I sighed. Everything here was so normal that it was like the things in the Gorge had never happened at all.

Chapter Sixteen

We retired to our respective recliners in front of the fire. All the residual terror and tension soaked out of me on alder-scented warmth. Our son crawled out of her lap and over to Harry, sprawled by my chair, and rolled over on his back to use Harry's rib cage for a pillow. Harry blew out a gusty sigh and my son yawned widely and almost fell asleep before his mouth closed.

"He needs a bath something terrible," she said. "Couldn't you *smell* him? I took him right back and changed his diapers, but it wasn't that."

My mind was far away. "Wasn't what?"

"Poo," she said primly.

"Not much smells worse than baby shit," I said agreeably.

"You're half-asleep! I said it *wasn't* that. And yes, it did smell worse."

That stench had been around me so long up there in the Gorge, and I had been so utterly focused on other things, my mind must have shut off the receptors as irrelevant to survival. I bet my old Filson up in the cabin stank with it. Now that she had forced it to the top of awareness, I smelled it rising off my son and the dog—a thin, sour shadow of its full-blown reek, right in my home.

My rage against that Goddamned monster roared back so hot it choked me. I didn't feel I could speak past my knotted vocal cords. I started trying to breathe through it, like she did in our Lamaze natural-childbirth class. She heard it.

"Are you all right? Are you having chest pains? Your face is all red."

"I'm just really, incredibly tired," I managed to get out. "Far too tired to sleep."

"Will you go talk to Bob in the morning since he's so worried about his story?"

"I'm not taking my son back in that Gorge!"

"Why are you yelling?" she said. "You woke Harry up. You're going to wake our son up."

"I'm not yelling," I said.

"Were too."

"Maybe a little," I said. "I'll call Bob."

"What on earth has you so upset?" she said. "Did somebody really throw rocks on the roof of that cabin to try to scare you?"

"Who would do such a thing? I'm trying to write a story about their glory days!"

She sighed. "It wouldn't be the first time Gorge kids pulled a stunt on outsiders. They don't like outsiders."

"Thanks for the warning." My sarcasm was heavy.

"Just as well you don't go, with you in this mood," she said. "We can tell Bob the roads are too icy."

"That's not going to fly," I said. "Bob knows I have a fine air conditioner in my truck."

She gave me a dangerous look. "What are you talking about?"

"Why, that air conditioner should get me over black ice better than any four-wheel drive like *I* wanted to buy."

She jerked upright abruptly. "I hate you when you get

like this!" Her lower lip trembled. "And I was looking forward to a *happy* homecoming. Bring the baby when you come to bed. Asshole!"

She swept off down the hall. I didn't feel too bad about deliberately pushing her buttons. I couldn't let her get into her compassionate, caring mode. When she got in her compassionate, caring mode, no trained interrogator was better at worming out all the details.

And I wasn't going to give her the details. Not about this.

We had built a pretty decent marriage based on love and mutual respect and honesty. But I was not going to tell her that I slaughtered a lactating female skook that stole our child right out of my keeping. I sat and stared at the flames for a long time. After a while, my son woke up and climbed unsteadily to his feet.

"Mo?" he said.

"Gone to bed, son. Go crawl in."

"'Kay, Da." He toddled off down the hall. My hearing still seemed unnaturally acute. I heard every soft footfall down the carpet, heard the door open quietly, heard him speak, heard her answer—instantly awake like mothers everywhere—and then murmurs as he settled in with her.

The fire burned down to red-hot embers before I moved again, to add split alder. My face baked in the heat near the fireplace. I went to the kitchen and replenished my coffee. The house creaked, settling in the cold. The wind picked up. Everything seemed safe, sane; normal. Sheer illusion: I wondered if I would feel safe or sane or normal again in my lifetime.

I could hear Joe Consonants' cracked pipe organ of a

voice against the Gorge wind: *"The kind of human that made Neanderthal extinct."*

He sounded sad, not accusing.

But he had come running out of the night with his Yeti rifle, and told the Carbonado boys skooks were on the prowl.

"You are a changed man."

Was I? I didn't know about that. The old saying goes that circumstances don't make the man, they reveal him. Under the rock siege in the Gorge, I stood revealed to myself as well as old Joe. I walked back into the living room. Harry had appropriated my recliner, curled in a comfortable ball. I saw his eyebrows twitch, and read it like plain English: was I going to evict him now he was comfortable? It lightened me a bit.

"Stay right there, Harry," I said. "Stay in Dad's chair. You earned it tonight, in spades."

I detoured to my office, flipped on the overhead light and started browsing my bookshelves. We probably had five hundred volumes in there, from big hardbacks to twenty-five cent Pocketbook Westerns my uncles gave me when I was a kid. Books everywhere: on shelves along the wall, a shelf above the wide door, on low shelves under the picture windows facing the foothills. I was looking for the book that jumped into my mind when Ralph the shell-shocked Montana cowboy tried to emulate Bigfoot speech. I wasn't sleepy, and I didn't want to sit and consider why a lactating beast had stolen our son.

I would kill her again in a heartbeat, extinction or not. But my peculiar divided mind couldn't ignore the tragic implication of the theft, or my son nursing at that alien breast. Best not to think about it at all. And especially not to talk about it. Not with anyone.

I found the book I was looking for: *Wildfowl Decoys* by Joel Barber, "140 illustrations with 4 in Color." I sat at my desk to scan the chapters. My peculiar brain had a memory chip that told me just about where to look, though I hadn't cracked that particular volume in years. Page 46— I dog-eared the page so I could find it again. Chapter VIII, *The First Decoy.* Barber had been tracing the earliest published references to the use of decoys along the Eastern Seaboard, and quoted from "Sporting Scenes and Sundry Sketches," published in New York, 1842, by somebody named J. Cypress, Jr.

His purpose in quoting Cypress was to describe the hand-made decoys Cypress found in use by a Fire Island duck gunner, handed down by his great-grandfather who came down from Massachusetts after the Revolutionary War to take a small farm on shares. "The most of his time, hows'm'ver," the hunter told Cypress, "he spent in the bay, clammen and sich like. He was putty tol'r'bl' smart with a gun, too, and he was the first man that made wooden stools for ducks..."

Then this: having lain out overnight in his skiff with his decoys out, not many years after Cornwallis surrendered, "putty well hid, for 't was th' fall of th' year, and the sedge was smart and high" the old man heard splashing in the shallows and peered out of his hiding place. What he saw was "a queer-looken old feller waden 'long on th' edge o' th' flat, jest by th' channel, benden low down ... and his eye upon gr't gr'ndf'ther's stool. 'That feller thinks my stool's faawl,' says the old man to himself, softly, 'cause he expected the feller was an Injin, and there wa'n't no tellen whether he was friendly or not, in them times..."

The stranger waded among the decoys, picking them up and uneasily smelling of them. But he overcame his nervousness, yanked every decoy up by its anchor, slung them over his shoulder and started off. That was too much for the old man. "He didn't like this much, but he didn't want to get in a passion with an Injin, for they're full of fight...then he could see plain enough it was a merm'n ... so he sung out to him, putty loud and sharp, to lay down them stools, and he shoved the skiff out the hassack ... and got his old muskets ready...

"Well, the merm'n turned around, and sich another looken mortal man gr't gr'ndf'th'r said he never did see. He'd big bushy hair all ov'r 'im, and big whiskers ... He hadn't stich clothes ont' 'im, but the water was up to's waist, and kivered 'im up ... the merm'n began to talk out the darndest talk you ever heerd. I disremember 'xactly, but I b'lieve 'twas something like 'norgus porgus, carry Yorkus....'"

And there it was, in bald print from 1842, the exact phrase Ralph from the Soldier's Home had uttered tonight at the Pick 'N Shovel in Wilkeson. The book was silent on the outcome of the confrontation, but since the decoys were still there to inherit, they spoke for themselves. Almost two hundred years later, I recognized that silence. I wasn't saying anything about my confrontation either.

"The kind of human that made Neanderthal extinct."

I closed the book and leaned back and tried not to think about anything at all.

Chapter Seventeen

I buried poor brave Paka at about mid-morning the next day. The storm clouds had rolled into the mountains, which were bedecked with fresh snow, and the sky was blue and cold. I left the boy in his high chair in the kitchen with Harry, both with food to distract them, and the blinds drawn.

I emptied one of my canvas decoy bags for a shroud. She had stiffened into the sleeping posture I placed her in the night before, so I disassembled the kennel to avoid disturbing her rigor and tucked her snug in the bag. I punched through a couple inches of frosty mud to get to the rich black dirt behind the fireplace. Once I had the grave roughed out I spaded deep into the gray lahar mud; I didn't want anything disturbing her final sleep. When I got the dirt tamped back down I leaned on the spade, my throat tight. She deserved some last words.

Finally I just told her, "You always loved to lay by the fireplace, girl. So I put you on the other side of the chimney. What a brave girl you were last night. We got him back okay, baby. But who's going to fetch his alphabet blocks now?"

Grown men aren't supposed to stand by a dog's grave and cry. Screw that. Rudyard Kipling was a grown man when he wrote that poem about giving your heart to a dog, to tear. I cried for her again there in the bright sunlight, and then put up the tools and moved her disassembled kennel into the garage. That took all my remaining energy for the day.

I hadn't slept for more than a couple hours in my recliner before my wife's strident 6 a.m. alarm went off. She came shuffling out and we held each other and murmured, mending the hurt feelings around my unexpected homecoming. Then she headed off to shower and go to work and I went right back under. The boy woke me next, crawling into my lap.

He smelled all clean and soapy and well-powdered, and rubbed his head against my shirt. "'Zat *smell*, Da? He wrinkled his nose.

Some of that thing's stink had soaked into my shirt when I tucked my son under my coat. My late-night cigars while I sat in my office pondering the Barber book had killed my ability to notice until he brought it to my attention. I got him settled in his high chair with a bottle of chocolate milk and some banana slices, put food down for Harry, and left them to deal with Paka's burial.

When I got back inside, I could smell traces of that stench in my recliner. I was going to have to scrub Harry down, spray smell-good stuff on the chairs and carpets and double-wash my clothing. And clean my rifles ... The list just seemed to grow. After dealing with Paka, I couldn't face any of it.

My son had smeared banana chunks all over his clean shirt and half the kitchen table. He had apparently ingested enough milk and banana to occasion a horrific dump. For once I was glad to smell it—it chased the stench of that beast out of my nostrils. I wasn't sure that thing *did* smell worse than baby shit, as my wife claimed. But baby shit was familiar and normal.

I went through the motions of cleaning him up again like a sleepwalker, and went back to sleep in my recliner almost as soon as I sat down. My son was playing quietly with an ancient set of Lincoln logs from my own childhood. So far he hadn't seemed to notice Paka was missing, thank God. I had no idea how I was going to deal with that.

I was dreaming of Paka's first retrieve, a ruffed grouse she flushed from alder thickets up in the foothills when she was only six months old, when Harry woke me with his Hound of the Baskervilles roar. Before I was even awake, I had my Remington out from behind the recliner where I'd leaned it this morning. My mind was all twisted up between the shattered happy dream and a violent flashback to the skook.

Early dusk had descended. My son was curled up on his mother's recliner, sound asleep. Somewhere he had found his Binky and was sucking away in a steady rhythm.

I got all the way awake and realized I heard a truck in the driveway. I looked out the kitchen window, and saw Bob Petosky. I realized I had forgotten to call Bob. Joe Consonants was with him. There was a rifle in the window rack behind the pickup seat; Joe's Yeti rifle. I told Harry to hush, unloaded my rifle, and went to the door.

"You okay?" was the first thing out of Petosky's mouth.

"More to the point, is your boy?" Joe added.

Joe had traded his galoshes for low-topped round-toed boots like the ones Li'l Abner wore in Dogpatch. I guess that meant it was officially winter in the Gorge.

"We're fine," I said. "Come on in, the coffee's on."

Skook

My son was awake now, struggling down off the
recliner. Harry wagged at Bob and started forward but
stopped in mid-stride and studied big Joe impassively, his
tail out stiff. Joe's wind and rain smell had been
augmented by a tracery of skook. I told Harry to down and
stay in the living room, and we all trooped into the
kitchen. I brought the boy with me, got out cups and we
sat around the table.

"Did you get my message?" Petosky asked.

"I meant to call but I forgot."

Petoskey sighed. "That cabin is a mess."

"A bunch of big rocks came down on the roof, and one
came through the back window," I said. "Just like Ape
Canyon in 1924. The so-called experts said back then that
was students on a camp-out, giving the miners a hard
time. My wife said kids in the Gorge weren't above giving
an outsider—that's me—the same kind of hard time."

"God damn it," Petoskey said. "When I find out who
did that, if their parents don't kick their ass, I will!"

"It wasn't kids in Ape Canyon," Joe said flatly.

"You sound pretty sure about that," I said.

"I was there."

"That was fifty years ago!"

"I wasn't hatched yesterday."

"That's a yarn I never heard you spin," Petosky told
him. "About being in the siege of Ape Canyon."

Joe shrugged. "And it wasn't kids last night."

Chapter Eighteen

Petoskey helped himself to more coffee, and topped up our mugs. "Well, *something* sure happened up there last night," he said, "and it wasn't a land slippage." He sipped coffee and kind of smiled. "Joe tried to tell me it was skooks. But the only big footprints I saw at the cabin were his. The galoshes made 'em look even bigger."

"The snow covered skook sign," Joe said.

"Yeah, yeah, there's always some reason nobody ever quite sees one, or their tracks, except you," Petoskey said tolerantly. To me: "Joe said you went out of there like your tail was on fire. When you didn't call, I decided to come see if you're okay. I picked up Joe on the way. He was walking down here to check on you too."

I looked at Joe again. "Carrying your Yeti rifle."

"When they get that stirred up over something, it's not a good idea to wander through their territory unarmed, even for me."

"For God's sake, Joe," Petoskey said. "Quit trying to scare the guy to death. And try not to shoot some idiot kid by mistake, okay?"

"I am always careful with firearms," Joe said coldly.

"Sure, Joe, I know. Just kidding." To me: "Your son sure is fascinated by Joe."

"What?"

"Hasn't taken his eyes off him since we came in. Has he, Joe?"

Joe smiled in his whiskers. "He recognizes a kindred spirit."

"A kindred spirit?" I said.

"We each have been marked by skooks. Myself, when I was somewhat older than the tyke here."

Petoskey grinned. "Nah, he just thinks you're Santa, with all those grey whiskers."

Joe didn't even crack a smile. "Loss of your offspring is the most awful thing a sentient being can confront," he said to me "As you well know," he added.

I met his gaze. "And if I say I have no idea what you're talking about?"

"Keep saying that. It's the right thing to do. I know young Mildred told you what she saw last year. The lost youngling, chased to its death on the rocks by wild dogs."

"That was a retarded kid from the State School," Petoskey said. "They try to hush those things up, all right."

"Mildred thought otherwise," Joe said.

Petoskey shrugged. "Mildred was really upset when her dog was killed. Didn't believe wild dogs could have killed a full-grown Husky. We're going to have to do something about those wild dogs." He drank coffee. "The guy at the stone quarry thinks he's figured out where they den, up by the park boundary. We need to go in there and clean them out before they get one of our kids waiting for the school bus."

Joe nodded. "I can find them for sure. No more youngsters must suffer because of humanity's cruel neglect of its pets."

"Mildred told me everybody up there uses skook as a nickname for Bigfoot," I said.

"Chinook word was *skookum*," Petoskey said. "We shortened it over the years."

"Skookum," I said. "Skookum he-man: big and strong. An Indian word that entered the language, like hammock and other words Columbus and his crew picked up in the Caribbean?"

"The Southeast tribes had their own jargon resembling Chinook," Joe said. "Did you know that? Lost to history in the European conquest."

"Skookum gets used a lot in the Northwest," Petoskey said. "Businesses use it as part of their trade name. Skookum Off-Road Tires and so on. Accepted meaning, like you say, is big, strong and potent. But originally it meant ghost, evil spirit or demon. Each tribe had its own word for Bigfoot, usually meaning wild man, same thing old Mr. Tuchi calls them." He grinned at me. "It was an old-time newspaperman who standardized on Sasquatch, from a Vancouver Island tribe."

"Trust a newspaperman to invent a catchy name," I said.

Joe graced us both with a sad smile. "There have always been stories about skooks stealing babies. But a skook that would try to steal a baby from this man is a tragedy. On both sides."

Petoskey shook his head. "Steal his baby? You making up a new tall tale for the tourists, Joe?"

"The bedroom window was shattered by a boulder. You did notice that, didn't you?" Joe said. "And the blood on the outside wall?"

"I thought it was blood," Petoskey admitted. "Did you or your boy get cut by the glass?" he asked me.

I just shook my head. "You're quite the crypto-zoologist," I said to Joe. "But your only warning to me was to keep my dogs close. Even old Mr. Tuchi warned me about wild men. Not warning me is the next thing to enemy action, where I come from."

"I have no desire to be an enemy of such a lethal man." He didn't sound as if he were being ironical. "But you are correct: what happened up there was my fault."

"Why," said Petosky, "do I get the feeling that there are at least two more conversations than I know about going on in this room?"

"You were well-armed," Joe said. "Well-guarded by your brave dogs. Incredibly brave dogs."

"I don't think I want you talking about my dogs," I told him. "You don't have the right."

He rubbed a big hand over his face. "The habit of staying unknown is centuries-bred. I thought you were perfectly safe. So you're right to chastise me."

Before I could think of anything to say to that, we heard the loose shocks of my wife's Pontiac thumping and bumping down the potholed driveway. I looked at the kitchen clock. She was home early.

"We'll be going," Joe decreed, standing with an easy grace that belied his years. He bent his gaze down on my son. "Be well, young man. You have many interesting years ahead of you." It sounded like that Chinese curse. To me he said, "We will talk again. We must. I have an obligation now."

"I guess we're going," Petosky said, and sat his cup on the drain board. "Don't take Joe's ramblings too seriously," he muttered as he left. "Sometimes he can't seem to turn off his tourist patter."

Chapter Nineteen

Way back before the Second World War, Dashiell Hammett, who created Sam Spade and the Maltese Falcon, told a story about how people adjust their expectations when their world turns upside down. Hammett had been with the Pinkertons, assigned to look for the guy who inspired his story.

Simply told, this man was walking down a city street one day when one of those old-fashioned enormously heavy safes was being lowered from a building. The rigging broke. The safe buried itself in the sidewalk beside him with no warning, *ka-boom*. One moment he was a married man with an ordinary job and an orderly, predictable existence—the next he was a man who lived in a world where a safe could fall out of nowhere and erase him.

He walked away from his life without looking back.

The Pinkertons' search was fruitless. Years drifted by. Eventually the man was located in a city not much different from the city where the safe fell; married again, with an ordinary job again, once more leading an orderly, predictable existence.

Hammett said this guy adjusted his predictable life instantly to a world where safes fell from the sky by becoming so unpredictable not even the famous Pinkertons could find him. After enough years with no more falling safes, the guy adjusted his life *back*.

By my second night out of the Carbon River Gorge, I

was prepared to re-adjust to a predictable world where mythological cryptids don't steal your child and force you to kill them with real bullets. So far Joe Consonants was the only person who knew what happened up there. And I wanted to forget it. Particularly the pathetic dribble of wasted milk from the dead skook's mammaries. I didn't need years to wall off the terror to a far corner of my mind. I was already doing it. The events were taking on the hazy quality of a vivid nightmare.

My wife assumed Paka was killed in the rock-fall at the cabin. I let her assumption stand. Such an accident could occur in the normal world I was determined to re-enter, and foreclosed questions about something I was busily walling away. She was upset about Paka's death, but grateful the rocks missed Harry—let alone our son, or me. In her own way, I suppose, that was her adjustment to falling safes.

I still had one more interview that had been scheduled before I went to the Gorge. A federal Bureau of Mines geologist had put me in touch with an Olympia attorney who represented Japanese industries. The Japanese had been interested in Gorge coal for some time. I thought such an interview might round out the piece with a glimpse of a potential future for the coalfields to balance the poignant closing of the last mine.

After dinner, we moved into the living room to sit by the fire—we didn't even own a television. She had decreed our home a TV-free zone until our son learned to read, without being distracted by the idiot box. I didn't miss television. My formative years had been spent sans TV. I was almost fourteen years old before my family spent any money on that new-fangled contraption, in our case a twenty-one-inch black-and-white Muntz. My youth had been divided into pre-TV and post-TV eras. I tended to remember the pre-TV era as more fun, with checkers and chess and Parcheesi, and *Our Miss Brooks* on the radio. But I thought it was going to be interesting when our son started school with kids who spent their time at home glued to the TV.

Not that we talked about the absence of a television set that night. It was just part of the normal background cogitation that floats below deliberate recall, the everyday thoughts of a man whose life did not include the slaughter of a terrifying child-stealing cryptid.

My wife was interested in the Japanese angle to the coal story, so we talked about that a little. The Olympia attorney—his name was Watanabe—had agreed to meet me this Saturday, in Puyallup, which I thought was very accommodating. She considered his selection of a meeting place ironical, since state fairgrounds in Puyallup were used as a concentration camp for Japanese residents during the Second World War. I hadn't known that, and said I wasn't about to bring it up on Saturday.

"I bet he knows," she said.

"And I'm not going to compare Japan's desire for coking coal now to its purchase of all our scrap metal before the war," I said. "Nor what use they put that scrap metal to."

"Aren't you just the diplomat," she said, "in your advancing years?" But she was smiling.

We talked for a while about this and that, things that happened in her day at work, how Bob's wife took the news that his coal-mining days were behind him, whether we should consider shopping for a new pup to distract our son from the loss of his block-fetching playmate. As we talked, I was building that whole traumatic Gorge experience into a deep cellar in my brain, trowel by trowel, as surely as Edgar Allen Poe's protagonist walled up the costumed jester looking for Amontillado. I did say Joe's winter brogans made me think of Li'l Abner. She said she noticed he was wearing his shoes today, as sure a sign of winter as migrating geese.

"I missed you," she said, when the talk wound down. "I don't like sleeping without you. I did too much of that when you were on the road."

"I missed you too," I said. "It was good to know you were right down the hill, not on the other side of the country."

"You still look utterly worn out. Come to bed."

"I've still got rifles to clean..."

"They'll wait," she said. "This is the night you were due home in the first place. I had plans for you tonight. They involve getting you in bed when I'm awake, even if this is a work night."

Our biorhythms had never meshed that well. I was a night owl and she was a morning person. With me not working, we had fallen into a habit of different bed times except on weekends. Depending on when she turned in, I could sometimes coax her half-awake later for some deliciously sleepy lovemaking. Other nights she would growl that she was sleeping, dammit. I had become reasonably adept at knowing which night was which. Tonight, she left no doubt.

"I'm going to take a shower first," I said. "I haven't bathed since I got home."

She gave me a heavy-lidded look that had nothing to do with sleep. "I'll get the bed warm. If I'm already asleep, wake me." She stood and stretched, arching her back, and I could see her engorged nipples tenting her old maroon robe. The sight brought me instantly erect. "Don't be all night." She trailed her hand over my crotch as she walked by.

I followed her down the hall taking off my shirt. She paused at the bedroom door and looked back. "You know, I just figured out what that awful smell must have been. All those different gunpowders Vern gives you in those little paper cups. Some of them give off a strong odor. You were tinkering with those powders, so the smells got in your clothes and then the boy's clothes. Mixed with your cigars." She wrinkled her nose.

"I guess that makes sense," I said. "I won't be long."

She winked. "I won't start without you."

Chapter Twenty

By the time my Saturday appointment with Tetsushiro Watanabe rolled around, I was well along the way to blanking the events in the Gorge from my mind. A couple of days of seeing my wife off to work, working on the coal story, splitting a few alder logs and stacking them on the deck and feeding the three of us until Mom got home from work was helpful. So was another weather front off the Japanese Current that snagged its clouds on the Plateau, resulting in a steady familiar winter Washington rain.

I made it to the Puyallup diner at the appointed hour and stood by the cash register looking the patrons over; I didn't see any Japanese.

"H'ep you, hon?" The dishwater-blonde waitress at the register, pencil in her ear, smacking gum, was old enough to be my mother.

"I'm meeting someone," I said. "A Japanese gentleman?"

"Huh," she said. "What makes you think Ted is a gentleman?"

"Ted?"

"Ted Watanabe." She smacked her gum. "C'mon, he's waiting for you in the small banquet room."

I followed her past the kitchen. He stood as I entered—taller than I had expected, almost six feet, well-dressed in a well-cut dark suit and shiny tassled loafers. He might have been in his early forties or late thirties. Black hair brushed straight back from a broad forehead, strong features that reminded me of a photo of Sadaharu Oh in his prime, the Japanese slugger who hit more home runs than Henry Aaron. Watanabe looked fit enough to take a couple of cuts at a fast ball right now.

"Found this fellow out front looking for what he called a Japanese gentleman," the waitress said. "Guess you'll have to do."

"Oh, Maud—you wound me!" He grinned as we shook hands. "I'm afraid they know me too well here."

"Ever since he was a boy ducking outta farm work to sneak down here for a banana split," the waitress said fondly. "Don't know where he puts the calories."

His handshake was firm and practiced and went with his attire; Olympia lobbyist at work, even on a Saturday. There already was a carafe and coffee cups.

"Would you think me terribly decadent," he said, "if I had my trademark treat while we talk?"

"Think it or not, it's being made right now," Maud said. "Don't get too big for your britches, Ted, with them fancy words."

As if it were a signal, a fireplug-shaped waitress with a tight iron-gray perm sailed in with an enormous confection brimming in a real old-fashioned glass banana-boat. I hadn't had a banana split in I didn't know how long; not something you can easily manipulate with a flailing boy on your lap.

"I might join you in one of those," I said.

"Bin a long time, Ted," the second waitress said. "How's your folks?"

"My folks are doing well, thank you. I just came from a

visit with them. And your husband?"

"Fishin' the Cowlitz today. Fall Chinook."

"Remind him I'd like a booking when the run really gets good. He has my phone number."

"I will." She looked at me. "Big boy, aintcha? Okay, looks like you can handle a Ted-size banana split." She clomped away.

"To state the obvious, they know you here," I said.

"Almost all my life." He glanced out windows along the side of the room. There was a large sign there that advertised the Puyallup Fair Grounds. "Not while I was a guest of the government over there, of course."

So much for discretion. "You were interned at the fairgrounds?"

"I don't remember much—I was so young I spent a lot of my time in a sling on my mom's back. Like a Japanese papoose." He chuckled. "And toddling around after other kids. I never really understood we were prisoners of war."

"I can't get over Americans doing something like that," I said.

"The politics of war hysteria." He shrugged delicately. "My folks ran a small truck farm over by Fife, so we weren't transported far away, like many were. A nice Norwegian family kept an eye on things for us and didn't let anybody steal our property. After all was said and done, I wound up graduating from the University of Washington. In the complex little world of state politics today, sons of men who pushed the internment legislation now owe me favors."

"What goes around comes around?"

He smiled. "Karma I suppose. My folks still live in

Fife. They grow a lot of flowers now. My younger brother has quite the green thumb. He manages a very successful flower stall at the Farmer's Market in Seattle. The city dwellers pay well to bring a touch of natural beauty indoors. Sometimes I envy him his simple life of the soil." He used an expressive sweep of his hand to brush all that personal history off the table. "But you are not here for *my* biography. You are telling the story of the Gorge coal towns. How is that coming along?"

"You're my last important interview, a glimpse at possible future markets in Japan. Something hopeful to counter Bob Petosky's last little mine being shut down."

"I just learned of that. Government out of control." He shook his head. "It's how I make my living, trying to curb government excessiveness that harms clients. I wish I had known Bob's predicament. Maybe I could have moved that exemption for mom-and-pop mines out of committee."

"All the way from out here in the sticks?"

"It's a matter of who you know, and of timing, as I'm sure you know," Watanabe said. "One asks the staff of whoever is blocking things if their guy really wants his name on the measure that grinds a small business out of existence. Especially with the largest newspaper in the region about to publish a lengthy feature on the colorful past of that business."

"Would that have an effect in the other Washington?"

He sampled the whipped cream on his banana split. "Yes. Particularly couched in terms of a show-and-tell for visiting Japanese businessmen who might want to invest." Then he concentrated on his banana split, taking a second spoon of whipped cream, blended with pineapple topping.

Then a careful spoonful of the chocolate ice cream: the banana-split ceremony.

The waitress reappeared with my banana split and I tasted my whipped cream. It was fresh-made, not commercial; the kind my mother used to whip for strawberry shortcakes when I was a kid. We enjoyed our treats in mutual gratification for a few quiet minutes.

"Excellent banana split, yes?"

"Beyond excellent." I laid down my spoon and flipped open my notepad. "Some of the mine bureau people told me Japan is interested in those coal reserves. How interested, would you say?"

"Very interested, I would say, in the high quality of that coal as well as the sheer quantity close to a Pacific shipping port." He took another spoonful. "I am not speaking now for any particular client, you understand. But I have facilitated exchanges of information between geologists here and planners there. The quality of that coal is very high. The quantity is almost surreal. The Butler and the Wingate fields represent enormous natural wealth. Carbonado is potentially one of the richest towns in Washington, because one coal company donated all its mineral rights to the town. And Japan needs a lot of high-quality coal to keep pace in world markets."

I scribbled. "I've got figures here from 1963," I said. "Our Bureau of Mines estimated Japan could use anywhere up to a million annual tons of that Gorge coal."

He nodded. "And that was over ten years ago. The need has certainly expanded. Did you also see that byproduct energy would produce 115,000 kilowatts of power, which could be plugged into the Bonneville Power

Administration's nearby transmission lines?"

"But environmentalists would pitch a fit now about mine-mouth coke ovens."

He considered. "They would also pitch a fit if a major mining operation was opened that close to Mt. Rainier National Park."

"But Japan still is interested?" I started on my strawberry ice cream under the whipped cream.

"In a word, yes. Mitsubishi contracted with an American coal company back in '61 to deliver 800,000 tons, using hydraulic techniques and a new tunnel-boring device. The equipment did not hold up and the experiment failed. But the interest remains. And the coal will wait."

"The coal will wait. Good line." I swirled a chunk of banana with a spoon of vanilla ice cream in pineapple chunks; delicious. "Bob Petosky says Gorge coal is hard to get to."

"It has shaped the character of the residents, wouldn't you say? Like the coal itself, they are right at the surface and accessible one moment, and the next moment remote and mysterious."

"Interesting idea," I said. "As I understand the geology, when the Cascades formed, they punched up through Eocene Age coal beds and pushed some seams up on end, cut others apart, shifted them this way and that. This was before the big Mt. Rainier explosion. It's like a jigsaw puzzle for miners. Move the wrong piece, the land slipped, the emergency whistles blew and there were funerals in those little churches."

"Jigsaw puzzle." Watanabe smiled. "The Japanese are good at puzzles. Hydraulics has come a long way since '61.

My bet is the technology will soon be in place to remove the overburden safely and economically. Technology will solve environmental issues as well by restoring the site."

I had the rhythm now for interviewing while partaking of one of the best banana splits of my life: take a bite of ice cream with topping or banana, or both, ask a question, take two bites while the answer came, scribble a note or two, pick up my spoon again.

"Nature has pretty well restored the site from the old mining operations without any help," I said. "Have you been up there?"

"I *have* been up there." He reached into an inner coat pocket. "I kept this for a souvenir of my visit."

It was a postcard. The broad face of Joe Consonants grinned up at me out of his wild tangle of beard. On the back a sentence described him as a "famous Gorge resident." In the message space was a scrawling signature in blue ink.

"Excuse me," Watanabe said. "You look as if you've seen a ghost."

"Joe's no ghost," I said. "He was at my kitchen table this week. You actually asked for his autograph?"
Watanabe seemed a little embarrassed. "I paid him five dollars. To commemorate meeting this legendary character in the flesh."

"What did he have to say about starting a big Asian mining operation up there?"

"He said the great karmic wheel turns. Asians labored in those coalfields in the last century to feed their families. Now Asians may return to bring prosperity to a new Gorge generation."

"Sounds like Joe all right. He told you about the Chinese coolies being burned out by an angry Tacoma mob?"

"He did. I was curious as to the lack of reported casualties. He told me the Gorge protects its own. The coolies went about their business in the mines. They were acceptable. Bringing violence to the Gorge was not."

"I didn't see anything about casualties either," I said. "Did Joe say that *Kung Fu* TV series was true and a Shao-Lin monk was up there kicking Tacoma ass? Joe is quite the yarn-spinner from all I hear."

Watanabe carefully spooned the last drops of syrup out of his banana split dish. "He is a curiously well-traveled hermit. India, Nepal, visits to temples and monks. He was more familiar with Japan's animist religion predating Buddhism than I am. That particular pantheon includes mystical beasts that the weak can call upon to protect them from violence. Joe said the Himalayas harbor such a protector." Watanabe raised his eyebrows as if expecting me to laugh at him. "And he said so does the Gorge."

Chapter Twenty-One

When I got home from Puyallup, my wife's Pontiac was missing from the driveway. I didn't think anything about it until I was in my office, putting together the scraps of my coal story and thinking about how Watanabe's contributions would fit, and wondering what kind of bill of goods Joe Consonants had been trying to sell him about the battle for Chinaman Slope.

Then I heard Harry bark. It was a single woof from the garage, and sounded forlorn. I went to the kitchen door leading into the garage. There was a note Scotch-taped to the door: *We're at ER Room. Harry in garage.*

The closest Emergency Room was in Enumclaw, the same hospital where her mother died. She didn't like that hospital, never had. If she had gone there, something damn serious must have happened.

I let Harry in. He danced on the kitchen tiles, needing to go out. I let him out the back and waited impatiently for him to do his business, then loaded him in his kennel and headed for Enumclaw. Through the remnant of rain clouds, the sun was well into the western sky; it seemed later than it was. Massed cumulous bulged high above the unseen Olympics; another cold front on its way in. The things you notice when you are trying not to surrender to dread.

Enumclaw was Saturday-quiet on the last weekend before deer season drew city hunters from Seattle and

Tacoma to the mountains. I found her Pontiac in the ER parking, parked as close as I could, and went in. Every time I have ever been in an emergency room, there seems to be a group of bedraggled people that look as if they have been there long enough for cobwebs to gather. I've never seen one of those TV-set emergency rooms where doctors and nurses rush back and forth with gurneys shouting obscure medical words.

My wife and son were not among the dozen or so refugees from suffering. When I pronounced my name to the woman at the receptionist desk, it was like a jolt of energy went through her.

"Right this way," she whispered urgently.

I followed her, trying to stifle my alarm. Through double doors there were individual rooms and a few curtained-off alcoves. All seemed occupied. My guide led me to one of the rooms with the door closed.

My wife and son were there. He looked pitifully small in the big bed. His face was heavily flushed. He was asleep, with a thin green plastic oxygen tube tucked in his nose. A monitor counted off electric green numbers that didn't mean anything to me. The receptionist backed out and my wife came into my arms, her face blank, stunned.

"What happened?" I said.

"He woke up from his nap with an awful fever," she whispered. "He was burning up. It just came on all at once! They're trying to get it to go down."

She was not one to panic over a degree or two of fever. "How high?" I said.

"It was one oh four when I checked it at home. It was another degree higher when we got here!"

142

"Jesus Christ! What has he got?"

"It's not flu," she said. "It's some kind of infection."

"Blood poisoning?"

Growing up in the South, it was the first thing that occurred to me. I looked at his small pudgy arms above the sheet for telltale red streaks, remembering stickers on brush up in the Gorge. I survived a bout of blood poisoning when I was a teenager; not a pleasant memory.

"Are there any red streaks on his legs?" I asked.

"Not that I saw. He's so hot, honey! So hot!"

Her voice trembled as if she had been holding herself together until I got there and tears might come now. I stroked her back and made the wordless sounds you make.

"He needs liquids," I said.

"I know. They're getting ready to give him a saline solution."

I couldn't think of anything else to say. I was as stunned as she looked. You go along in life unsuspecting. Then, twice in a single week, it looks as if you're about to lose your son. This time there was nothing I could shoot to save him. There can be no more impotent feeling on earth than looking at your very sick child and not knowing what the hell to do.

The door popped open. A nurse rolled a rack holding an IV bottle into the room. She went right to work setting it up. She must have had a deft touch because he didn't rouse or yell when the needle went in.

"Fluids and antibiotics. This will help," she said kindly. "The doctor will be right in."

It turned out that I knew the guy. He had drawn blood from behind my kneecap after I tweaked a ligament playing pickup softball at a neighborhood picnic. Short, red-bearded, with intense blue eyes, he was a sturdy pocketsize Norwegian who seemed to know his stuff. I remembered he had played football at the University of Washington, but not his name. He took the boy's temperature, pushed down the sheet and looked his body and limbs over carefully, listened to his chest.

"Okay," he said. "The fever hasn't gone higher. It should come down with the saline and antibiotics. I'm using broad spectrum until we narrow the diagnosis."

"Thank god!" my wife breathed. "But we don't know yet what it is?"

He blinked. I saw it. "Not yet," he said. "But the antibiotics should begin to knock it down, whatever it is." He looked at me. "Your wife tells me that you and your son spent some days up in Carbon Gorge earlier this week, is that right?"

"You think he picked up an infection in the Gorge?" It had been my first thought.

"Possibly."

"Blood-poisoning?"

I had blood poisoning on my brain; I was hunting squirrels in a Florida swamp when I contracted mine via scratches on my hand.

"I don't think so," the doctor said.

My boy stirred restlessly in his sleep. The doctor stepped quietly away from the bed. "Could you come outside with me for a minute?" he asked me. "I want to talk to you about where you were, up in the Gorge."

"Go," my wife said. "I'll be right here."

He led me past other patient rooms through another

set of double doors into some kind of staff break room with burned-smelling coffee on a burner next to a small refrigerator. He picked up a big blue coffee mug and drank, made a face.

"I have one thing that scares the hell out of me, in cases like this," he said. "Call it my personal nightmare. Forgive the lack of bedside manner, but I really need you to concentrate on what happened up there, because your boy can't tell me."

"You're sure this has to do with the Gorge?"

"God, I hope not. Did your boy handle any small wild animals up there? Chipmunks, like that? Kids love to chase things. Did he catch one? Was he close enough to any for a flea to jump to him? I didn't see any flea bites, but still..."

"A flea? What are you saying? *No*, he didn't chase any small animals. And no, he wasn't that close to any."

"You're sure? Was he under your constant observation at all times?"

"...not every single second, no."

He nodded. "My personal nightmare is *Pastuerella pestis* getting loose in the Cascades."

It was as if frozen water coursed down my spine and turned it to ice. "Bubonic Plague?"

He held up a cautionary hand. "Not so loud. Even these days, those words could create a panic. I'm surprised you recognize the Latin."

"I'm a reporter, for God's sake. You think that's what my son could have? *How?*"

"We're culturing his blood as we speak. It doesn't always show in the blood. But I'm starting broad-spectrum antibiotics anyway. If we tried to wait to get a definitive tissue sample, it might be too late—if it's *Pastuerella*. I really, really hope it's not."

"Why would that even occur to you?"

"Because," he said, "in past decades of this modern century, it has failed to occur to admitting physicians across the Western mountains more than once. People died who didn't need to, because it didn't. *Pastuerella* has been dormant in the Western mountains for a long time. In this state we have specific protocols that kick in with a suspect infection."

"It's like you expect this to happen."

"It's not a matter of *if,* it's a matter of *when,*" he said. "The old-timers tried to stop it at these shores with quarantine of inbound ships. But rats didn't honor the quarantine. *Pestis* jumped into wharf rats, probably, and eventually migrated into small rodents in the mountains. You're sure your son didn't get too close to any chipmunks up there?"

"Don't take my word for it," I said. "Do whatever you have to do to keep him safe."

"Don't worry, I'm doing it. Even if this is my nightmare, I think we caught it in time. I've alerted the health authorities. You will need to show them everywhere you went up there, if this is *pestis.*"

Chapter Twenty-Two

My wife and I settled in at the hospital. We took turns getting fresh air or taking body breaks. His fever dropped another degree by six p.m. and I thought he didn't look so flushed. I was afraid to say anything for fear it was wishful thinking. The doctor was in and out between his other patients. Down the hall a youngster was crying his eyes out for what seemed like a long time; furious, angry wailing.

"Splinters," the doctor said when I asked.

At some point I began to feel light-headed and realized that the banana split with Watanabe had been my last food. I asked my wife if she wanted anything from McDonald's before it closed, and she said *no* so emphatically it seemed like an accusation: how could I think of eating at a time like this?

I drove over there and got a bag of their cheapest cheeseburgers and some fries, along with a giant-size Coke and some coffee. I sat on the tailgate in the hospital parking lot and shared some of the meat and cheese with Harry; he disliked the soggy buns and the pickles, so I finished those off.

"It's something to do with that damn thing that took him," I whispered to Harry, though nobody was around the darkened lot. "I know it is."

Harry wagged at me and crunched another French fry. He seemed perfectly happy and healthy; I wondered if I should take him to the vet. He'd chewed on that thing pretty good; was he infected? But how could I tell the doctor my suspicion? He would conclude that I was losing my grip because he had mentioned bubonic plague as a possibility. Were cryptids carriers of the dread disease? That was one of those questions that—once asked—put you beyond the pale of sanity in the mind of whoever heard it.

Not that I would give a damn what they thought—but they wouldn't act on it, wouldn't look for anything that thing might have been carrying, or transmitting in its milk. No more than if I said I shot a lactating Martian, so the bug must be extraterrestrial. If whatever it was was bacterial, the broad-spectrum antibiotics should stop it; I just had to hope the doctor knew what he was doing—not a comforting thought.

That night I was keeping a lot of secrets.

The doctor had advised me not to mention bubonic plague to my wife until and if they were sure. So I was keeping the doctor's nightmare from her. And I was keeping my secret fears from both of them. All I could do was wait it out and pray. I hadn't been a churchgoer in a long time, but I understood the desperate desire to bargain with a higher power: *Save my son, and I will...*

What could I offer? To range those mountains like an avenging fury and hunt down and destroy every child-stealing monster that was left? The Old Testament deity might have accepted that for a valid oath, based on all the blood and gore when He was on speaking terms with God's Chosen People. The New Testament God seemed to ask for kinder, gentler oaths, but I didn't feel kinder and gentler.

I definitely was losing it, to be thinking like this.

I finished my big Coke and took Harry for a walk on his leash. He did his business and I put him back up with a last handful of French fries to munch while I drank my coffee. The Norwegian doctor came out the emergency room exit, looked around, and walked over to me, lighting a cigarette. His name finally surfaced in my memory: Thorson.

"Taking a break," he said.

He must have seen the surprise on my face; already in the seventies I had begun to equate all doctors with the nicotine Nazis.

"Yeah, I still smoke," he said wryly. "Something's got to kill you, because none of us gets out of this life alive." He exhaled a perfect smoke ring. "Your son's temp is down another degree. All his vitals are positive. I just came from telling your wife."

"Thank God!" I fumbled out my pipe and makings and built a smoke of my own.

"The blood work was negative for *Pastuerella*," he said. "No safety pins."

"What?"

"They call how it looks under a microscope a safety-pin look," he said. "No safety pins in his blood. And no seizures, no chills, no vomiting, no cramps—all symptoms of the infection, along with the high fever."

"Good god."

"It's an ugly thing, *pestis,* but I'm betting against it now. We'll keep him on the antibiotics to be on the safe side."

"Antibiotics will stop it?"

"When you move fast enough. Your wife did the right

thing to bring him straight in." He stepped on his cigarette butt, grinding it into the pavement. "Well, back to work."

I took a couple of circuits of the hospital parking lot while I smoked my pipe. My emotions were all over the place. Was the crisis past? Thorson being Norwegian, the way my brain works I recalled the Scandinavians had called the bubonic plague a goddess named Hel, an old bitch with a broom who swept their cold countries empty of human life. I had wondered when I read that about the Four Horsemen of the Apocalypse: War, Death, Famine and Pestilence.

"And Hell followed with them," the Bible passage said.

Hell or Hel? Most Bible-readers apparently assumed the Black Death was the fourth horseman. I'd never read any theories about who Hell was, other than the obvious pitchfork guy. Now I wondered half-crazily if Scandinavian legend crept into Bible translations in the fourteenth century, when the Pope's census of the European death toll counted nearly forty-three million dead from the plague. *Forty-three million*—how many ICBMs and how many megatons would be required to spawn that much death?

In the five centuries following that dreary toll, the plague came back century after century. In the nineteenth century, U.S authorities tried to stop it with their month-long (hence "quarantine") prohibition against ships coming ashore. But Thorson said it had jumped to mountain rodents, to lie in wait.

Bewildered medieval populations under the terror had supposedly blamed its recurrence on everything from comets to strange miasmic vapors to sin. An earlier pandemic that nearly depopulated the Roman Empire was blamed on the sins of the Emperor Justinian.

Nowhere had it been blamed on cryptids.

I finished my pipe and took a fish sandwich, bag of fries and a large lemonade in to my wife. The boy's color was definitely better.

"Doc says the fever's still coming down," I said. "You need to eat to keep your strength up."

She took the greasy sack. "Fish sandwich?"

"Yep."

"It's cold. What took you so long?"

"There's a microwave in their break room," I said. "I'm sure they won't mind you warming it up." Sometimes it was better just to ignore her snipes when she spoke with that accusing note. This was one of those times.

"Where's the break room?" she said.

"I'll show you and come back and sit with him."

When I got back, the boy's eyes were open. They still had that glazed look of a fever.

"Da?"

"Right here, son."

"Mo?"

"She'll be back in a minute." I laid a hand on his forehead. He was still warm but not burning up. He closed his eyes again.

"Hawwy? Paka?"

"They're not here, son. Only people allowed here."

"Why?"

"Just because."

"'Kay..."

He was drifting off again. I stroked his forehead,

thinking how sick he must be to not question "just because," when my wife came back.

"Did you eat?"

"I guess I *was* starving. Gobbled, is more like it." She rattled her cup. "They gave me more ice for the lemonade."

"He opened his eyes and spoke for a minute."

"Oh, God, I shouldn't have left!

"Told him you were coming right back. Then he wanted to know where Harry was...and Paka."

"Oh, my poor baby." She replaced my hand with hers on his forehead. "He's cooler. Isn't he?"

"His color is better too."

"What on earth could it have been?" Her voice sounded less stressed, thinking the crisis was past. I hoped she was right.

Chapter Twenty-Three

Ralph Lincoln was a lean, fit-looking individual who moved with that unconscious grace of somebody in good shape. He appeared to be in his forties, which probably made him some kind of exercise fanatic, handball or jogging at a guess. He didn't particularly look like a bureaucrat in his plaid button-down shirt and chinos, but he was; a medical bureaucrat from the state Department of Health. He showed up about dawn, fighting a big black bumbershoot in the gusty rains that came with daylight, and came into the ER lobby stamping his feet. I was getting a Coke out of the machine for my wife and saw him fold his umbrella, speak to the receptionist, turn to look at me, and then head my way.

He held out a hand, introduced himself. "I understand you're the father of the boy they brought in?"

I said I was. He glanced around at the careworn people waiting to be seen. The cast of characters had changed overnight, but not the forlorn mood.

"Perhaps we could talk in your son's room? I'd like to examine him, with your permission. I'm an MD."

"Doc Thorson had him moved to a private room from the ER," I said. "Let's go."

My wife was in a chair by the bed, eyes half-closed. She started awake as we came through the door. My son was asleep again. His color was lots better, but they still had him on fluids and oxygen. My wife of course wanted to know why a doctor from the state Department of Health was there.

He looked a question at me. I shrugged. "Doctor Thorson hasn't given him a diagnosis."

"Just what the hell does *that* mean?" She was up out of her chair, ready to do battle.

"I'd like to examine your son, if I may?" he said softly, seeing the anger and responding to it gently. "We were afraid he might have picked up something infectious in the Gorge, you see."

"What?" she said flatly. "What do you think he picked up?"

He kept moving, to the side of the bed, eyes on my son. "May I?"

"You're a doctor?"

"I am. I came straight from Olympia."

"Do you know what's wrong with him?" Her tone suggested he might be the cause of whatever that was.

He folded his hands patiently. "If I could just look at him for a minute..."

It looked like she was biting her tongue. She gestured curtly. "Go ahead. Then tell me what the hell is going on!"

He nodded and gently raised first one of my son's arms and then the other, focusing on his armpits. Despite Thorson's reassurances, my blood ran cold again. Sometimes it doesn't pay to be too well-read; Lincoln was looking for buboes. Next he examined his feet and hands closely, and his arms and legs: looking for fleabites.

"Mo?" came a sleepy little voice.

"I'm here, son," she said tightly. "The doctor is examining you."

"Da?"

"I'm here," I said.

He looked sleepily up at Lincoln. "Hi," he said.

Lincoln broke into a wide smile, "Hello, little guy. How do you feel?"

"Ummuck," my son said. Lincoln looked at us for translation.

"Stomach," I said.

"What about your stomach, little man?" Lincoln asked him.

"Owie!"

"Your stomach hurts?"

"Ummuck. Owie!"

He lifted his pudgy little knees toward his chest. Cramps—the doctor has said cramps were one of the symptoms. Before I could panic, he thrust his legs straight with a grunt and his face turned red—but only for a moment. Then his face relaxed, the color retreated, and he let out something like a sigh. An incredibly foul odor washed into the room. I was so far gone I almost broke out laughing. My son had just taken a power dump, the awful reek of baby shit probably intensified by the antibiotics they had been pumping into him.

"Oh, my," Lincoln said. He almost laughed too. "My, oh my, little man." He patted my son's hand. "Feel all better now?"

My son wrinkled his nose. "Ugh."

"He hadn't gone potty all day yesterday," my wife said.

"Well, he certainly has now," Lincoln said.

"Oh, God—I left the diaper bag at home."

"Not to worry. I'll get a nurse in here to clean up." He

thumbed the call button by the bed.

A nurse poked her head in and jerked like she'd hit an invisible wall. Lincoln did laugh then. "Our little man needs to be cleaned up and re-diapered," he said.

"And maybe gas masks for the grownups," she said brightly. "Doctor Thorson is on his way up."

Lincoln looked at us both. "If that's not a healthy stool, I don't know what is. I'd say we're well on the road to recovery here."

Thorson showed up about the time the nurse got back to tend to my boy. Things got a little confused for a few minutes because the room got really crowded. My wife insisted on supervising the cleanup, which didn't earn her any points with the nurse. Not that she gave a rip.

"His poo never smelled that bad before!" she told Thorson, like it was his fault.

"Sounds like he was a little constipated yesterday?" Lincoln put in, using his bedside voice again. "That could explain it."

"And the medications to knock his fever down," Thorson added. As soon as they had my son dry and comfortable, he put a stethoscope to his chest and then his stomach. "Lungs still clear, stomach sounds normal."

"Ice cweem?"

Thorson's turn to laugh. "Opportunist! Maybe in a little while, slugger."

"Tunis?"

"You just rest now, okay? You've had a big day for a big boy."

While this was going on, I noticed Lincoln step into the hall to speak to the nurse, saw her nod and head off carrying the soiled linen at arms' length. Lincoln stepped back in.

"You asked me some questions when I came in, ma'am," he said. "I'd be happy to answer them, but I think it might be best outside the hearing of little pitchers."

"I don't want to leave him by himself!"

"Completely understandable. I can talk to you one at a time, and one can stay here."

She was already moving to the door. "You stay here." If you've ever been in the Army you recognize a direct order when you hear one. They all trooped out together.

"Ice cweem, Da?" as soon as they were gone.

I pulled the chair up to the bed and held his little hands. "Just as soon as Doc says okay. Promise."

"Hawwy too?"

"You bet. Harry can have some too."

"Paka?"

My heart ached from being turned over again and again and again in the past few hours. "You rest now, son, get better, and we'll get that ice cream."

"'Kay..." His eyelids were fluttering. That enormous dump must have exhausted him.

I held onto his hands and watched him sleep and ignored the cramp in my side from the awkward position. I noticed the can of Coke sitting forgotten on the side table and thought about drinking it and then thought better of it. My wife was probably going to storm through that door and brain me for holding out on her, and I would regurgitate Coke up my nose.

She was gone for what seemed like a long time. I was dozing when I felt her hand on my shoulder, and felt my balls tighten in expectation of her recriminations. But when I looked up, all that showed on her face was shock.

"Are you all right?" I said.

"Oh, god, honey. Oh, *god*. The damned *plague*?"

"Shh-h-h," I said. "Evidently not. They were just being careful."

She bent over our son, touching him gently on the forehead, the arms, everywhere. A mother's touch. In my sleep-deprived state I flashed back to my own mother's touch on my hot forehead when I had scarlet fever. I was so young I had no idea how serious it was, but I knew that soft hand on my brow was going to keep me safe somehow. I could feel the silken touch of her palm and the tiny hard calluses from a lifetime's toil...

My wife said something. I had been drifting. "What, love?"

"Doctor Lincoln would like to talk to you now, about where you went in the Gorge. Just in case, he said."

"Whatever this turns out to be," I said, trying to wake up enough to get on my feet, "always remember that you saved our son by moving so fast."

She squeezed her eyes shut and shivered. "Oh, my god."

"You gonna be okay while I go talk to Lincoln?"

She nodded mutely. I hugged her, hard. "Hang in there, babe. The worst is over." I hoped it was.

"It better be. I can't take much more."

Chapter Twenty-Four

I found Lincoln and Thorson in the ER break room, drinking that burned coffee. When Thorson offered me a cup I didn't turn it down. I had tasted worse on various newspapers over the years—but not much worse. At least it was bitter enough to prop my eyes open.

"So it looks like a false alarm," Thorson said. "Thank all the saints."

I was surprised, figuring a Norwegian for a Lutheran, but didn't comment.

"Still, everybody did the right thing here," Lincoln said. "Your wife, bringing him in right away. Dr. Thorson, looking at the symptoms and hearing where he'd been, and putting him on broad-spectrum antibiotics. Whatever caused that fever has been knocked out. All vital signs are good."

"My first thought was blood poisoning."

"You must have had a bad experience with that, for that to be your first thought."

"I did."

"Around here?"

"Florida."

He nodded. "I know you noticed me talking to the nurse after your boy had that enormous stool. Just to be utterly sure, I want fecal cultures run to see if any antibodies show up."

"We're going to do a preliminary in the lab here,"

Thorson said. "If there's anything suspicious, we'll send it to the state Health Lab."

"But we've got a lot in our favor here," Lincoln said. "For one, October is the wrong time of year for *pestis*. Usually it's summer, kids getting too close to infected animals. Domestic cats can carry it, if they get out roving and catch infected rodents."

"How about dogs?" I said.

"Coyotes pick it up from infected rodents, so dogs could too. But you told Dr. Thorson the boy hadn't been near any chipmunks or ground squirrels up there, right?"

"Come to think of it, we didn't even see any."

"H'mm." His brow furrowed. "That's *not* a good sign. Let's hope it's coincidence and not from a die-off late summer. We'll have to send a team up there checking."

"It snowed while we were in the Gorge."

"Right. Not the time of year to expect *pestis* to jump to a human. And it doesn't look like this is *pestis*. We'll check anyway. This is not something to play around with."

I drank some bitter brew. "I'm curious: is it just small rodents that carry the infection? How about bears, for instance?"

"Did you have a close encounter with a black bear?" he said quickly.

"...no," I said. "But there are bears around. I saw scat."

He nodded. "For some reason bears seem to ward it off. You'd have to either shoot one or dart it, and check the blood for antibodies, to find out if it had been exposed."

"Look," I said. "How likely is it the plague could crop up?"

"*Pestis* is out there," he said flatly. "When's the next

time it will find a human victim is a crap shoot. That's why we jump all over a situation like this. If your son had come back positive, you all and your dogs would be in quarantine. So would whoever you encountered up in the Gorge."

"Jesus H. Christ."

"You told me you're a reporter," Thorson said. "That you were up there working on a story?"

"Freelance now. But yeah, a story on the coalmines."

"What coalmines?" Lincoln said.

So I gave him a nickel preview of my story. Lincoln was very interested, particularly in the historic angle about Tacoma's coaling docks and the Chinese workers.

"Maybe you'd be interested in doing a story sometime about *pestis* in the Northwest," Lincoln said. "Answer some of your questions and inform the public about risk factors. I'm afraid it's not very newsworthy until there's a confirmed case, but there's a lot of history there."

He said it casually, but I could see it meant a lot to him. I just wanted to find some place to curl up and sleep for about twelve hours. But this guy had saddled up immediately and come all the way from Olympia. He was part of that unseen safety net we all take for granted in this country. I had encountered many people as a reporter with that wistful hope that someday their unsung keeping of the watch would be recognized in print. Telling those untold stories was part of what I liked best about being a reporter.

"My wife needs a little time alone with our son," I said. "Tell me a little bit of that history. Maybe I can pitch the story to the *Times* when I turn in my coalmine piece."

"Really?" He sounded surprised.

"Sure. If I could prevent one parent going through what we just went through—except for real—it would be worth doing the story."

His eyes lit up with the fervor of a true believer. What a hypocrite I was; I just wanted to move him away from remembering I had asked about large omnivores carrying the plague.

"Did you know," he asked, "that ship rats brought *pestis* to Seattle from Asia in 1907?"

"That recently?" My turn to be surprised.

"Oh, yeah. Five people died before they caught it."

"Only five? They didn't have these antibiotics then. How..."

"Well," he said, sitting back with the satisfaction of someone who has set the hook, "it's quite a yarn, really. Seattle passed the first rat-control ordnance in the United States as a result of that outbreak, for one thing. The predecessor to my agency—the state Board of Public Health—was created that year, 1907, because of *pestis*. In a way, those rats gave me a job seventy years later. Not only that, the U.S. Public Health Service was born and grew out of their ship-jumping."

"You're kidding. This actually sounds like a good story."

"You mentioned the problems the Chinese coolies had up in the Gorge—that they were burned out. Ironically, so was Chinatown in Honolulu, in 1899. In their case, it was a public-health decision, because of *pestis*. It got into the islands from China, and they thought the only way to contain it was to burn out the infected areas. But the fire got out of hand and Chinatown was leveled. The plague came on across the ocean to San Francisco, and then to Seattle eight years later."

"And the rats infected other rodents and *pestis* escaped into the mountains," Thorson said. "Now some kid playing with a sick squirrel in a park, or some ranch hand handling a coyote carcass with fleas from infected rodents, is my nightmare. It's out there like some evil genie, just waiting to be let out of the bottle."

"There wasn't a single fleabite on your son," Lincoln put in.

"I guess a miss is as good as a mile," I said.

But I was remembering Harry as a pup, happily chasing chipmunks around up in the big timber where I was trying to teach him to hunt blue grouse. He never came close to catching one as they scampered up trees and under deadfalls. And me having no idea that if one proved too feeble to escape, and he brought it back to me for approval, it could have been curtains for both of us.

Nor of course knowing that mythic cryptids lurked in the same dark timber I ambled through with a sixteen-gauge bird gun loaded with low-brass 71/2 shot—not exactly a monster slayer. The Northwest I had been so pleased to move to was proving haunted by more horrors than I could have imagined. Florida gators and water moccasins were looking pretty tame in comparison. I became aware of Thorson speaking again.

"...are you okay? You just kind of faded away there."

"It's been a longish kind of weekend," I said. To Lincoln, "But I still am interested in that story of yours. Once all this is behind us."

The break room phone rang. Thorson answered,

listened, and said, "You'd better tell Dr. Lincoln, he's right here." He handed off the phone. "Our pathologist," he said.

A series of expressions chased each other across Lincoln's face that I couldn't read as he listened; he darted a glance at me. *That* I could read. When he hung up, he stared at the phone for a longish moment. Then he looked up.

"This is preliminary," he said. "I'll be taking a sample back to our labs to double-check. But the oddest thing: your son's fecal culture? He passed a parasite of some kind. Either your son's natural immune system or the antibiotics killed it and ejected it. Dr. Wu postulates his immune-system reaction to the parasite might be what caused his high fever."

"A parasite, but not plague germs," I said.

"No, no, nothing like that. No antibodies indicative of that either. Just an intestinal parasite of some kind. The thing is"—he paused—"Dr. Wu says he's never seen one like it, or even heard of one. It's a parasite of unknown taxonomy, evidently maladapted to a human host, or susceptible to broad-scale antibiotics, or both." He shook his head. "What on earth did your son get *into* up there in the Gorge?"

Chapter Twenty-Five

The hospital discharged my son Monday afternoon, when his temperature was back to normal and all vital signs were healthy. My wife's boss turned out to be a pretty good guy, telling her to stay home until she was sure the boy was okay. We caught up on our sleep and drifted around the house in a kind of walking daze. In-laws dropped off casseroles and pots of stew, and some hand-made elk sausage from one of her sister's boyfriends, almost as if someone had died.

Tuesday morning when Ralph Lincoln called the house, he sounded very happy our son was none the worse for wear. He had a couple more microbe hunters with him, headed for the Gorge, and wanted to know if I would show them where we had been. My wife said go ahead, she and the boy would be fine. I met Lincoln where the county road from the Gorge entered 410; he was driving a white Suburban four-by-four with exempt plates, a whip antenna and a small Department of Health logo on the rear glass.

"Thanks for doing this," he said.

"You still worried about a chipmunk die-off?"

"We're going to check. But that's strictly precautionary. What I'm really curious about now is that mysterious parasite."

"I have no idea how he could have picked that up." I was lying in my teeth.

In some ways it seemed a hundred years since I

crossed the high bridge into Burnett above the Carbon River. A glimpse of turbulent green water far below made me think about the inbred clan led by the albino mutant who was always on the lookout for government vehicles. I wondered if the official-looking Suburban would trigger his CB alarm and halt spearing of the protected fall salmon run.

It was raining steadily in the Gorge. The early snow had melted though the surrounding hills were white. There was nobody on the street in Wilkeson when we went through. A half-mile past Wilkeson, a big black bumbershoot bloomed like an alien toadstool on the left shoulder. When I got closer I saw a familiar form slouched in what looked like a rocking chair, big bare feet stretched out in front of him. I pulled into the oncoming lane and dropped my window. Lincoln stopped behind me.

"I thought now it was winter you'd be wearing shoes," I said.

Big Joe Consonants reached under his rocker and held up his brogans. "Got 'em right here. But my feet like to breathe, and it's not that cold today."

"You know, my wife told me you had a rocking chair right by the road to wait for tourists to drop by, but I'd never seen it."

"Actually, I got three," he said. "Spread up the road in likely places for tourists. Tuck 'em back in the brush. Nobody around here bothers 'em. Who's that with you?"

"State health-department people. They want to go down to Petosky's cabin, look around for dead chipmunks and such."

"Hell, there ain't no chipmunk die-off. I'd know if

pestis was active." Of course he would; he was the self-styled close watcher over the Gorge.

"Maybe you should tell them that," I said. "How's the road down to Petoskey's cabin?"

"Pretty mushy, after all this precip."

"Thanks." I drove to the muddy track down to the cabin, pulled past and stopped. Lincoln stopped behind me and ran up through the rain. "The cabin we stayed at is down in there," I said. "It's probably locked. I can give you the owner's phone number if you need to get inside."

"You're not going down there?"

"Joe says the road's pretty mushy. I'm not sure I can get back up out in two-wheel drive."

"That was Joe in the rocking chair back there?"

"That was Joe."

"He lives around here?"

"In a cave, supposedly."

Lincoln squinted at the rain. "We're farther away from Olympia than just miles, aren't we? Is there a place you can park so you can ride down with us?"

"Back in Wilkeson is best."

We drove back to town, I parked near the Pick 'n Shovel and walked back to the Suburban carrying my Remington in its scabbard.

"Is that—a gun?" The little crew-cut guy riding beside Lincoln was staring wide-eyed.

"It is," I said.

The third member of their group was a woman, with hair pulled back in a severe twist and black-rimmed glasses. She leaned forward from the back seat.

"We can't allow firearms in a state vehicle," she said

primly.

"Then go on your own," I said.

"Is it that important to you, carrying a rifle down there?" Lincoln said.

"I never go anywhere in these mountains anymore without a rifle."

He eyed me shrewdly. "Is there some danger we should be aware of? Marijuana growers, for instance?"

"This is the Gorge," I said. "You never know." I could feel the eyes in the establishments along the street boring into us; anything unusual in the Gorge drew immediate and focused attention.

"We could call in a state trooper," the crew-cut guy said. His prominent Adam's apple bobbed up and down. "Is it—are there—that is, are they like old hippies? Growing dope to survive, like moonshiners made whiskey back in the Smokies?"

I didn't bother to tell him that illegal stills in the Cascades caused some revenuers to call them Smokies West. "These hills are full of ex-flower children," I said. "And survivalists. And cranky old-timers whose feuds make the Hatfields and McCoys look like suburbanites. One state trooper alone won't venture far off the pavement, if at all."

"We need to get started," the woman said impatiently. "Are you coming with, or not?"

"Not without my rifle."

"Oh, for goodness sake! That's out of the question."

Lincoln was watching me closely. "I don't want to expose my team to any danger. Survivalists? Hemp farms?"

"Plus a pack of wild dogs that has the locals stirred up," I said. "They chased a child off a cliff to its death last year. People are worried about their kids waiting for the school bus."

"I never heard anything about that!" the woman snapped.

I had about had it with her. "Then of course it's not true, if *you* didn't hear it."

"Hey!" the crew cut guy said.

"What else?" Lincoln said.

"Bears and cougars and the odd Sasquatch."

"Oh, for crying out loud!" the crew cut said.

"I've got state two-way radio," Lincoln said. "If I get stuck down in there, is there a wrecker dispatch can call?"

I gave him Boots Rubery's phone number. "Have them call the Pick 'n Shovel when you're done and I'll take you to Mildred's. Her road is gravel, so I should be okay."

"I'm sorry about these rules about firearms," Lincoln said. "Ever since the Black Panthers marched on the capitol with guns, bureaucrats are nervous about private firearms."

"As I recall, all their guns were unloaded," I said.

"Still," the crew-cut said. "A swarm of Afros big as Jimi Hendricks', carrying guns to the legislature? Give me a break!"

"Let it rest," Lincoln told him. To me, "Okay, you were around the Petoskey cabin and all through the old township and the woods down to the river?"

"Don't fall in the hotel cellar."

He put the Suburban in drive and left. He didn't look happy, caught between disapproval of his team members and my refusal to play by their rules. I put my rifle back in my truck and drove back to where Joe lounged beneath his big umbrella.

"Want to grab a coffee at the Pick n' Shovel?"

"Shore."

He put on his Li'l Abner shoes, not bothering with laces, and dragged his chair and folded umbrella back into the brush. At the Pick n' Shovel, he greeted several locals eating late breakfast. The slim waitress brought coffee and two cups without asking, patted Joe's big shoulder and gave me a smile.

"You see that gov'mint truck, Joe?" one of the men eating breakfast asked him.

"Shore did." Joe stuck a big thumb at me. "He says they're health-department folks lookin' for bugs."

"Yeah?"

"Yeah."

The man turned back to his steak and eggs, curiosity satisfied.

"Heard your boy took'n real sick," Joe said. "Is he okay?"

"He ran a bad fever, but it's over now. He's home."

"Good, figgered so." Joe tipped his chair back. "Them health people lookin' for chipmunks means you still ain't tellin' tales. That's good. How come you didn't ride down with them?"

"No firearms in state vehicles, they said. I won't go down there without my rifle."

"Oh, for the lova Mike!" He lowered his voice to a bass rumble. "Things is calm now. They should be okay."

"I noticed you didn't have your Yeti rifle."

"Boots Rubery keeps it at the gas station when I'm waitin' for tourists, till I head for m'cave."

"You actually live in a cave?"

"Yep." He let his voice lift to something like normal. "Started out as a coalmine, but played out. They nailed it shut instead of blowin' it. I just took the boards down and rearranged 'em and took a door off a scrap heap. Good stout timbers shorin' up those first couple dozen yards into the hill. Plenty of room for an old coot like me, and plenty of odds and ends of coal for warmth."

It was my turn to speak quietly. "I know you must have followed the tracks that night. What did you do with the carcass?"

He dropped his voice to the rumble again. "I didn't do nothin' with it. They came and got it."

"Skooks did?"

"They got centuries of practice hidin' from Cro Magnon." He gazed out the front door at the rain. "Huntin' season comin' on, so they'll be plenty scarce. Berry season is always touchy. They do love their berries."

"Berry pickers ever run into them?"

"Occasional. Berry pickers mostly don't talk about it, tired of being taken for fools. Footprints mostly, 'cause skooks don't always take time to fox their trail when they're gobblin' berries." He let his voice drift back up to conversational level. "Around here, folks that find big bare footprints just figger it's me out roamin'. I got a size-sixteen foot, ya know."

"Jesus," I said. "I thought my feet were big." I leaned my elbows on the table and spoke quietly again. "That why you go barefoot so much? To give them a cover story?"

He gave me a look. "Now you're th' fust ever suggested that. You got a devious mind."

"You seem way too familiar with skooks to my liking."

He was gazing out at the rain again. "Not by choice," he said so softly I almost couldn't hear him. "No more choice than you and you boy." He paused. Then, "They can stay hid for years. For decades. It's better so. They can't be tryin' to steal Cro Magnon *tenas*, no matter how bad a momma aches with the loss of a young'un. *Mesashie mitlite*."

"More jargon?"

He blinked. "Sorry, my tourist talk gets to be habit. *Tenas* means papoose—little kid." He was speaking louder again. "*Mesashie mitlite* is a compound of bad and dangerous. A dangerous place where bad is. Or vicey versey."

The two men at the closest table scraped chairs back and started putting coats on. "Good to hear you're working on a story about our coalmines," one of them said to me. I was becoming a local celebrity. "Don't let Joe pull your leg too far outta shape with his tall tales." They walked up to the cash register laughing. Joe smiled in his whiskers.

"I don't see anything funny about this," I said. "You know what happened out there, don't you?"

He sobered. "I recognized her track. She's the one lost her baby to the wild dogs last year." There wasn't anyone else close enough to eavesdrop, but he still pitched his voice low. "So she took yours," he said. "You shot her up and tracked her down with that black dog and took him back." He shook his head. "Even Cro Magnon females been known to steal babies from hospitals when they lose their own."

I shivered, reliving alien milk bubbles on my son's chin.

"A year is a long time to lactate with nothing to nurse."

"There are more things in heaven and earth than are dreamt of in our philosophy," he said. "Not all mammals follow a human schedule."

"Shakespeare," I identified. "You must read a lot up in that cave of yours." There still was no one close enough to pay us any mind. "So why does everybody call your old Winchester your Yeti rifle? Did you shoot an abominable snowman with the late colonel and his trigger-happy lady?"

His rugged face seemed to turn to stone—it didn't have far to go. "I never. Them's just ugly rumors. You ain't funny."

"I wasn't trying to be."

His face relaxed. "I guess you wasn't at that. Reporters must get used to askin' folks things to their face nobody else will. When folks found out the colonel was hirin' me to outfit him, Boots Rubery's daddy said Joe, you takin' your Yeti rifle? It kindly stuck."

".45-70 or .45-90?"

"Ninety. I load my own shells. Too spendy to buy commercial, even if you can find 'em."

"I suppose it would kill a Yeti," I said. "Or a skook. Did you kill that one in Ape Canyon? Since you said you were there."

His face hardened again. "You ain't interviewin' me."

"Wrong answer, big man. You forget you apologized for getting there too late the night I shot that thing. So you knew something bad was going to happen. And at my house you told me we need to talk."

He stared in his cup. "What are them health-department people really looking for? They must know by now your boy didn't contract *pestis.*" Like Thorson, he used the Latin.

"They're looking for a parasite they've never seen before. They found it in my boy's shitty diapers at the hospital."

"Your boy nursed from her, for sure. Nothing to fret over. Harmless to them, harmless to Cro Magnon."

"He ran a terrible fever!"

"His natural defenses, throwing off an alien but harmless organism."

"You sound pretty certain of that."

He held up a big hand. "Don't even think about askin' me how. Not here."

I was getting irritable. "They'll collect any stool samples they find."

"They won't find the right kind. A fundamental principal of hiding forever is to bury your shit deep. Even that Ishii, in California, knew that."

"Ishii? Is that more Chinook jargon?"

"Nope, name of an Injin. Last survivor of his tribe. He stayed hid a good long time with none the wiser."

"You seem to know an awful lot nobody else knows about skooks, including their toilet habits," I said.

He sighed. "And you need to learn."

"I don't want to know."

"Well, it's too late for that."

"What the hell does that mean?"

"I did say we need to talk. But not here, and not now. Let's get these health-department snoops done and outta the Gorge. Then come see me."

Chapter Twenty-Six

Eventually the Health-Department people went away disappointed, finding no trace of the peculiar parasite; Lincoln said the information would be filed away in case it ever showed up again.

In the meantime I made my first visits to the coalmine cave Big Joe Consonants called home. To everybody in the Gorge he was just the local colorful character; harmless, eccentric and good for the fledgling tourist business. But I couldn't ignore the fact he showed up the night I shot the skook.

The story I wrote about the vanished coal towns was good for their economy too. The Sunday Magazine editor gave my story the cover; it created a mild tourist bonanza. A trickle of city people walked the streets of the remaining towns, shot pictures of the little Orthodox Church with its small blue onion domes, and asked about the coke ovens.

Mildred Fenton, the VA nurse, was aggravated by strangers showing up at her cabin searching for coke ovens. But she took it with weary good grace since my story brought them; she figured she owed me. I found that out when I ran into her with Ralph at the Pick 'n Shovel having ice cream despite the hard freeze of dead winter. She walked outside with me to speak privately.

"Thank you," she said softly when we stopped at my truck.

"For what?"

"For taking revenge for King," she said calmly. "Joe told me the whole story. Maybe poor King's soul will rest better now, wherever he is."

My throat tightened. "I lost a dog, too."

"It sounds corny but maybe your dog told King, wherever they are, that we got one back for him." Her remarkable violet eyes were cold as glacier ice. "I never was able to get a bead on one of those things. If I ever do, I'll repay my debt for *your* dog."

"I hope Joe's not spreading that story," I said. "Too many people think skooks are cute and fuzzy."

"He only told me because of King," Mildred said. "He's not going to make it part of his tourist shtick."

Joe had two old firehouse chairs he appropriated somewhere to bracket the sheepherder's stove that warmed his cave. One chair for solitude and one for company, he said, quoting Henry David Thoreau. That first winter we sat by the stove smoking our pipes while I explored the off-center geography of his mental universe, convoluted as those Gorge coal seams.

He seemed glad for the company, and at first I wondered if he was just lonely. Then I wondered if he thought I was interested in his biography, because he rambled quite a bit, from skook lore to holy men in Nepal to the time he met Mahatma Gandhi and back again. Sometimes he'd just stop talking and his big head would slump down into his whiskers. Sometimes he would doze, snort awake and start off on a different tack. He kept a pot of cowboy coffee brewing on the stove that had a real kick.

The day I told Joe what Mildred said, he nodded gravely.

"Mildred saw the young'un that died when the dogs chased it," he rumbled. "She's a good nurse and a fine lady. She understands the whole tragic thing, why the female came for your boy an' all, after its young'un was killed. But Mildred loved that King with a passion and he was a fine dog and wholly innocent. A woman can be mighty unforgivin', more so than a man. I doubt she'll rest until she puts a crease in a skook personal."

"You think she might?"

"Well, they do tend to be creatures of habit, like all mammals. She might. This Gorge has been one of their homes ages since. The river Injins mostly left it to 'em in the old days before coal. They don't cotton to evil spirits."

"The Gorge is only one skook hangout?"

"They range..." His far-seeing eyes stared out the smudged little window he'd installed beside the salvaged door to his cave.

"How far do they range?"

He shook himself slightly and his attention came back to me.

"I'm not sure. A male cougar now, he'll patrol a beat pret' near a hundred and fifty miles when his paw pads start to itch. Females maybe half that. Onliest reason I know that, one of the Game Department guys who did a study tole me. And bears, now." He wagged his big head. "Black bears ain't the cuddly little Smoky Bears that city folk think. Soon as a boar bear gets to puberty he's at risk of life an' limb from the old boar whose range he's born on. It's move or die. That's why so many young bears wind up in dumpsters and people's yards as so-called civilization spreads out. Big boar pushing from his backside, humans in his face."

"Bears are omnivores, like you say skooks are," I said. "You think skooks treat young males that way?"

"Oh, hell no! Young'uns is their pride an' joy 'cause they breed so few. Life they live ain't conducive to a lot of young 'uns. They gotta stay scattered to survive. Only once in a while do they hanker to congregate. Up in British Columbia years ago, some bands came together on this one mountain every four years and built a great big bonfire, like a ceremony. Always wanted to go see that, but never got around to it." He puffed his pipe. "Never seen these 'uns use fire. But it's not beyond 'em, I don't think."

"You're saying they're more than just animals. Love their children and are capable of building fires."

"Only if you can say mankind is more than just an animal." He knocked his big homemade applewood pipe out on his horny palm. "Every time I read the headlines, I get less sure I can agree to that."

He wasn't being deliberately coy, he was just being Joe. It was almost an afterthought when he said they never forgot a scent.

"That sounds like some kind of warning."

"They won't ever forget your boy's smell," he said. "Now he's been nursed by that grievin' mama. Your house ain't all that far from the foothills, and a breeze off the river might just bring 'em down for a look."

"For God's sake! You think they might come into town?"

"Towns don't scare 'em none. They been in towns before. But you scare 'em. You're quicker on the draw than most."

"Then they should stay away," I said flatly.

"Death in your voice again," Joe said. "They know you now. They'll be a lot sneakier when they come."

"What are you telling me?" I didn't like it, whatever it was.

"You took me to task once, for not warnin' you about skooks. So I'm warning you now: might want to pay special attention when the wind shifts up off the river bottoms."

Chapter Twenty-Seven

I thought Joe was certifiable and would have disbelieved his rambles—but for the skook that stole my son. So I couldn't disregard his frightening pronouncement that they might be back. I pondered ways of trying to gauge river-bottom winds and hit on the old brass elephant bell. This was before the digital revolution, remember. There were no digital trail cameras to link to a home computer—or for that matter, home computers. Maybe the military had appropriate surveillance gear, but I didn't know about it and couldn't have afforded it if I did.

I was a bundle of nerves each time that bell chimed. If it chimed at night, I would sit in my office by the light switch that threw floods out over the deck, with the window unlatched and my Remington in the corner. I wanted to go out prowling but was afraid some neighbor seeing the rifle would think I was getting ready to poach an elk in my apple trees.

If we could have afforded to move, I would have suggested it. But I knew my wife liked living in her mother's house. I would have a hard time prying her loose without telling the truth—and then I might wind up in a rubber room. My thoughts went round and round, poisoned by Joe's ramblings. Even nights when the bell was quiet, I had insomnia.

I was off my feed so bad my wife noticed. I told her my old stress reaction from the years of learning to write on newspaper deadline seemed to be coming back because my fiction writing was bogged down, and she accepted that for an explanation.

Right on the edge of sleep, I would suddenly be terrified for my son, and have to get up and go check his room. Then I'd be awake but exhausted the rest of the night, only able to sleep in the daytime after my wife went to work. Since I had always been a night owl, my wife didn't find that odd; she assumed I sat up mulling story lines even when she didn't hear the typewriter.

Those waking nights, the wild dogs make more than one kill down in the river bottoms. Mildred Fenton was right: they sounded more like hyenas than dogs, or even coyotes. Their cackling yapping caterwauling was enough to make your blood run cold when they pulled down a deer. But Joe said skooks were afraid of them, I was glad they had migrated into the bottoms now the Gorge riflemen had thinned them out up by the park. Their presence made it unlikely skooks would circle out of the foothills into the riverbed behind us. Thinking like that made me wonder if I was certifiable myself.

The days and weeks and finally months dragged by. Six months before the skooks came that July afternoon I went to talk to my friend Vern, the cranky old gunsmith. He was in the middle of one of his many odd projects that day, building a matchlock from scratch. The hand-lapped barrel was complete, polished to a high sheen, and he was applying stain to the lovely walnut from which he'd fashioned an authentic stock. When I told him what I had in mind, he put away his rubbing tools, sawed off a fresh bite of chew and squinted at me as if sighting down a rifle barrel.

"How big a pistol you interested in?"

"Something that would stop a bear."

"Huh. I thought you knew more about guns than that. Ain't no pistol made can compare to your rifles."

"Those bear hunters with hounds usually pack a pistol," I said.

"Well, shore. But shooting a treed bear don't take any real snoose. Even a .30-30's got more snoose than a .44 Magnum. You plannin' to take up bear huntin'?"

"No. I just want a powerful handgun to carry around on my property. I don't want to spook the neighbors or the town clowns by walking around out there with a rifle."

Vern snorted. He was the one who taught me "town clown" for city cop. That was the day he showed me a local cop's revolver so heavily nickeled by some mail-order house that the cylinder wouldn't spin; the cop thought his gun was broken.

"You got bears girdlin' your apple trees," Vern said. "Is that it?"

"Not exactly."

He was still squinting at me. "Word is, you've been hanging out up in the Gorge with crazy old Joe. His tall tales got the wind up?"

"What makes you think that?"

"Petoskey stopped by to sight in that old Model 99 of his for elk season last year. Said old man Tuchi told you about his salmon-catching wild men. And said you had some rocks come down on the cabin you stayed in up there. Could be you suspect them wild men. They're said to be big on tossin' rocks. Funny old Tuchi hit on the same name for 'em that all the Northwest tribes used in their different lingos. All but one meant wild men. That one tribe called 'em clam-eaters."

I had a strange *frisson*. According to my Joel Barber book, the wild man who tried to steal the first duck decoys was prowling East Coast clam beds.

"Is everybody up here a student of skook lore?" I said.

"Skook, is it? Hell, son, Joe's got you talkin' like a native."

"You ever see one of those things?"

"'Fore I stopped hunting, I seen a lot of things in these mountains." Vern expectorated a brown stream into his spit can. "Blue wolves, now. All the so-called experts say we ain't had wolves in these parts for years. But I've seen 'em."

"I thought blue wolves were a myth."

"So are Sasquatches," Vern said. "Hang on."

He went into his house, alongside his shop. I heard him talking to his wife in there and then he came back. "Wife says howdy." He was carrying a big black revolver and a box of shells. "C'mon out to the range."

He had a two-bench shooting range alongside the shop, with targets a hundred yards away against a berm. He had to trust you before he'd let you shoot there, because an electric wire fence crossed in front of the targets so his horses could get to the barn behind his house. He led me halfway to the targets. The horses were at the far end of the pasture, near the highway.

"Here." He handed me the pistol, a long-barreled three-screw Ruger Blackhawk. "Lemme see your hands." I held the gun up. My hands engulfed the walnut grips. "Remembered you havin' big hands," he nodded. He slipped open the box of ammo, big fat .44s. "You know how to load a single-action? Good. Load 'er up."

I half-cocked the hammer and opened the loading gate to feed the big shells. "Ever shot a .44 Magnum?" he said.

"No."

"Let the barrel roll up in recoil. It's gonna surprise you." He stuck his fingers in his ears.

"I don't have hearing protection," I said.

"Just gonna pop a couple to see how it feels," he said.

"Okay." I lined up the sights. Even at fifty yards, the paper targets looked small. The gun had a big boom, even in the open pasture. It kicked and twisted in my hands. "Jesus! Felt like it sprained my wrist."

"Don't try to out-muscle it. Just let it ride up. Try her again."

So I did. I fired five more rounds, getting the hang of it, wondering if I was developing hell's own flinch. My ears were ringing.

"Good enough for now," Vern pronounced. "Don't bother to go look at the target. You pulled most of 'em clear off the paper." He headed back for the shop.

I had seen gouts of dirt jump out of the berm too. "Now what?" I said.

"You know where the cleaning tools are. Clean her up. Go buy yourself one box of .44 Special and one box of Magnum and come back when you can. Use the short .44s and get up within twenty-five yards so you can hit. Learn the gun. When you've run through the light loads, go back to the Magnums and we'll see what's what."

So I got familiar with the big Ruger. I switched it up some by mixing loads, so I wouldn't know if a Special or a

Magnum was next under the hammer. Concentrating on my sight picture, letting the shot surprise me. Before I ran through all 100 cartridges, I was able to keep a cylinder-full on paper. I even began to shoot decent groups. I was there the day Vern tried out his matchlock. From the bench he scored touching holes in the target at a hundred yards, proving to himself ancient firearms were capable of such accuracy.

Then Vern introduced me to a stainless .454 Casull.

"Took it in trade for a custom Model 70 with an Al Biesen stock," he told me. "Damn fool bought this pistol without ever having fired one. He managed five rounds before he wanted rid of it." He spat tobacco juice. "Small hands."

The big Casull took a lot of getting used to, even after the Ruger .44. The shells were shockingly expensive. Following Vern's guidance, I used the same technique to learn the gun: ordinary .45 Long Colt to start with before full-throttle loads. I wrapped my wrist in an Ace bandage the first few times I fired .454s and started doing wrist curls with thirty-pound dumbbells to strengthen my wrists.

Vern told me the .454 generated the same power as a .30-06 at any range I'd have a right to expect a hit. So I had to adjust to equal and opposite reaction from a handgun weighing less than half a high-powered rifle. I've had more fun shooting, but I was motivated to tame the beast. The price almost stopped me, but all I had to do was remember that damn bell's hesitant chimes when the wind shifted.

I almost utterly drained my secret stash of mad money

and never did tell my wife how much I paid for the Wyoming-built revolver. Vern, being Vern, reloaded all the .454 empties for me with a good heavy bullet and refused to charge me. The day I took delivery on the gun and loads, he grinned at me.

"Got yourself a portable skook slayer now," he said. "And know how to shoot it, too." I just looked at him. He busted out laughing. "Big Joe ever decides to take you huntin' some of them myths of his, you can tell him your Casull trumps even his old Yeti rifle for snoose."

Chapter Twenty-Eight

The day after my boy almost made it through the pasture fence, I had a lot of thinking to do. For all my sleepless nights, it had never occurred to me they might come in the daytime. Nor that he would go out to meet them. How the hell did he know they were out there?

Maybe I was overreacting. Maybe my wife was right on that score; maybe he just decided to go for a ramble, and that laid his scent more strongly on the uphill breeze and drew them in. Maybe. Even though I slept damn little that night, there was no way I could sleep after she left for work. I couldn't stop pacing and fulminating.

Finally I loaded our son and Harry in the truck and drove around to where Spiketon Road goes toward the foothills and dead-ends at Carbon Creek; the bridge from the coal-mining days long since vanished. On the far side of the creek, a muddy two-track is all that was left of the road on that side, climbing into second-growth Doug firs. A little over two miles up the track, the vanished town had been named after a coal man named Spike, of all things. Later the town's name was changed to Morristown for another coal man who came later. But the locals, nothing if not averse to change, still called our end of it the Spiketon Road.

I parked facing the creek and stayed in the truck, looking into the dense woods across the sun-sparkling ripples. The big Casull was a comforting bulge under my leather jacket. I was long-bodied enough the long barrel didn't protrude beneath the jacket, and barrel-chested enough an extra lump under my left arm wasn't noticeable by town clowns. Not that it mattered; my concealed-pistol paperwork was all in order.

If I could get across the creek, would I find giant naked footprints coming down the muddy track? Probably not, if those things had the habit of stealth. Too much chance of some guy in a Jeep coming down behind them. The Bonneville Power maintenance road cut across the foothills to White River, and local Jeepers liked to ford the creek here going to and coming from the power-line road. If I was really curious I could go up to Burnett, cut back on the power-line road and scout the two-track. I wasn't that curious. I rolled down the window to see if I could catch a trace of skook stink. All I smelled was resin from the firs.

"Goin' fishin', Dad?" In the last almost two years my son had mastered the second D.

"No, son. Why?"

"Big fishes in there."

"There are, huh? How do you know?"

He pointed. "See 'em. See?"

All I saw was sun-glint on dark water. I stared hard—and suddenly I could see log-like shapes in the shallows, pointed upstream. Then I couldn't again.

"See?" he said.

"I did—for a minute. Boy, you've got sharp eyes."

"Sharp eyes? Like a knife?"

"It means good eyes—means you can see really well."

"Oh!"

"Salmon, I reckon," I said. "Looks like some got by

those wild men down under the Burnett Bridge."

"Wild men?" He thought about it. "Norgus porkus?"

"No, son, not those kind of wild men."

"But Raff said!"

"You remember Ralph, do you?"

"Sure! Ne-o-poln!" He was gaining on pronunciation of his favorite dessert. "Raff likes it!"

"Your memory's good as your eyes."

"Gonna *see* Raff?" He clapped his hands.

"Not today, son." I thought about what he said for a minute. "Say, son? You weren't headed off to see Ralph by yourself yesterday were you? When Harry got you by the seat of your britches?"

He scowled. "Hawwy bad! Stop me 'splorin!"

"That's why you were out there, exploring?"

Still scowling: "Mom said! 'Splorin."

"Yeah, little guy, she did say that. But you didn't say. Not a word."

"Mad at Hawwy. Mad at *you*. You told him good dog!"

Harry was curled on the floorboard beneath my son's booster seat. I could see those fine antenna-like hairs above his eyebrows flicker as he followed the conversation.

"Harry *is* a good dog." I drew a deep breath. "That's the second time he's found you for me. I don't suppose you remember the first time."

"Wanna see Raff!"

"Okay, okay. I'll call Mildred and see when we can go see Ralph."

"'Kay." His brief thunderstorm was past. "Play cheggers!"

I backed around to head out. The change in angle

brought the breeze that was whipping down the creek through the open window. Harry uncurled and put his forepaws on the seat, nose working. His lips wrinkled back from his teeth and he growled. Well, he had a way-better nose than me.

"Quiet, Hawwy!" my son said firmly.

Harry's ears drooped. But he didn't stop growling.

"It's okay, Harry. We're leaving," I said. "Good dog. I thought they must have come this way."

"Dad? How come you tell Hawwy good dog when he gwowl?"

"He smells something he doesn't like," I said. "He's warning us."

"Smell 'zat bad smell back there?"

Icy fingers played my spine like a xylophone. "What bad smell, son?"

"Hawwy smelled it too. Ugh. Be-uh, Dad? Be-uh come eat the fishes like on TV?"

I drove back up the Spiketon road. "We don't have a TV. Where'd you see bears fishing?"

"Mattie does!" Mattie was the Montessori teacher my wife had found for our boy. "We see nachur shows!"

So much for a TV-free household; I had to smile. "So you know bears fish for salmon," I said. "That's in Alaska, which is far away from here. I don't know if bears around here catch salmon that way."

"How come?"

"Different sort of bears."

"How many kinds *is* there?"

"You know, I don't rightly know. Maybe you can ask Mattie."

"'Kay. Where to now, Dad?"

"I've been craving a hamburger and a milk shake. Wanna go to Enumclaw, see what we can find?"

I didn't have to ask twice.

Chapter Twenty-Nine

We were skating pretty close on finances, but I figured we could afford burgers and shakes. After we finished our food at a worn little Enumclaw eatery whose food was way better than its décor, we walked around the little downtown park in the bright mild July sunshine. I pushed our finances a little harder and paid $12.95 for a Chinook Jargon Dictionary at an independent bookseller's, among one of the most eclectic I'd seen anywhere; of course he had the dictionary at his fingertips.

A dozen or so artists and artisans, including a small independent coffee company, were showing their wares along one edge of the parking lot. I bought a cup of strong Costa Rican and sat to page through the dictionary for a few minutes before my son got restless and wanted to look at everything.

I was struck by some oil paintings done by a woman that depicted totem poles chopped off at the base, lying in crushed ferns in front of what looked like a long house. In one of the paintings, the poles were on fire. The juxtaposition of splintered, bright-colored faces with the black blistering of the flames as they consumed the wood was startling.

"Kind of grim topic," I said to the painter.

"Even worse in reality," she said. "Good Christians did this, to break the natives of their superstitions."

"Really?"

"Oh, yeah." She surveyed her work. "A tribesman came

by once when I was showing these. You know what he said?"

"What?"

"They thought they had the right. That's all he said: they thought they had the right."

The salmon-river tribes of the Northwest had been developing their myths and culture and trade lingo for more than thirty centuries when Europeans showed up to set them straight, based on a Johnny-come-lately religion from the other side of the world. Somehow she had captured that whole tragic culture collision in her paintings.

My book said the various tribes addressed the strange pink men in trade jargon, of course. They were strangers and that was what Chinook Jargon was for: to interact with strangers. The jargon adapted quickly, and Americans became "Boston men" from Boston *Illahee*, meaning Boston Land, an unwitting tribute to far-roving sailors from New England. The English were "King Chautsh men" for King Charles. Every other brand of white-eyes but the French were called Dutchmen. French were Pasiooks. The artist lady got a kick out of that one.

"I've often thought the same thing myself about the French," she said with a smile.

She was a nice lady, and her rendition of the Christian destruction of the totem poles spoke to me strongly about follies of religious hubris. I was wishing I had the wherewithal to buy one of her paintings for my office when my son let out a whoop: "Dad! Look!"

He dragged me in front of another portable awning where a little old grandmotherly type was busily at work on a large canvas back in the shade. My son planted himself in front of another big canvas, and stared.

It was a god-damn skook, tromping through the *salal*.

"Don't be afraid, son," I said. "It's just a picture."

"Not *afwaid!* Look! Must be eatin' bewwies!"

The gray-haired lady bestowed a fond smile on him. "That's right, sonny, they just love those big blue berries."

She wasn't a poor artist; you could see dew glisten on the plump *salal* berries. The skook was faithfully reproduced but for one thing: somehow she had made its alien mug as open and guileless as a child's. As this child of mine, staring at it in fascination.

"You painted the thing as harmless," I said.

"Why of *course* they're harmless. Just big old softies, that's all they are. Berry-eaters."

"You sound like you know them personally."

"Well...no." She looked at me strangely. "Of course not. They're just legends, you know. From all the way back to superstitious Indian times. But the Indians like *salal* berries, so I figured why not?"

"Different kind of be-uh, Dad?" He held his nose. "Kind that smell bad?"

"Why bless your heart, honey, it's a Sasquatch!" the little old lady said.

"Smell bad!" he told her, still holding his nose. "Pee—you!"

"Well now, that *is* part of the legend," the little old lady said, surprised. "Aren't you the smart one, to know that about Sasquatches?"

I was shocked how quickly I had relaxed after the burgers and shakes and mild sun in the slow pace of a small peaceful town: for a few moments I had almost forgotten Enumclaw was the last stop before Chinook Pass, on the edge of the vast Cascade Wilderness, where our personal trouble came from. Even though our trouble had come calling just yesterday.

I noticed my son was trying to pronounce the strange word, trying to sound it out. My throat tightened just to watch him. "Try skook," I said.

"Skook, Dad?"

"What is that, that word you used?" the grandmotherly artist reacted to the tone of my voice; her lips pressed together.

"Skook," I said. "Short for skookum. Chinook Jargon for evil spirit."

"Oh, my—you can't call a Sasquatch evil!"

"Let's go, son," I said. "Time to be headed home."

The old woman gazed after me with a troubled look. I was pretty damn troubled myself. No matter where we went, we couldn't seem to escape the damn things.

Chapter Thirty

I had to wait until Saturday when my wife was off work to go talk to Joe Consonants about skooks coming toward our house in broad daylight. She and one of her sisters planned to take the kids to some kind of children's activities in Seattle, so I didn't have to worry about leaving my son at home.

After they headed for the city, I headed for Joe's cave. Even midday, the Gorge was shadowed from the sun and it was cooler than the lowlands. Joe wasn't answering his cave door, so Harry and I walked back toward the county road. I heard a vehicle stop and a door open and close, a mumbled exchange, and the car went away. Harry wagged his tail and woofed that little woof with a question mark on the end, and I knew Joe must have bummed a ride from somebody. Harry and Joe had reached a rapprochement of sorts on previous visits, cemented with grilled bits of rabbit from Joe's snare line.

The big man came soft-footing from the highway with an open-top pasteboard box under each arm. He was wearing an old hickory logging shirt with sleeves scissored off above his impressive biceps and faded black logger's jeans supported by bright red suspenders. The britches were staged off at his shins to accommodate a rigger's high boots. His feet were bare, of course; no logging boots for Joe.

I took one of the boxes, full of a stack of old

newspapers, and followed him back. The other box held a big blue can of Maxwell House coffee and assorted canned goods. He unsnapped a leather flap on the cave door, exposed a long-shank bicycle lock and spun the combination one-handed.

"I didn't even know your door locked," I said.

"Yep." He pulled open the door and picked up a length of steel rebar with a center-drilled hole for the padlock. A steel bracket with a corresponding hole was bolted on the center of the door, other brackets on each side of the frame.

"Pretty tricky," I said.

"Too complicated for a teenager to bother with anyway."

He put his supplies on his kitchen counter; a slab of warped Formica somebody had discarded doing a remodel. He struck a big kitchen match on his thumbnail and lit his kerosene lamp, then took the box of newspapers.

"How come you're collecting old newspapers, Joe?"

"Good fire-starters." He reached for one of his handmade pipes. "Plus, I like to let my news of the world age a little. Less stressful that way. Then I burn it. A little ritual, like. See?"

"It's one way to do it."

He touched off a bowl of his personal *kinnikinnik*. The word meant smoking weed in the Jargon and stood for bear-berry, a shrub with reddish bark, evergreen leaves and bright red berries. Indians cured the leaves for smoking and ate the berries. Joe blended the leaves with inexpensive Carter Hall drug-store tobacco. He expelled a cloud of smoke, sat and stretched his long legs toward the cold stove.

"*Elip kloshe.*" He rolled up a handful of newspaper. "Means 'better'. Take a load off." He struck another match and pushed the newspaper in the stove with some cedar kindling. "Be ready to brew coffee in no time," he said. "Coffee aids talkin'. What brings you up to see me?"

I sat and leaned forward. Harry curled up beside me. "Skooks came into the pasture behind mine," I said. "Just a couple day ago. In broad daylight!"

He squinted at me. "You saw 'em?"

"No. But I heard one scream."

"A-huh! Wind off the bottoms?"

"Just like you warned me," I said.

He moved a handful of newspapers to reveal a paperback book and laid it aside: *Jaws*, by Peter Benchley, published to a lot of fanfare right after the New Year. I was surprised it already was out in paperback.

"Summertime reading, Joe?"

"Waitress at the Shovel said she's not gonna surf the Oregon coast anymore after the nightmares she got."

"You need more nightmares?"

He chuckled. "Well, I ain't no surfer. Great White Sharks hold no terror for me." He scanned headlines as he twisted more sheets of newsprint into tight spirals.

"Lookahere. Another Jap soldier came out of the brush in the Philippines, been hiding for twenty-nine years. They been finding those guys off'n on since the war got over. Like that Ishii guy in California I tol' you about. If Injins and Jap soldiers can hide from us, I don't see why a person is so surprised skooks can."

"Joe, they came in broad daylight!"

"But you didn't see 'em. Did anybody?"

"Not that I know of."

"Why do you think one yelled?"

"Those bear dogs on Ryan Road went crazy when the skooks got upwind of them."

"A-huh! They're afraid of those packs. I suppose they ran when the dogs winded 'em."

"They did. But dammit Joe, my son sneaked out his bedroom window and was almost through the back fence when I caught him. It was like he was going to meet them!"

He nodded solemnly. "To be expected."

Chapter Thirty-One

I leaned back. "What the hell do you mean, it was to be expected?"

He added small splits of alder as the kindling began to crackle. "Tol' you he was marked by 'em," he said calmly. "He'll always know when they're around. Just like me." He went on reading. "Huh. Some things don't never change." He read aloud: "United Mine Workers president found guilty of first-degree murder for ordering assassination of union reformer, his wife and daughter."

I felt like strangling him—if I could have got my hands around his thick neck.

"Joe..."

He looked up. "I did read your coalmine story. You left out the big UMW strike in 1919. Some blamed the union for the fire that destroyed Melmont, after a miner was tried in Tacoma for plantin' dynamite under his foreman's bed in a Melmont boarding house."

I had missed all that; primitive fragging in the coalfields before anybody ever heard of Viet Nam. Another time I would have been bothered about missing it, but not now. I felt like yelling at him. He was still reading.

"They find Patty Hearst yet?" he said.

"What the *hell* does that have to do with skooks in my pasture?"

"Nary thing. Says here the cops and FBI burned up them SLA terrorists in a fire. But Citizen Kane's progeny

203

didn't get cooked," he added thoughtfully.

"Joe, are you going to talk to me about these skooks or not?"

He consigned the SLA news to the flames, got down his old enamel coffee pot and primed the pump on his recycled sink; he'd shown me the Rube Goldberg plumbing he devised to bring creek water indoors on my first visit. With the pot on the stove he relit his pipe and studied me.

"Death in your voice again," he said. "Reminds me of me, back when I took to killin' skooks. I wasn't any more ready to think about anything else than you are now." He turned back to his newspapers. "My, my—*India* testing an atom bomb? Bet my old friends in Nepal don't like that!"

I controlled my building anger by a sheer act of will. Joe was acting no differently than ever, though it was the first time he had admitted to killing skooks; it was me that had changed, because the damn skooks were back.

"Muster your patience," he said as if reading my thoughts. "Way they operate it coulda been a dozen years before they showed up."

"But it wasn't," I said.

"Tell me what happened," he said.

So I went through it for him while the coffee perked. When I was done, he poured two cups. I accepted one automatically. He settled back unhurriedly.

"Young feller made it all the way to the back fence, huh? Strong young'un. Determined, too."

"If Harry hadn't grabbed the seat of his britches..."

He smiled down at Harry. "But Harry did. That's some dog you got there." Harry's tail thumped slowly. "Yeah, yeah, I'll get you some rabbit in a minute," Joe said. "After your boss gets it all off his chest. You had your big old pistol with you, I expect," he said to me.

"You're damned right."

He nodded gravely. "They won't be back, not for a long time. They know you, don't think they don't. They're afraid of you. And you surprised 'em by reacting so quick. Believe me, they got the message: your place is off-limits for visits."

"*Visits?*"

"A-huh. Just to get a glimpse of the boy, see. He's special to them now, since he spent time with that female."

"You need to tell me about this marking business," I said. "Sooner rather than later."

He gazed into the shadowy ceiling of his cave for what seemed a long time before he answered.

"I was six years old in nineteen and ought eight, the year I was marked," he said. "I'm two years younger than this century. I've done put *sinamokst tahlum* behind me."

"Joe," I said, "No jargon please."

"What?" He looked at me. "Oh. Seventy. I'm already past seventy *ikt cole*. Years." He paused. "'Ought-eight was the year the skooks came for me."

"What? Skooks kidnapped you when you were six years old?"

"Not perzactly. They found me. I was lost in the woods."

"At six years old?"

"There was lots more people in the Gorge then remember, when coal was king," he said. "Thousands, prob'ly. Lots of kids like me. And boys like to do stuff. Hoyt and me went huntin' mushrooms. Had some, too.

Kept goin' deeper in the woods and got turned around."
He sipped coffee. "Hard to remember now I didn't always
know every wrinkle in these hills."

"What do you mean they marked you? And marked my
son?"

He gazed at me levelly. "You know damn good and
well your boy nursed from that 'un before you caught 'em.
How you think he came up with an unknown parasite?"

"We were scared to death, he was so sick," I said.
"Another score for me to settle with these damn
monsters."

He flinched. "Such cold rage," he said softly. "It hurts
me to hear it. Mostly because I was the same way for a
long time, after I got away from 'em. It pains to admit it,
but I shot more than one to death as a young man. They
were too easy for me to find, see—because just like your
boy, I always sensed when they were around."

"Did you shoot that one in Ape Canyon in 1924?"

"You never turn loose a question, do you? I was
twenty-two that year," he said slowly. "A man full-growed.
Or so I thought. That 'un wasn't my first either. I've got a
lot on my conscience. I'm glad you scared 'em this time.
They'll stay gone now for a long time. Maybe I can help
you avoid gettin' too much on your conscience, too."

"You claim you were grabbed by skooks, you hated
them for it, and you hunted them. But now you're an
apologist?" I was getting angry. "Let me worry about my
own damn conscience."

He wagged his big head and drank coffee. "I swear,
you remind me of me back then. Almost the same thing I
tol' ol' Ronnie Satiacum when he tried to put me straight

about skooks. He said I wasn't all that great shakes as a stalker, they let me find 'em see, because they kind of trusted me at first."

"Who the hell is Ronnie Satiacum?"

"A real-old Injin who lived up here in the Gorge. Older than I am now back when this happened. Half Nez Pierce and half Puyallup, talk about your unlikely marriages. He didn't like river fishin' for salmon like his daddy's people, wanted to be a horse Injin like his mama's kin. Best hand with horses I ever saw. He opened a livery stable in Fairfax for coal folks who might want to rent a horse or a buggy, and he trained saddle horses for a lot of people."

"Okay. What did this ancient horseman know about skooks?"

He got up and offered more coffee. I hadn't touched mine. He refilled his mug and sat cradling it and his gaze got lost in the cave shadows again.

"About all there was to know," he said slowly. "Ronnie's the one who got me back. Shot the big' un carryin' me right through the brain with that old .45-90 o' mine. Left it to me when he passed at age ninety-eight."

"So he was a local hero. But how did he know that the skooks kind of trusted you, as you put it?"

He gave me an embarrassed look. "Besides him, I ain't ever told another living soul this: before Satiacum got me back, one o' the lactatin' females fed me. Only way she could. Just like that 'un was tryin' to feed your son even as she died."

Something I had been trying to forget. Now I said, "Joe, you were six years old!"

"Sounds kinda perverted, don't it?" He ducked his

head. "You wonder I never told nobody?"

"It sounds...Never mind how it sounds." I had been going to say it sounded crazy but that was a given, talking to Joe. "Did you get sick?"

"Damn near died. Parasites in my shit? Don't know. The local sawbones for the mine company wrote it off to exposure, being wet and lost all night in the woods. Same reason he gave for cause of death when the hounds found Hoyt's body."

"Wait. Your friend died?"

"A huh. I was too sick to go to his funeral. But I knew it wasn't exposure, see. We got separated that night. I knew the skooks scared him to death. Like they almost did me."

"They scared your childhood chum to death," I said.

"My best friend." He nodded. "I spent a lot of years tryin' to get even, before I finally understood ol' Satiacum was right, I was marked by them. Picked out for a special bond."

Chapter Thirty-Two

Joe told me a lot more before I left his cave that July afternoon. From any twentieth-century perspective it was utterly insane. But Joe had the complete conviction of the utterly mad that skooks and early Indian tribes forged some kind of ancient pact of coexistence that was handed down from generation to generation. He was absolutely serious that he had been abducted when he was six and rescued by this Ronnie Satiacum and his father, tracking the skooks with his father's hounds.

In the early seventies, Sasquatch literature was not the drug on the market it later became, complete with idiotic movies and television commercials. Nothing I read came close to Joe's tale—or to my own experience. There was nothing about parasites passed to humans. The few stories about abductions reported muteness or madness in returned abductees, from tough fur trappers to women, attributed to "hysteria." Evidently a catch-all phrase for something akin to post-traumatic stress syndrome.

On the Track of the Sasquatch, a new paperback published the year before by a retired Canadian newspaperman, assembled some Bigfoot stories. He reported that British Columbia tribes had legends about "mountain giants" who had been around thousands of years.

But his most detailed account came from a statement sworn before "the commissioner for oaths in and for the

Province of Alberta." A lone hunter attested that night-stalking hairy giants rolled him, his rifle and his bedroll up in his tent and made off with him. They unrolled him in a remote camp and gave him to understand he was a prisoner. They utterly ignored the rifle he had clung to like grim death. He concluded in his affidavit they had no idea what a firearm was. When he made his break for freedom and they swarmed after him, a single shot into rocks above their heads scattered them and they broke off pursuit...

There was nothing about this hunter being forced to nurse from a female. And of course, nothing about him being "marked" in such a way as to always know when skooks came around.

"That's totally illogical," I said when Joe told me about his and my son's alleged marking that July afternoon.

"You mean it don't make scientific sense in the outside world," dismissing the outside world as beneath notice. "But I always knew they were around. I hated and feared 'em after what they did to Hoyt. When I was old enough, I tracked down and killed my first one with my daddy's .30-40 Krag. Then I went to ol' Ronnie Satiacum for a horse to pack it out. He tol' me forget it, the carcass would be gone by the time we got there. And it was."

"Joe—they came at my place in broad daylight!"

"They couldn't hardly resist, with the wind off the bottoms. Not to grab your son again." He held up a big hand. "Just to look at him. They came around a lot when I was still a kid. I could always sense 'em. More people saw 'em back then, too. Fishin' for salmon an' all."

"But you went from killing them to apologizing for them," I said. "Because of this old Indian."

"Ol' Satiacum said the exchange of mother's milk sealed the treaty between them and us for centuries. Ever since they walked over here together from Asia in prehistoric times. Humans forgot. But they never did. I never really b'lieved him till I fell in with them holy fellers in Nepal and found out it's the same with Yetis."

"And how could this would-be horse Indian have known that?" Let alone Nepalese and Abominable Snowmen; but I could only follow one thread of his insane tale at a time.

"Ain't it obvious? Ronnie was marked before I was. He was their human contact since Civil War times. Tryin' to watch over them. He had to kill that 'un to get me back, to prevent my daddy burning down these mountains to kill 'em all. Watchers have to do hard things sometimes. Like I thought I'd have to kill that 'un that took your son. But you beat me to it."

"I wondered how you knew to come down there," I said. "Don't tell me skooks warned you."

He smiled faintly. "Okay I won't. You got enough to digest as is."

"This old Indian was nursed by a skook too? Back in the last century?"

"Spent near a month with 'em, when he was about eight. His Nez Perce mama said she'd scalp that baby skook one o' the Puyallup squaws nursed if one hair of her baby was hurt."

"I don't believe any Indian mama would suckle a hairy little chimp," I told him. "If that's what you're trying to sell me."

"I ain't sellin' nothin'. Somehow after all the forgotten

centuries, skooks in the Gorge still cotton to a need for a secret contact with humans. Satiacum was it for a long time. Then when the tribes forgot, there was me." He put down his coffee mug. "And when I'm gone, the most likely candidate will be your son."

Chapter Thirty-Three

The skooks didn't come back around our house again that summer as far as I know. I watched my son like a hawk, and he took no more unexpected jaunts toward the foothills. After Joe Consonants shrugged off the incident as not worth worrying about, because the skooks had marked my son out for a special relationship dating back centuries, I stopped going to talk to him that summer. I was afraid if I spent more time around him, my own grip on reality would slip; after all I had slaughtered a lactating female to rescue my son. Sometimes I wondered if I hadn't been hallucinating the whole thing.

The rainless mild days bled into one another and August came. My orchard's tree-fruit ripened and the wild blackberries along the fences turned deep blue-black and juicy. Meanwhile, the outside world went about its business: Nixon resigned his Presidency that August to avoid impeachment.

When I wrote a story about *pestis* in the Cascades for the Sunday Magazine, Lincoln at the Health Department told me he was keeping an eye on professional journals for reports of an unidentified parasite like they found in my son's stool sample; so far, nothing seemed suggestive. I wasn't about to ask him if he thought an unknown parasite could transmit extrasensory perception via a cryptid mother's milk.

I tried to keep life as normal as possible. With

Mildred's help, I took my son to see Ralph at the Soldier's Home in Orting, and they had a happy reunion. I promised to bring him to Wilkeson for Tillamook ice cream the next time Mildred brought Ralph to her cabin. Mildred reported no new skook sightings but said she was keeping her rifle handy in the Gorge. Mildred's unrelenting hatred was one of the few things to reassure me of my own sanity.

My wife kept working for the jet-engine guy, and enjoyed learning all the ins and outs of clearing the New Zealand motors through Customs. She brought home trunk loads of New Zealand pine slats from their crates for me to split into kindling.

After I failed to get a job as Seattle bureau man for a string of weeklies because the editor didn't believe I could find enough gas to get to work in the aftermath of the Arab oil embargo, I answered a newspaper ad for temporary weekend work at an outdoor publication headquartered in Seattle and wrote brief stories about salmon fishing at Westport and trout fishing in Eastern Washington.

I hadn't told the editor of the weekly chain that right through all that even-and-odd nonsense during the Embargo, and a limit of five gallons even where there was gas, my wife and I always had plenty of fuel. It was yet another Gorge secret: Boots Rubery had some kind of arrangement with independent tankers.

My wife's connections to the Gorge—and my writing about the coal towns—meant she could always get to work in Tacoma and I could put forty gallons in my dual tanks for a dime a gallon more than the pre-embargo price. All we had to do was keep our mouths shut about where we got it, to prevent a run on his tanks that would make the bank runs of the Depression look like an Easter parade; Rubery's words. I was in the habit of keeping my mouth shut, so I missed out on the first job, but wound up liking the second one better anyway.

One reason I liked it was that I worked weekends only, and my wife was home with our son. But my first days away from the plateau were tense anyway, worrying the skooks might somehow know I was gone. My wife promised not to let the boy wander off, the first weekends passed, and the skooks stayed gone. Our finances eased, and I began to relax by degrees; skooks might exist, and I might have shot one, but that didn't mean their behavior represented some inhuman intelligence that would lead them to conform to a demented hermit's elaborate imaginings.

In mid-September I had a Saturday free and took Harry and my shotgun up in the Cascades to look for grouse or band-tail pigeons. My wife grumbled about it, but I told her that now I was officially an outdoor writer, I needed to get outdoors. That got an eye-roll, but I went anyway.

All the chipmunks I saw looked healthy and frisky, and seemed to delight in teasing Harry. He damn near climbed a Doug fir chasing one. He bumped a couple of ruffed grouse out of an alder bottom, and I got a clear shot on one and dumped it with the left barrel of my old Winchester 24. Later, way up in the high country, I found a blue grouse that looked big as a young turkey perched in a fir and made a head shot with a .45 Colt round in my Casull. The only band-tails I saw were flitting along the far side of a canyon. We were coming back down in mid-afternoon

215

when I saw fresh sign crossing the road atop my tire tracks.

Big bare feet, with lots of weight on them.

They came down the cut bank on one side of the road and climbed the other side. I slipped a couple of rifled slugs into the Model 24, never having lost my old Florida habit of carrying big-game loads for my shotgun, and tried to follow them to see up the bank. My boots dug in, causing mini-avalanches with each step and I slid back before I reached the top. The bare feet had caused no such disturbance.

It looked like the Yahoos were back.

When I was a kid, Fess Parker played Davy Crockett on TV, "King of the Wild Frontier." Being contrary, I thought Daniel Boone was really the frontier king, always westering out ahead of what passed for civilization, returning with hair-raising tall tales for the stay-at-homes. He was a long-hunter well into his crippled-up old age after most men would have traded their saddle for a rocking chair.

One of Boone's tales was that on a hunt into uncharted lands he killed a ten-foot tall "Yahoo," bigger than a bear and twice as woolly. Too good a yarn to die, it trickled down through generations of wilderness campfires and eventually into tall-tale collections; after all, this is the nation of Pecos Bill and Paul Bunyan.

Some historian postulated the whole Bigfoot myth originated with Boone's windy, which seemed as good an explanation as any. But not anymore, now I had shot my own Yahoo. And not today, with big bare footprints atop my tire tracks. All my tension came back as if it had never been away.

When I made it back down to pavement, I decided to go see if Joe Consonants was home.

Chapter Thirty-Four

There was a clapped-out old Plymouth station wagon parked near the path leading to Joe's mineshaft. I left Harry in the truck and took the blue grouse with me. Joe was hunkered comfortably outside the door to his cave puffing on his pipe and talking to one of the most Mongoloid of the kids from beneath the Burnett Bridge.

"Brought you some dinner, Joe," I said.

He stood up with that amazing ease. The boy stayed hunkered. I never could hunker worth a damn but Joe looked capable of catching a double-header, even at his age. "First grouse o' the season," he said. "I thank you. This here's one of Aaron's boys."

Aaron was the albino outlaw with the CB to warn his poaching clan if the law showed up.

"You look like you ran into an unfriendly Indian," I told the boy. His usually bushy hair had been buzzed so short he resembled a boot-camp trainee.

He gazed up at me with his narrow almost-lidless eyes. "Too hot."

The Gorge had probably topped at around seventy that summer, a veritable heat wave. "You'll need a warm cap pretty soon. Fall steelhead showing up yet?"

"Some. Wanna come spearin'?"

"See you're acquainted," Joe said. "He brought me a nice one, already smoked. With steelhead and grouse I'm gonna eat like a king tonight."

The boy stood up as easily as Joe. It struck me that with his new haircut he looked just like that banjo-playing hillbilly kid in the movie *Deliverance*. "Better git," he said.

"Say hello to Aaron for me," I said.

He nodded. "Come spearin'." And he was gone.

Joe was studying me. "That boy don't trust many. He likes you."

"Showed me his favorite spearing spots one time."

"Quite an honor." Joe hefted the grouse. "Nice and plump, and already drawn. I thank you."

"I stopped by to see if you'd been up roaming the high country today," I said. "Big bare feet on top of my tire tracks."

"Warn't me. I'll just put this bird on the sink and put on the coffee." When he came back, he was lugging one of the chairs from beside the stove. "I noticed you ain't much for hunkerin'," he said. "Take a load off."

"So it was a skook." I sat.

"Imagine so. It's berryin' time. You and Harry musta got upwind and spooked him, for him to leave tracks in the open thataway. Told you, they know you." He resumed his catcher's squat. "They'll be down to see Aaron soon."

"What do you mean, down to see Aaron?"

The big man shrugged. "Him an' his have a sort of agreement. They don't get run off the creek for spearin' skooks' fish. In turn, they dry-cure fish and jerk pemmican—venison an' dried berries—for the skooks, so they can stay out of the creek and hide from people like you an' old man Tuchi."

"Of the things you've told me," I said, "that's close to the hardest to believe. And that's saying a lot."

"Disbelievin' don't make it not so," Joe said. "Huntin' season's comin'. Skooks cain't fish for winter supplies like they usta before the coal towns crowded up the Gorge."

"You're telling me old Tuchi really saw them fishing for salmon like bears do?"

"Tuchi warn't the only one. Men goin' fishin' run some off the creek a time or two. Some got rocks thrown at 'em, and ran themselves. They didn't talk about it much."

"Tuchi said skooks resented the miners taking their fish. Caused cave-ins to kill the offenders. I have reasons of my own to know they're handy with big rocks."

"That's...possible," the big man said. "Warn't that many good ways to find out what caused a land slippage in them days. And just because Mr. Darwin never met a skook don't mean they stand outside the natural processes he figgered out. Aggressive displays an' such—like throwin' rocks--can turn deadly outside yore own kind if you're defending territory that's been encroached on. They never had a pact with miners, see."

"Except maybe the Chinese miners in Burnett?" I said. "You told some Japanese tourists the Gorge looked after its own when the Knights of Labor came to burn down their tent city."

"Well I didn't say that perzactly," he said. "We was talkin' about animist religions as I recall."

"Like a belief in giant screeching animals slinging boulders the size of a basketball ball at every raider who raised a rifle?"

"You're developin' quite an imagination," Joe said. "Giant screechin' animals that smell like they crawled rottin' from their tombs, I bet you was about to say. Not that I was there, mind. I ain't *that* old."

"But your mentor, Ronnie Satiacum, was."

He smiled sadly. "Ronnie was some taken with a Chinee girl, daughter of one of the laundry fellers in Fairfax, because she respected him as an elder. He come to respect them hard-workin' men in Burnett after she tole him how they was workin' for their destitute families back home. Took it strong amiss when them white boys from Tacoma marched up the Gorge."

"And being Johnny Weissmuller of the Skooks," I said, "he let out a Tarzan yell and they all came running, boulders in hand."

"You ain't old enough to remember Johnny Weissmuller."

"I watched a lot of Saturday movies when my folks got their first black-and-white TV."

"It's all ancient fairy tales anyways," he said. "More ancient than Mr. Burrough's original Tarzan books. Bloodbaths averted don't make history, as a rule. But they can become part of fairy tales."

"With you as the chief tale-spinner," I said. "But we did kind of wander off Aaron being the commissary for skooks."

"I don't wonder you have a hard time takin' it all in." He hunkered again. "The Injins would say Aaron is touched by the gods. But modern-day society just discarded him to that damn state school because they decided he wasn't all there."

"Aaron was in the state school? He's no more a boy than me."

"He was just a boy when he escaped, though. Kids are

always escapin'. Sometimes they drown in the river. Sometimes they get caught again. Sometimes they die of exposure."

"He's odd, Aaron," I said. "But I never thought of him as retarded."

"Aaron's got plenty of brain cells. He just uses 'em different, like. He tries to look after his kin."

"You call the skooks his kin?"

"Well," Joe said slowly, "screwin' one and makin' babies does create a kin-relation."

"For God's sake, Joe!" This was just taking it too far. "Hypertrichosis doesn't make those kids of Aaron's part-skook. Not unless skooks have the right number of chromosomes."

"My, what a fancy word for havin' a lot of hair." Joe smiled a little sadly. "I sometimes think fancy words are what we use to hold reality at bay. Far as I know, nobody ever counted chromosomes in a skook."

I changed gears. "If I was still a newspaperman, there would be a story in what you say about kids escaping the school and coming to harm," I said. "Official neglect, and so on. Now you tell me Aaron was an escapee a long time ago."

"Don't seem that long to me, but yep. And didn't drown or freeze to death or get recaptured." Joe pulled a face. "But he did get found."

Chapter Thirty-Five

We moved inside Joe's cave so he could prepare his repast of smoked salmon and fresh grouse. Once more, he had set the hook in me with his claim of Aaron's kinship with skooks. I probably should have ignored the big barefoot tracks and gone home. But now I wanted to hear this part of the fairy tale. If that's what it was.

"Aaron escaped the school when he was a boy," I said, "and made his way up the Gorge to you?"

"Not perzactly. They found him and brought him to me because he was so terrified." He paused. "A feelin' I clearly recall from when I got grabbed. A feelin' you clearly recall, for a slightly different reason."

"Skooks you're talking about."

"Yep."

"Skooks didn't build him that cabin or buy him a CB radio and those beat-up old .22s."

"Well, no. I did that."

"And taught him to drive and use a CB?"

"He already knew how to do those things. Taught him to shoot. But he's kind of a savant with electronic gadgets. I got him that old car from the wrecking yard."

"Of course you did," I said. "I suppose it's registered to you."

"Nope, to the wrecking yard. They like all the salmon and venison Aaron supplies. If it breaks down for good, he can just walk away. They'll haul it to the scrap-metal yard

223

in Tacoma and I'll have 'em fix him up another'n. My social security check's good for some things."

"It's like a damn secret society," I said. "The skooks, Aaron, the chop shop and you. But that doesn't make those kids who live with him half-skook."

He was plucking the grouse. "Maybe their mama was one of them girls from the school that got with a skook male. I try not to pry into my neighbors' sexual habits."

"I've never seen females at Aaron's."

"'Spect he keeps 'em hid from pryin' eyes. Let the school people keep thinking they drowned or froze or caught a bus to Tacoma to sleep over a heat grate."

"You make the school sound medieval," I said.

"There's a whole movement these days claims that institutionalizin' the mentally retarded is little better than medieval." His big hands were surprisingly deft; he deposited each handful of feathers into a paper grocery sack under the sink and few fluttered loose. "I'd think you know that, as a reporter."

"Started back when JFK was president," I said. "Word was he had a sister who had been lobotomized in the dark days. Before somebody lobotomized *him* terminally with a full-metal jacket." I shrugged. "There's always a movement for something these days," I said. "And there are plenty of rumors in town that the school will close down one of these days. Until it does, they should take better care of the kids. When I was a working reporter, I would have considered it criminal for even one kid to escape and die of exposure. I still do."

He pulled a couple of random grouse feathers off his shirtfront. "Getting' stuck in the ass end of nowhere as keeper of lost souls ain't good for a climb up the bureaucratic ladder. All it can get you is ignored if you do it right an' grief if somethin' scandalous happens on your watch. So bein' human, you cover it up so nobody knows."

"Some disgruntled employee or upset family member would talk," I said. "They always do."

"Kids with family actively involved in their care, that come take 'em on day trips and such, don't tend to go over the fence." He began slicing off servings from the fish Aaron's kid brought him, releasing that smoky mouth-watering steelhead aroma into the cave. "It's ones they warehoused an' forgot, like Aaron. Some act out, violent-like. They'd be the last to get moved into a community program like the newspapers talk about. If thos'uns go over the fence, the school prob'bly says good riddance, lose their files, and hope they don't get brought back."

"That's almost the same as hoping they drown or die of exposure!"

"You try to dig into it, you gonna find Plateau people is almost as resistant to outside snoopin' as the Gorge is about skooks."

I thought about that. "Any story about school escapes would have to involve Aaron," I said. "I'm enough of a maverick to think he's happier free. He's basically deinstitutionalized himself. He's created his own little family to belong to."

He favored me with a wide smile. "I knowed you was a good 'un. The skooks got lucky when that 'un nursed your boy. Blood runs true. He's gonna make a fine watcher."

Back to that again. I decided not to take it up. Joe ran a long smoke-blackened spit through the plucked grouse and set the spit in brackets welded to the sides of his stove. He sat to turn the spit, and took up one of his apple-wood pipes.

"After I got Aaron all set up with a place to live an' all, he took to sneakin' around the school watchin' for other runaways," he said. "Like you say, he's doin' his own deinstitutionalizin'. The Gorge protects its own, and they're happier free. Sex habits? None o' my business." He lit his pipe. "Sadly, most skook-human babies don't last."

"You act like such miscegenation is a matter of course. I've never read anything like that!"

"Depends on the languages you read." He basted his bird with an ancient brush. "Roosians call 'em Almasty. The Mongols call 'em Almas—wild man—just like old Tuchi did. They range the Altai Mountains between Russia and China. Back in Czarist times, Roosian villagers captured a female for a sex slave. Any offspring that lived was raised by the village. The record was pretty thin about how many survived."

"Daniel Boone called them Yahoos," I said.

"Did he now?" Joe paused in his basting. "I missed that one."

I told him the theory Boone's tale was the root of the Bigfoot legend.

"They got the thing ass-backwards," Joe said. "All he did was report the truth. Dan'l musta been better read than I realized, to call an unknown critter a Yahoo. You know where that comes from, right?"

"No idea."

"*Gulliver's Travels*. Yahoos were strange, unsettling, uncouth critters that liked pretty stones and were always diggin' in the mud for 'em."

"The only stones I know connected to skooks are big rocks and boulders," I said. "Plain old ugly rocks, used as weapons. Did they throw pretty stones at those miners in Ape Canyon in 1924?"

Joe seemed amused. "Nope. Plain old ugly rocks."

"Why were you there? I thought you were too big to fit down a mine shaft."

"A couple of those miners came up th' Gorge talkin' about seein' apes. Since I started huntin' skooks, they had made themselves scarce around here." He focused on his cooking. "Local Injin legend was that them at St. Helens ate human flesh. I believed it because I believed all of 'em was evil incarnate."

"But now you don't," I said.

"Not since I went to Nepal an' India with the colonel and his lady. Fell in with some of them holy fellers who helped me get over my urge to kill 'em all. Did I ever tell you about the time I met Mahatma Gandhi?"

"More than once." I stood up.

"You hungry? There's plenty here."

The roasting grouse and smoked steelhead aromas filled his cave. "I'd have to be dead not to *get* hungry," I said. "But I promised my wife I'd be home an hour ago."

"Best get a move on then. I ain't quite ready for the undertaker, so we have plenty of time yet for yarn-spinnin'. I'll try to be around until your son is ready to take over."

There wasn't a damn thing I could say to that. I left him slowly revolving his dinner over the stove.

Chapter Thirty-Six

The rains came back right as the Puyallup Fair ended that September and a typical Western Washington autumn settled in. The only wild creatures that came onto the plateau were coyotes after the neighbor's bantam chickens. The pack of wild dogs still hunted the river bottoms, still sounded like hyenas when they made a kill, and I still was glad they were there to block that line of approach to skooks.

The publication I worked for on weekends printed weekly editions for eight Western states, aimed at providing hunters and fishermen the latest possible news on good opportunities for the following weekend. Being from back east, I had never heard of such a publication; it bridged a gap between the Big Three monthly outdoor magazines and skimpy outdoor columns in daily newspapers.

When deer season opened and the regular editors took their vacations, I agreed to work weeklong vacation relief in Seattle. I could drop my son off at the lowland daycare my wife found, and she would pick him up on the way home from Tacoma. I left Harry forted up in the garage. I was pretty sure no skook would risk the wrath of the Ryan Road bear dogs without the fresh scent of my son to attract them down from the foothills—or invade the residential lowlands between Seattle and Tacoma searching for him. I was all too aware that even thinking like that made me a candidate for a rubber room. But that didn't stop me.

The weeks at work and the nights between passed uneventfully. I enjoyed talking to outdoor-loving people all over the west. With the winding down of the fall Chinook runs, bottom-fishermen from California north were combing ugly but delicious varieties off the ocean reefs; rock cod, ling cod and others.

There was a lot of anticipation of fall steelhead runs, and I knew Aaron's tribe would be hard at work again on their illegal fishery. The wrecking yard was selling bright fresh salmon out the back door. Between chop-shop regulars and Aaron's allegedly supplying winter pemmican to Gorge skooks, I wondered how long the supposedly protected creek runs could hold out.

A lot of my outdoor writing that fall was concerned with sportsman anger at depletion of migratory fish runs by tribal net fishing; nobody knew about Aaron's spearmen, working runs supposedly off-limits to everybody. The Gorge looked after its own. If I dropped the dime on Aaron to the Fisheries Department, it might alleviate pressure on the Gorge fish runs. But if Joe was telling the truth, it would amount to an act of war against Gorge skooks, like destroying the buffalo herds and providing smallpox-infected blankets to Indian tribes. Not to mention Aaron and the others would probably wither away and die if reinstitutionalized.

I found myself mulling these things on my commute to and from Seattle. Despite everything, the Gorge had drawn me into its conspiracy of silence. The longer I lived on the Plateau the more secrets I had to keep. From time to time I was sure I was losing what little sanity I had to start with.

When two of the outdoor editors came back from vacation to tender their resignations, planning to open their own fly-fishing magazine, I was offered a full-time job, and took it. The pay scale was about seventy percent of a journeyman reporter's at the Seattle and Tacoma dailies, but the publisher offered fringe benefits I could never have imagined back east. He traded advertising space for free hunting and fishing trips with favored clients, and handed the junkets out freely to his employees. It more than compensated for making less than journeyman wages. I should have felt like Br'er Rabbit landing in the briar patch. But my particular briar patch included Goddamned skooks and there didn't seem a thing I could do about it.

But now that our son was being cared for well away from the plateau, we both could safely continue work and gain some financial ground lost while I tried to write fiction. The babysitter's husband was a woodworker, very taken with our son's quick grasp of spatial relationships; said he made a good apprentice young as he was. The boy often came home smelling like wood shavings and shellac.

In between all the angst and activity, I finished my L.A. novel. I wasn't satisfied with it. My wife liked it a lot and started typing a clean draft. In the meantime, nights and weekends I started work on a new science-fiction novel about an alien beast that deliberately hid its intelligence from pioneering humans. I invested this creature with the secretive nature of the skooks and for dramatic purposes added the ferocity of grizzly bears. I called my invented alien creature a skook for lack of a better name, and placed him on a faraway frontier world. I thought maybe I was trying to create psychological distance from my skook fears by caricaturing them.

My wife, reading the new material, pronounced the work satisfying and noticed I was using Pacific Northwest scenery as the alien-planet backdrop. Since she never liked terror-filled thrillers that tried to outdo each other since the advent of *Jaws,* it appeared I had given my fictive skooks a sympathetic aspect, though not quite the gentle berry-eater depicted in that old lady's painting in Enumclaw that had entranced my son.

I had weekends off now, which given the shortness of the state's elk season meant I had four days to try for one. I visited Vern Smith and sighted my Remington with 175-grain loads to be sure it still held its zero. Vern looked at the target and grunted.

"Okay for an amateur," he said, and I agreed: just under two inches at a hundred yards.

I fired the Casull from twenty-five yards to keep my hand in, left-handed with .45s and right-handed with full-throttle loads. My left-hand groups were twice as tight as my right-hand ones, probably due to the recoil of the big .454s.

"Good enough for a charging skook," Vern allowed with a touch of sarcasm.

I opened my elk season with two loggers from Wilkeson. We went up high, where they had been employed by a gyppo logging outfit and spotted animals almost daily before the operation shut down for the winter. Dave had a 1966 Toyota Land Cruiser, his "Tote" as he called it. Like goat with wheels he said; and it handled the rough terrain like a mountain goat. J.R. had just discovered he was diabetic and had to keep food handy at all times, and pack an emergency insulin kit; but that didn't keep him from hunting.

In the pre-dawn we bumped a big cow elk and yearling right off the landing where the logging company's equipment was parked; they moved off unhurriedly, not spooked, into the clear-cut. I was loading my .454 by feel as we went up the road and the prospect of all that winter meat, legal or not, was powerful in my brain; but I didn't say anything. Dave and J.R. spoke regretfully later about all that elk meat we didn't get; our rifles were still cased and they hadn't been sure enough of me to suggest I take a shot.

Later, another big cow circled J.R.'s stand and bedded down right in front of him. He was tempted sorely but again he didn't know how I might react, since I was only connected to the Gorge by marriage. None of us saw so much as a glimpse of a legal bull. So there went a good winter's supply of meat for all of us; they were laid off for the winter and hated to ask for public assistance.

When I said at the end of the day I was really tempted to put a .454 slug between that big cow's ears, since we were behind a locked gate to which the Game Department didn't have a key, we all had a good laugh at our mutual uneasiness. I was thinking more and more like a Gorge outlaw, and they approved.

Sunday we didn't see a cow to tempt us, let alone a shootable bull. Dave shot a grouse with his .30-30 and led us to a large high-country beaver pond with a massive dam that had been growing since he was a kid. Big trout, probably Dolly Varden, swirled at flies hatching in the mid-day sun, even in November. It was plain beautiful. I decided then and there I was going to put that dam in my skook novel, built by parallel-evolution beaver-like creatures on my imaginary planet.

Dave said he was getting too old for gyppo logging, but hated the idea of a different line of work that would put him indoors. Even with his newfound worry about blood sugar, J.R. agreed with him. They both allowed that working the high country with Mount Rainier for a backdrop amounted to a privileged state, and I couldn't disagree.

After we walked ourselves out Sunday, I turned down a chew of Red Man and a beer, sticking to my pipe and coffee. They chewed along companionably while we swapped hunting yarns, and had two beers apiece, something new in my hunting experience since I don't think alcohol and firearms mix. They seemed about as affected as if they were drinking Coke. The dusk came down and we admired the high bright sun on Rainier's cone. Even though they were life-long Gorge denizens who spent most of their time outdoors, they didn't mention skooks once, and neither did I.

Chapter Thirty-Seven

My second two days of elk season ended without me filling a tag or even seeing a bull. I had yet to catch a steelhead either, whether drift-fishing legally on the Puyallup River or spearing in the Gorge with Aaron's kid, who got a kick out of my inability to develop the proper wrist flick. But the couple times I went out with him, I always came back with fresh fish; a gift from Aaron whose smoker was busy enough to follow its scent-trail to his hidden cabin.

The albino wasn't a big talker, and I wasn't about to ask him if he really supplied Gorge skooks with their winter rations. When I tried to refuse a pair of particularly fine fish as too much, since I hadn't contributed to the bag, he got grumpy.

"The daddy of Joe's heir gotta make sure to feed that boy right," he said flatly. "When Joe's gone, the Gorge gonna need your boy big and strong and ready."

Some things just aren't worth arguing about. Some people it's useless to argue with. Like Aaron, when he got his mind made up. I took the fish. But I didn't go back all winter. Having two of the Gorge's madder inhabitants taking as a given my son's ascendancy to skook guardian of the Gorge was not a happy thing.

I did catch resident Chinook or "blackmouth" off Westport charter boats wintering inland on Puget Sound, on free trips provided by my employer. Plus some six- to eight-pound samples of the ubiquitous rock cod. We ate well that winter.

The outdoor publication's news crew made a pilgrimage to an Eastern Washington duck-hunting resort, all expenses covered by an advertising trade-out. The Pacific Flyway had a seven-duck limit in those days and I shot more big mallards in two days than I ever bagged in my life. Harry stifled his aversion to water and got a real workout. Roast duck a l'orange spaced out baked steelhead and salmon feeds, and deep-fried cod feasts. I say again, we ate very well that year.

To top things off, there were no skooks or rumors of skooks. I felt nervous about leaving my wife alone with the boy those nights I was away on a junket. Occasionally I would jolt awake in a motel room with my heart racing, unable to sleep until I found a pay phone to call home for reassurance. Despite my lingering dread, nothing terrible happened.

Life seemed so normal, with me staying out of the Gorge except to buy gas at Boots Rubery's after I quit spearing with Aaron's kid. I avoided the Pick 'n Shovel for fear of running into Joe and getting sucked in to more wild tales. My wife visited the Petoskeys and a couple other families she knew in the Gorge, but I always managed to beg off and keep the boy home with me. I used my new novel as my excuse; and told her she needed some time for herself with her friends. That kept the boy out of the Gorge.

My wife finished clean-typing my L.A. novel, griping all the way about not having the fancy IBM Selectric she used at work. I sent it off to a publisher with my fingers crossed. She was certain it would sell, but I wasn't. I secretly feared I had been typecast as "only" a science-fiction writer. In those pre-Star Wars times, science-fiction had to struggle for respectability despite the talent of men like Heinlein and Herbert who wrote it.

Spring rolled around with no alarms and excursions. The first publisher rejected my L.A. novel, as I had expected. At least they sent me an individualized rejection letter. And of course mentioned my previous science-fiction success; if I had anything like that they'd love to see it. I consoled my wife in her disappointment at their failure to see the brilliance of my mean-streets story and sent it off again. I wrote back that I did in fact have science-fiction in the typewriter, thanked them for their interest, and went back to my skook story.

The days lengthened into summer. Right around the start of July, the rains dried up and the hay matured and I sold it to the Morgan-breeder again. In August, my employer gave me a raise and a week's vacation for my son's fifth birthday, to celebrate my almost-year of employment; his generosity touched me deeply. He had started his outdoor publication in his garage after he got disillusioned trying to teach high school journalism. The company had legends about him setting egg-timers to control long-distance costs, pacing around the writers' desks and hanging up for them in the middle of a sentence if they went over three minutes. I never did know if that was true.

When I worked for him he owned a top-end Mercedes-Benz, a big sailboat and a city condo besides his big home in the county, and traveled to England annually for bird shooting. Advertising revenues were pouring in. Circulation across all eight states was climbing steadily. If an employee wanted a new Remington firearm, he or she could buy one a year, at cost, through the company. I made my wife happy by using my turn to buy a new rifle like mine for a high-school friend of hers whose house burned down with loss of all his hunting gear. I felt pretty good about being able to do it.

My wife's boss gave her the same week, and we spent it at the beach. Harry liked romping in shoulder-high waves after a thrown dummy. My son liked romping in the ocean, period. The Pacific was way colder than the Atlantic of my childhood but no one seemed bothered but me. I loafed a lot in our beachfront cabin, three long flights of wooden steps above the sand, editing my skook manuscript, and watched the three of them explore and play. The boom of the surf made for wonderfully peaceful sleeping.

When we got home, early rain had cut the stuffy inland heat of August; an early autumn gift. The apples and pears in the orchard were round and bright and delicious; the wild blackberries were lush and purple, bursting with juice. When the premature rains cleared off, everything had a freshly laundered look and the nights stayed cool. The coyotes sang on the ridges and the wild dogs hunted loudly in the bottoms. Deer and elk helped themselves to the orchard.

I went back to work refreshed and happy, marveling at the tranquility we seemed to have achieved in our little bit of heaven above the ancient lahar. October came in colder than usual, indicating an early winter, and there was already snow on the higher foothills of the Cascades. At work, I turned from talking to fish-camps and charter-boat skippers to hunting guides and game departments about early big-game seasons across the West.

My superstitious Southern grandmother would have warned me not to be fooled; the most tranquil landscape hides the deadliest trap. But she wasn't around, and I didn't remember her habitual warning until our tranquility was rudely shattered.

Chapter Thirty-Eight

It was an October Saturday when our peaceful time crashed down around our ears.

The winter rains were back. Saturday dawned with a steady downpour, but Western Washington residents never permitted a little rain to interrupt plans. We were planning an outing to one of the new outlet malls that had just begun to spring up. This one was about ninety miles away and we'd be inside a lot so after I gave Harry his morning constitutional, I put him in the garage with plenty of water and a bowl of crunchies to hold him.

My wife was finishing up a wicker basket with sandwiches and such for a picnic somewhere along the way and perking coffee for the half-gallon Stanley bottle. So I bundled up the boy in his new padded blue jacket and watch cap. The little yellow slicker, rain hat and boots from when he was two had gone to the Goodwill; along with winter jackets from when he was three and four. He outgrew them fast and was quite the little man at five.

We were taking the old Pontiac, which got better mileage than the truck and gave him the whole back seat to play with his little backpack full of various toys.

"I wanna start the car, Dad," he said. It was his latest accomplishment.

"Okay, son." I handed him the keys. "Remember the rules."

"Leave it in park, don't touch the pedals," he said

impatiently. "Even if the engine starts to die on me."

"Just right," I said.

"That old car *always* dies on mom first time."

"Let's see what happens." I squatted within the open door and pushed the gas pedal a time or two. "Okay, now try," I said.

The old Bonneville fired right up, ran hard for a couple seconds, then kicked down. His grin blazed. "Mom always forgets that!"

I stood up. "I think it'll warm up fine now." I saw her come out the front door juggling the picnic basket and the Thermos while trying to put the key in the lock and started toward her to help. She looked up at me. Then past me. Her mouth seemed to fall open. Her face reflected sheer horror.

She yelled. Not screamed, yelled. *"No!"*

I spun, thinking he had moved the gear selector.

Somebody was getting in the open front door of the car as my son's face twitched up toward him, shocked. Just somebody—that's all I noticed right then. Somebody putting his hands on my son, trying to push him away from the steering wheel. I saw my son's face change from shock to instant anger.

"No!" Just like his mom, he yelled it.

Big as the intruder was, he was momentarily stymied trying to pry my son away from the wheel. Or I wouldn't have made it back in time to keep him from shutting the door.

It was close, anyway.

He shoved my son, hard, all the way across the seat and grabbed for the door handle. But I was there and blocked it with my leg. He yanked it hard enough to hurt, trying to dislodge me. All I could think of was him daring to lay hands on my son. I reached in, grabbed him, snatched him out of the car and slammed him upright against the back door. His flimsy, filthy T-shirt tore in my hands and I staggered back.

The son-of-a-bitch was bigger than me. A lot bigger.

And strong, oh man was he strong. He used one hand to push me away like I weighed nothing. He didn't even look at me; he might have been swatting a fly.

I managed not to fall. In that stunned moment, I had just enough time to register that he must go six-four or five with a huge tangled mop of coarse black hair and a wild, matted beard that masked most of his face; beady little eyes devoid of expression. Beneath the tattered shirt, his broad chest was as hairy as his face.

And he was barefooted beneath ragged old pants.

In the next split second he dived with preternatural speed back into the driver's seat. Tried to slam the door. I blocked him again. I grabbed him again. I got one hand under an armpit. He stank almost badly as a skook.

He clung to the steering wheel. Those massive arms knotted and writhed with muscle. My son clubbed him in the side of the head with his backpack full of toys. He let go with one hand and swatted at my son. Missed.

Red killing rage suffused my alarm. He was coming out of that car, *now*. I didn't care if the damn steering wheel came with him. I snatched him out again and turned with him and gave him a judo hip like the Army taught me in unarmed combat. I threw him clear over the car.

"Get my damn gun!" I yelled to my wife.

Today of all days I hadn't put on the Casull's shoulder harness.

The intruder hit the ground beyond the car—and bounced up like a rubber ball. Raced around the hood of the car with that same inhuman speed. The bastard was *still* trying to get to the driver's door. As if I wasn't even there. His single-mindedness was terrifying.

"Get my gun!" I yelled again.

I blocked him with both hands up and open and drove my full weight into his broad chest. He rocked back, but didn't fall.

Harry had heard enough. He weighed in with a basso profundo roar and hit the garage door like he was coming through.

That got this asshole's attention. His flat dead eyes widened. The closest thing to an expression I saw the whole time crossed his ugly mug: fear of the dog. He spun and ran down the driveway. When he hit paving, he turned toward downtown. Then he really ran. How could somebody that big move that fast? I watched him out of sight before I checked my son.

"You okay?"

His eyes were still blazing but his chin quivered. "He was *strong*, Da!" The lost "d" was telling. I pulled him into my arms.

"So are you, son, so are you. You kept him from closing the door till I got here. And gave him hell of a whack! Good for you!"

"Peee You! He stank, Dad!"

"He sure did."

"Where'd he go?"

"He ran away when Harry started barking at him."

"He better! Harry don't like them stinkers, remember?

From down by the creek?"

I was watching to make sure the asshole stayed gone, so his comment didn't register then. My wife still was nailed to the spot where she'd first seen the intruder, eyes wide in shock.

"What the hell is wrong with you?" I yelled. "Where's my damn gun?"

She seemed to shake herself. "Is my son all right?" She rushed to the car and pulled him out of my arms. I let him go. So he was her son again; that usually meant she thought I had done something wrong. I didn't have time to worry about it. I was still scanning for the asshole.

"Go in the house and check him out," I said. "Now. That asshole may come back."

"He was stealing our car!"

"And our son with it," I said. "I almost couldn't handle him, he was so damn strong. I needed my gun!"

"It was just a kid from the school," she said, fussing with our son.

I drew a blank. "What?"

"They're always trying to escape. He just saw the open car door, and—"

"That was no damn kid! He was big as a damn linebacker and strong as an ox!"

"A kid in his mind," she said, not even paying attention to me. "Mentally they never grow up."

"That sonofabitch was stronger than me!"

"Well...the school has a weight room for patients."

"Just god-damned dandy," I said hotly. "Get inside in case he comes back." I shut off the car and pocketed the keys. "I'm calling the cops. Right now!"

Chapter Thirty-Nine

I got Harry calmed down and called the local police department. The dispatcher said the school had not reported a runaway that day. She said sometimes they were a little slow to do that, having to search the grounds first to avoid a false alarm. Neither of the two day patrols had reported a hairy barefooted giant running down Main Street, but the dispatcher seemed unsurprised.

"Pretty routine around here," she said. "A lot of people here don't lock their doors still. When they come home they find one of those kids in their refrigerator having a snack. Or asleep in front of the TV."

"This *kid* as you call him was a head taller than me," I said. "And he was a lot bigger than me, with a beard like an Old Testament prophet. He tried to steal my car with our son in it!"

"The beard sounds a little unusual, but sometimes those older kids do try to escape," she said, after making sure I didn't want medics. "I'm sure he wasn't trying to hurt your son."

Needless to say, we didn't complete our trip to the outlet mall. My wife kept holding and checking our son over and over, to his increasing disgust. When she was absolutely sure he was all right, she said she was going to take him to wash up to get the stench from the intruder off him.

"Smells like skook, Dad," he said. "P.U."

"Now where did he get such an idea?" she wanted to know. "Have you been filling his head with silliness?"

"Everybody knows skooks stink!" he told her. "Even Ramona." His baby-sitter. "But she calls 'em Bigfoots."

"Bigfeet," my wife said automatically. "Feet is the plural of foot." She took him down the hall.

When they got back with my son in clean clothes, she suggested we go ahead and have our picnic right at home; she was recovering well from her fright. My son was good with that. I let Harry in to cadge tidbits. For the first time in his life, he refused food. He lay down beside the boy and refused to move, facing the front door. His muzzle wrinkled in a silent growl. When he sniffed my hands where I had grabbed the intruder, the growl became audible.

"It's okay, Harry, I'll wash the stink off," I said. "He'd have been in real trouble if you'd been out there with us."

"See, mom," my son said. "Harry thinks that guy smelled like a skook, too."

"That's silly." Her tone was that of condescending adult to unreasonable child. "How would Harry know what a skook smells like?"

Before I could stop myself I said, "You'd be surprised what Harry knows."

"Yeah!" my son said. She looked at me peculiarly, reacting to the way my voice was freighted with unsaid things.

I ducked out and went to wash the stink off my person. While I did, I had the half-mad thought of getting Harry's leash and my gun, and putting him on the scent at the end of the driveway. If the local cops couldn't find this creep,

Harry certainly could. But I wasn't sure I wouldn't shoot him, given the chance, and that would be asking for trouble given the community's evident acceptance of this kind of nonsense.

I was in quite a state. I wanted to take some of my anger out on my wife. How could she live in a place like this? Forget the damn skooks; this business with a retarded giant trying to steal our son was the cherry on top. But she was so upset that I stifled myself. I did go around making sure all the doors and windows were locked and put on my .454 harness: locking the barn after the horse was out, so to speak, before we had our home picnic. She didn't give me attitude about wearing the gun, eloquent as to how scared she had been.

Later in the day, the dispatcher called and told me the school had all patients present and accounted for. If our intruder was been one of theirs, he'd made it back before they missed him. The school administrators were concerned about his attempt to steal a car with a child in it; that was far more serious than wandering into an unlocked house to raid a refrigerator. Well no shit was my thought.

The dispatcher gave me a phone number and name of a school bureaucrat who wanted as good a description as I could furnish, so they could keep a special eye on him if it had been one of theirs wandering off the reservation. At least they were making some kind of effort.

So I called this guy. Right off, he wanted to make sure our son was all right. I imagined fear of lawsuits floating through his bureaucratic brain. I told him we were taking him to the doctor to make sure, since his idiot shoved my son pretty hard.

He didn't like the word idiot, but he was in no position to take exception. He had that unctuous tone of people who manage the disadvantaged that makes you think they think everybody is disadvantaged—especially you. He asked for a detailed description of the intruder. Said he was sure he'd misunderstood the police; the attempted car-thief couldn't have been that big.

"I'm six-two," I said. "He was taller than me. I go two-forty. He was a lot bigger and had a full, bushy beard. He didn't look like any kid I ever saw."

"Well..." A pause. "The local folks call all our patients kids, out of recognition for their mental challenges," he said. "Arrested mental development, so to speak."

"But not physical."

"Well...no. Not in every case."

"And you give them access to a weight room."

He didn't like my tone; his own voice tightened up. "We provide exercise opportunities for our patients. You've seen our facility?"

"No. My wife has. She grew up here."

"So you're not from around here then? I can see why this might be unsettling to a newcomer."

Give me credit; I didn't cuss this asshole out. "If you wouldn't be unsettled by some hairy freak trying to steal your car right out of your drive," I said, "and putting his hands on your five-year-old son, maybe *you* need a doctor."

He made a sound that I swear sounded like "tut-tut." It certainly had that intonation. "You have every right to be upset, sir. I did not mean to imply otherwise." Very formal now. "If you could just give me as exact a description as possible..."

So I did. I talked it seemed like ten minutes without interruption: size, shape, uncanny speed and strength, total lack of facial expression, crazy beard and hair, ratty shirt and pants—and barefooted. Silence on the line; when I noticed the lack of response, I stopped.

"Did I lose you?"

"No, no—I'm still here." He sounded different again—more guarded. "The thing is, sir, we have no patient at present who matches that description."

"It's a big school. You're sure of that?"

"I'm very sure. I make it my business to know them all. For one thing, we don't permit facial hair."

He should have sounded relieved it wasn't one his kids. But he didn't sound relieved. My old reporter's nose twitched as I replayed his comment.

"No patient *at present* who matches the description." My brain was beginning to function finally: Aaron and his band of runaways. I had never seen a hairy giant around his retreat under the Burnett Bridge, but his little band certainly ran to a lot of hair. "That must mean you did have a patient that matches the description," I said. "He could have grown a beard later."

He recovered himself. "I'm sorry, sir, I can't help you. We never had a patient like that." He was lying, or I never heard a liar. His voice was tense, evincing no relief at being able to honestly say his school wasn't involved. "I certainly hope your son is fine." He couldn't wait to get off the phone.

Chapter Forty

The local cops came out to examine the scene, took our statements, told my son what a brave little man he was, and petted Harry. Said the intruder sounded like some passing hobo that vanished into the river bottoms after his failure to grab the wheels; probably long gone. They'd keep an eye out, sure, and put the word out for any hitchhikers matching his description.

Then they left.

If they thought I was just going to let it go at that, they were badly mistaken. I marched into the police station, demanded an audience with the chief, and was put off—he was out of town for the weekend, supposedly. So I demanded an appointment for Monday and called in for a day off. It was midday before I got the call.

The chief was an old dog with sparse gray hair and a small hard-looking pot gut; a retiree from a Western Washington sheriff's department double-dipping the law-enforcement retirement fund. He was intimately connected with small-town politics; his wife was running for mayor. His main concern seemed about my connections to *The Seattle Times,* because of my feature stories.

"Word is, you were a hard-nosed reporter back east," he said after he gave me a cup of so-so coffee and we settled in his office. His name was Samuel Moore; he must have been pushing sixty.

"Small towns," I said. "Everybody knows everything about everybody."

"Well in this case I decided to check after you yelled at my young men." He smiled. "Pennsylvania State Police and the Georgia Bureau of Investigation say you always play straight, but not to piss you off needlessly. Have you talked to *The Times* about doing a story on this? I know you're a writer for that hook-and-bullet magazine in Seattle now. But a guy with your rep could get the real media stirred up."

"I probably could," I said. "What I want to know is why your men tried to pass this off as a wandering hobo. This asshole tried to steal my car. *He put his hands on my son.*"

"Surprised you didn't shoot him," the chief said. "I know you carry."

"I wasn't carrying yesterday. A mistake I won't make again."

"I understand you threw him around a little. Even if he was bigger than you."

"He was trying to abduct my son!"

He held up both hands. "Understood."

"Understand this, too. Your men screwed up."

He frowned. "Tough language. What do you mean?"

"If they really believed this asshole was a wild card— some unknown hobo passing through trying to steal a car—they would have been all over it. Printing my steering wheel, wherever I remembered him touching the roof of the car, taking our prints to exclude them, and then running him to see if he's in the system."

"We could still do that, if you want."

"Too late, chief. Way too late. You already know who

this asshole is."

"That sounds like an accusation." His face stiffened up; he was done making friendly.

"The bureaucrat at the school slipped up. He said they had no patient *at present* to match this creep's description."

"So you jump to the conclusion it's a former patient? How would that work exactly?"

"How that works exactly is that this asshole must be one of those patients who escaped the school and is living rough in the Gorge."

He blinked. "What makes you think something like that happens?"

"I know Aaron and some of his brood, Chief. And Big Joe Consonants, too."

He shook his head. "Knew about you knowing Big Joe. Not about you knowing Aaron. You been getting around quite a bit for a newcomer. I sure hope you're not going to turn this into a newspaper story."

"It's a story waiting to be told," I said. "Runaway kids drown in the river, die of exposure, or hook up with Aaron. Dereliction of duty by school officials, avoidable deaths—rumors of worse than incest in Aaron's clan."

He didn't pick up my slip of the tongue, but shifted uneasily in his chair. "Now, look here: every time we get a report on a runaway, we make every effort to find the child and bring 'em in safe. Call out local search and rescue and everything. Approved overtime—and my budget ain't that fat. But we do try."

I held up a hand. "That sounds like a newspaper quote defending your department. I hadn't even considered getting the newspapers involved." He started to say something but I talked over him: "Even if I did, the story's not neglect by your department. But I know damn good and well that big kid escaped from the school. And so do your men. So inventing a passing hobo was basically a lie. Lies get my reporter's juices flowing."

He pursed his lips. "That's pretty thin. Could have been a tramp. As for taking prints, any prints were probably smeared useless by your tussle."

"But it's sloppy-ass police work just to assume that." I held up a hand as he started to object. "Unless you already know more than you're saying. You forget," I added, "my wife grew up in this town. She volunteered at the school for several years before I ever met her. It was her son almost got hurt too. And she got a real good look at this guy."

"Recognized him, did she?" He eyed me narrowly.

"Not somebody you would forget," I said.

He gave me a hard stare. "Would she swear she recognized him?"

"You want to push this thing public, try her out, when he almost stole her son?"

He heaved a sigh. "What is it you really want?"

"How long ago did this big kid escape the school?"

"I never said he did."

"If they reported his escape like they're supposed to, you'll have a file—and it's discoverable."

"Discoverable." He said it like it left a bad taste. "Legal jargon. You planning to sue somebody? I'm getting a little tired of this conversation. If you weren't such a tough guy according to some pretty good cops, I'd show you the door."

I put down my coffee and stood up. "Okay, if that's how you want to play it..."

"Jesus!" He threw up his hands. "Calm down, I just don't think the Plateau or the Gorge needs this kind of publicity. We get along up here fine without outside interference."

"So it's okay for local children to be endangered, long as no outsiders show up?"

"I didn't say that! " He stood up too; didn't like me looming over him. But he still had to look up to meet my eyes. "You are a big'un," he said. "No wonder you could toss poor Adam around like that."

My turn to blink. "Adam? That's his name?"

"I'll deny it if you get anything printed."

"How long has he been loose?"

He rubbed his face. "Pretty near three years. He grew up at the school—physically at least. So he was there when your wife was. If that was a bluff you just ran, it was a good one."

"He sneak into town often?"

"Nothing like this. Food, clothes off a line, stuff like that. I don't know what got into him—but I promise you, he's gotta go back inside if he's dangerous."

It was the best I was going to get. "Is he one of Aaron's?"

"Who knows? I never see anybody but Aaron if I go up there. And he's in the county, so he's out of my jurisdiction. The county's not interested in going in the Gorge unless it's in force. You know why."

I nodded. "Aaron's not one of the pot-growers, so he's

of no interest to their task forces."

"And let the Gorge take care of its own." He picked up his coffee. "You going to ring down the press on us?"

"The school deserves it," I said. "But I like Aaron. He's made a life for himself and those kids. So no newspapers. I just wanted an explanation. I get really paranoid when someone endangers my son."

He drained off his coffee. "Can't say I blame you, after getting a rock shower up at them vacation cabins a few years back."

I just looked at him. "You heard about that too?"

He shrugged. "Petoskey said he never did find the kids did it. I was thinking Aaron's brood, probably. Nervous about strangers up there."

"As good a guess as any." One slip of the tongue about Aaron's brood was enough. I wasn't about to introduce skooks into this conversation or tell him I went spearfishing illegally with one of the runaways.

He put down his cup. "Adam really ain't all there in the head. But this ain't like him." He paused. "You don't have jurisdictional issues. Since you say you know Aaron, maybe you should go talk to him."

Chapter Forty-One

But I didn't go looking for Aaron. I went looking for Big Joe. When I drove into the Gorge that afternoon, I found him ensconced in one of his roadside rocking chairs, getting his picture taken with a couple of twenty-something women in flannel shirts and down vests, baggy shorts and hiking boots. The photographer was another fit-looking young woman with a Nikon. I parked behind their muddy Subaru wagon and stepped down.

"Right on time," Joe rumbled. "Ladies, this here is a gen-u-wine newspaperman. He can snap a pitcher of all three of you with me if you'd like."

They would like. The blonde with the Nikon handed it over and went to squat at Joe's knee. The two brunettes put their hands on his big shoulders. Three perfect white smiles bracketed his tobacco-stained grin. There is something wholesomely sexy about good-looking feminine legs set off by shorts and heavy hiking boots, but I was in no mood to appreciate it. He produced from his own baggy flannel shirt pocket some of his postcards, signed them and dealt them around. The driver beeped her horn as they drove away.

"I notice you didn't charge them for their autographs," I said.

"Hell, would you of?"

"I'm not a legend like you."

His tourist's smile had vanished with the Subaru.

"Been kindly expectin' you. Heard about Adam."

"Of course you did. Is he one of Aaron's, or a solo?"

"You been to Aaron's already?"

"I wanted to talk to you first. This Adam looked like a younger you. Right down to the bare feet."

"No relation o' mine. I got no progeny." He stood and lifted the old rocker one-handed. "Just as well you didn't waste time at Aaron's. He's prob'ly hidin' out. He knows how you get when somebody messes with your son."

I had just thought I was angry before. *Now* I was angry. "Is that what this was? The cops thought he was just trying to steal my car. So did I."

Reacting to the change in my voice, his face became sad. "Don't know for sure. But 'fraid it was the boy he was after." He carried his chair back in the brush.

My temples were throbbing and I bet my blood pressure was sky high. "I want this Adam locked back up," I said tightly. "I've got enough on my plate with your damn skooks. I can't be watching out for crazies too."

"Have to agree" He wagged his big head slowly. "At least you didn't say you plan to bury him somewhere in these here hills."

"Don't think it didn't cross my mind."

"You are a lethal man," Joe said. "But that would be murder."

"This Adam asshole is too damn strong and fast to run loose!" I knew I was almost shouting. "But the city cops have no jurisdiction up here. They won't level with the county or state, because he's not supposed to *be* loose. I'd get about much help from them as if I asked them to arrest a skook. I'm going to have to track this asshole down myself."

"Hard to do, up here. Adam's pretty good in the woods. Almost good as a skook."

"That's why I'm talking to you," I said, quieting down. "You're the self-anointed watcher over the Gorge. You'll know where he hangs out. From there, it won't be so hard." I nodded at Harry in the front seat of my truck. "Harry got a good nose-full of him from the piece of T-shirt I ripped off. Smells to high heaven, almost like a skook. And Harry doesn't like skooks."

"Harry could find him all right." Joe hitched up his suspenders. "But Adam's awful strong. And not all there. He might not respect a pointed gun. Then what?"

"Then I bend the barrel of my pistol over his head and you help me drag him to the road. I've got stuff to tie him up with."

"I could do that," he said. "But there's a complication."

"What complication?"

"He ain't at Aaron's. He runs with the skooks. To find him you'll have to find them."

"*Them* I don't mind shooting," I said.

"Death in your voice again," he said. "You're obsessed as I was when I was your age." He held up a big hand. "With just as good a reason, I grant you. Maybe more reason than you know, in this case. This is plain bad business. You don't even know how bad."

"Meaning what?"

"I'm pret' sure Adam was after your son, not the car. Aaron's got a car to use if Adam needed one. It's the *why* Adam was after your boy that makes it so bad. We better go down to Boots' place and get my rifle."

Chapter Forty-Two

Monday was too far gone for us to do much looking after I picked up Joe, though the old forest-service roads he guided me onto climbed high out of the cloud cover socking in the Plateau and Gorge. We had all the remaining sunlight there was, but the autumn days were getting short. We stopped at the heads of a few canyons that had nothing to visually differentiate them from other canyons. But Joe knew these mountains like the back of his hand.

"Skook cave up that 'un," he said once. "Too far for most hunters to hoof it, so they don't get disturbed."

I had Harry on a leash, to his disgust. I didn't want him winding this Adam and charging off where we couldn't follow. Even though Joe said no skooks were home, I waited at each place while Harry's nose sorted out scents on the changeable upland breezes. Nothing was fresh enough to raise his hackles. One of the roads led past where I'd seen those big bare footprints.

"I didn't know then another human troglodyte ran around barefooted up here," I said. "And you didn't enlighten me."

The big man had the grace to look embarrassed. "Didn't think it was any of your business at the time."

"Yeah," I said. "Well, now it is. Why would this retard want to steal my son?""

"It's kindly confused," he said glumly. "Near as I can

tell, him and a female skook had a baby, 'cording to Aaron. But it taken real sick and died. Somehow he taken it in his head that since your boy been marked, he belonged to be with this new grievin' mama."

My Georgia grandmother had a saying about that awful chill you sometimes get up your spine: *a fox running across your grave*. I literally shuddered; it felt like a skook had run across mine.

"That son-of-a-bitch," I said.

"Death in your voice again. You gonna kill him now?"

"I feel like it. But if we can hogtie him and take him in, I'll settle for that."

"Good enough."

We didn't talk a lot after that, except for directions. Joe knew all kinds of ways those old timber roads connected up there, including a lot of two-tracks that looked too overgrown to push through in two-wheel drive, but allowed shortcuts between canyon roads. Despite the shortness of the day we covered a lot of terrain. No barefoot tracks in the road—not that we expected any— and no positive scent reading from Harry. Joe shook his head as dusk came sifting down.

"Tol' you, I always know when they're around. They ain't. But they will be sooner or later. So will Adam if he's still with 'em. Can you come back tomorrow?"

I said I'd try to get Tuesday off. At dark, we stopped where a foot-wide stream came trickling down a sheer rock face. I smelled sulfur, a rotting-eggs odor, drifting off the trickle. Joe dismounted and bent over the trickle, drinking deep and smacking his lips. His big shadow, face pale in the backwash of headlights, reminded me just how alien this man was; drinking that stuff with enjoyment was just a confirmation.

"Mineral water," he said. "Drink up. Good for you."

"The last time I smelled that I was a teenager on the highway between Jacksonville Beach and St. Augustine," I said. "There was a spring and a pool the tourists liked. Rotten-egg water. I didn't drink it then and I'm not drinking it now."

We rode slowly back down to pavement with the windows open so Harry's nose could work, though Joe said it was a waste of time. I was thoroughly chilled by the time we dropped into the rain clouds. We closed the windows and turned on the heat. It was raining hard when I dropped Joe at his cave and headed for home, and raining harder down on the plateau. My wife and son were home, and she had a pot of venison stew simmering, courtesy of some in-laws. I was so famished I ate three heaping bowls before I called my boss. He had sons of his own, and had been outraged about mine almost being stolen right out of my driveway. He said go, do what you have to do to get that crazy bastard locked back up. I laid out some gear, packed a lunch, hit the sack early and was up and gone before dawn.

Joe was hunkered by the road at the path to his cave under one of his big bumbershoots. "Hope you brung coffee," was all he said when he got in.

"Two quarts," I said, and handed him the big old Stanley bottle. "Cup on the dashboard."

He surprised me by taking us out of the Gorge and up Highway 410 toward Chinook Pass.

"Told you they range," he said. "Roads is the long way round—they cut cross-country and ford the river where it's shallow."

Chapter Forty-Three

East of the wide spot in the road named Greenwater we turned off Highway 410 and climbed up past Twenty-Eight Mile Creek above the rain into snow. The roads turned to slush. I was surprised to see a couple of dark pickups parked along the edges.

"Bow season," Joe said.

I drove as high as I felt comfortable and turned back; easier to get started again if you're facing downhill. In the pale cold dawn, the steep drops on one side of the road seemed to fall off forever. We sat for a few minutes watching the dawn open out. An ancient Willys Jeep with a canvas top but no side curtains ground around the next downhill curve, pulled even with us and stopped. I dropped my window.

"I'll be damn, Joe, I thought that was you." The driver was a burly unshaven character with the consonants of Middle Europe larding his words. "What brings you outta the Gorge? Never took you for a stick-and-string guy."

"Howdy, Bill." Joe's chuckle rumbled. "I could say the same for you. I thought your .270 was the be-all and end-all for these mountains of ours." To me: "You are looking at a local legend, Bill Simp in the flesh."

"Simp ain't my real name," this character said. "Anymore than Consonants is his. Been over to First Hill and Mohawk Ridge, lookin' for shootable bucks for later."

"I actually know your whole name," I said. "My wife's

father was a timber faller with you back in the day. Before a tree killed him." I mentioned her maiden name. "You're supposed to be quite the yarn-spinner."

"Me?" He snorted. "I'm nothin' to old Joe there. Let alone you, if you're the writer married into that family. I liked your stuff on the coalmines and the plague. You got a good feel for how wide an' wild this country is."

"You can say that again."

"Yep. Its 114 miles from the last town on this side of the mountains to the first one over east. Not even Texas can say as much. Heard it's down to 90 miles between towns there."

We talked a bit longer before Bill Simp put his old Jeep in gear and headed higher, not seeming to notice how Joe had deftly deflected his curiosity. As we rolled downhill, we repeated our pattern of yesterday, stopping at the mouth of canyons Joe indicated. Here, they cut through black timber on the uphill side of the road. Each stop, Joe just shook his head, and Harry didn't smell anything of interest. The slush was so slippery I was glad to be back down in the steady rain before long.

We stopped at the mouth of another canyon.

"Maybe," Joe said. "Just maybe. I'm gonna take a stroll up this one. There's another about a quarter-mile down. You ease on around the bend there and take a stand. Don't go in too far—its tough goin' anyway. If somethin' runs from me up in here, they'll come down that 'un. Don't take your rifle, or the game warden liable to think you're rifle-huntin' in bow season, with Bill Simp out moseying around."

"What about you?"

He snorted. "I been walkin' these hills with this rifle longer'n you been alive. Nobody bothers ol' Joe."

Joe was wearing his uninsulated clodhoppers, but had conceded the weather by adding socks. I left Harry in the truck and eased up the timbered draw, clumsy-footed in felt-lined Sorel pacs. I found a comfortable stump in a timbered draw. It was very quiet. Time stretched. Far uphill I heard a wet pop of a rotten twig snapping. After a long time I heard another one. The sounds were so sporadic it took an act of imagination to envision something sneaking toward me. I eased my big .454 out of the shoulder rig under my Filson.

One instant he wasn't there and then he was, gliding into visibility: an Indian. Bareheaded, long black hair mink-shiny in the rain, dark face concentrated on his careful, graceful ballet through blow-downs and thickets. He wore an orange knapsack over a soaked Army field jacket and carried a 740 Woodsmaster with a big scope. An Indian with an autoloading rifle—in bow season. Indians had ignored state hunting regulations since they started winning all their federal court battles.

He was within twenty feet of me, and jumped nearly a foot, when I raised my hand in greeting. He looked pissed-off when I grinned at his momentary startlement, then grinned back and stepped closer.

"Anything come through ahead of me?" He hardly moved his lips; his voice was very quiet.

I shook my head. "Nothing."

He glanced at my pistol. "You hunting?"

"Not deer," I said.

"Saw some blue grouse up top," he said,

misunderstanding.

I nodded. He moved on silently, the best woods-moving I'd heard in a long time, like a wary buck, no unnatural sound; but he wasn't paying enough attention to his surroundings. I suspected skooks could move at least that well, but didn't know about Adam. If he could, I hoped he'd be like the Indian, too focused on quiet walking to monitor his whereabouts.

The rain poured, but a lot of it was blocked by the timber. I sat in drizzles and drips and waited some more. Given the overcast it was as dark in the timber as if dawn had never come. I was beginning to realize the size of the job I had bitten off, trying to find one woods-running retard in this vast country.

"Don't shoot," said a familiar voice—from downhill. "It's only me."

"God damn it, Joe." I stood up and stretched my cramped legs. "I could hear that Indian coming but I didn't hear you."

"Nice kid," Joe rumbled. "Muckleshoot. Talked to him down by the truck. Said you was invisible in plain sight, nice compliment. Good discipline on your part—and you didn't take a poke at him with that cannon either. I came around 'cause I thought you might be jumpy."

We started walking back to the truck. In the distance a chain saw started up and bit into wood. When we came out of the draw I saw a small silver travel trailer I hadn't seen on the way in, tucked into a fold of land off a piece. Low pale smoke from wet wood hung low over its lighted windows.

"Bowhunters," Joe said. "Talked to 'em after I walked

over the top and back around. They were mad I had a rifle, said they saw Bill Simp earlier with his rifle. Said they were gonna tell the game warden." He chuckled. "Told 'em game wardens had no interest in our pot farm, but Bill and me would take it amiss if they mentioned us to anybody with a badge."

"You're a card, Joe."

"Huh. Then they wanted to buy some. City men!"

We rested in the truck. He said if the skooks or Adam had been up top, Indian hunters had spooked them; there were a couple more Muckleshoots with a pickup on a road up there.

"Why do they rifle-hunt in bow season? Just to rub it in?"

"Their kind been huntin' these hills near four thousand years. Why change their ways because of white man laws?"

"Never mind."

I dug into my knapsack for sandwiches. Joe pulled smoked salmon and venison jerky out of his possibles bag. We washed it down with coffee and then headed for the Huckleberry Creek drainage on the other side of 410. When we got above snowline the only thing we saw in the road was fresh elk sign. I parked facing downhill and put on my pack board.

Joe slung his possibles bag and led out, high into the timber. We split up at a creek bed in the black timber and he went up a steep canyon while I side-hilled around until I broke timber into a wilderness of downed trees covered with hard-glazed snow. I started for the top but changed my mind when I floundered into soft snow above my knees. I tried a game trail up a slope, but it was so steep you could stand straight up on the trail—if you could find a wide-enough spot—and reach out and touch the rock in front of your face. I didn't want to fall off the trail if I got any higher; my feet were getting cold and clumsy even in the Sorels.

Getting back into the timber below was no mean feat. A well-beaten game trail ran just inside the fringe. A thin skim of snow distorted all sign. But something caught my eye a few feet away. At first I thought it was probably elk droppings, but closer it looked like bear scat. An awful lot of scat in one lump. Right on top of it, it was neither. Something had upchucked its stomach contents, reddish and full of half-digested berries, frozen solid.

I had never heard of bears eating until they threw up. That was more a human trait. Especially wild humans: Apache raiders were known to feast on a slaughtered horse until they threw up, then go back and feast again.

I felt my back-hairs stir. There were no tracks in the frozen snow—my own boots didn't make a dent. But the vomit was on top of the snow. I hatcheted some boughs for an insulated seat on the snow and backed up against a big Doug fir with my pistol in my lap. My binoculars opened up the woods all around, but nothing moved. After my eyes tired, I drank coffee and ate freeze-dried peach segments.

I could see a road far below, campfire smoke; hear chainsaws and see tiny men loading firewood in toy pickups. A light plane flew through the valley toward Chinook Pass—I looked *down* on it. I waited as long as I could, but the day was moving along and my feet got cold again. Finally I moved out. Plenty of deer sign lower, tracks frozen into the snow. Nothing else. I read somewhere that deer don't like deep crusted snow because it rubs their legs raw. I could well imagine.

When I got out of timber into seedlings, I still was higher than crowns of big trees in the canyon. A long hard hike, picking my spots, brought me across our boot-prints where the snow was softer, going up. When I got back to the truck I let Harry out for a constitutional and watched him closely. He chased a couple of chipmunks and generally behaved like he was on vacation; his nose told him nothing bad.

When Joe showed up half an hour later, he just shook his head. "Couple of their lay-up caves ain't been used. 'Fraid this wood-cuttin' and bow huntin' and all got 'em layin' low."

I told him about the upchuck. "Could be," he said. "Been and gone, I expect. They ain't around."

"Harry agrees with you," I said.

"Wastin' our time here," Joe said. "Let's go.

Chapter Forty-Four

I thought three days off in a row would be pushing my publisher's good will, given deadlines we had before the weekend. I told Joe I'd be back Saturday if he was willing to keep looking. He said he was—and would keep looking on his own until Saturday, maybe check with Aaron to see if he knew anything. It was hard readjusting my brain to the traffic rush of Seattle on my way to work, and not easy to keep my mind on the stories about bow-hunting and fall fishing and early rifle-hunts I ground out.

At home that evening my wife said the police chief had called to assure her they still were on the lookout for Adam. He'd hinted around, trying to get her to admit whether she remembered him from the school. But I had briefed her on our conversation and she gave back as good as she got, and thought he was even more worried when he hung up. I told her that was all to the good—meant they'd really keep an eye out. I hadn't told her what Joe told me: that the theft attempt was aimed at our son, not the car. And I wasn't going to.

Friday, at work on the Montana edition, a guy who ran a store called The Powderhorn in Bozeman reported that sheepmen who bought ammunition from him swore Sasquatches had been at their flocks, leaving nothing but tattered wool and gnawed bones. I mentioned the old veteran Ralph saying he saw Sasquatches on Montana summer range. He laughed about the old cowboy's tall tales and shrugged off the sheepmen's claims; game wardens said it was bound to have been coyotes or a big cat. Sheepmen didn't live out on the range with their flocks like they did in the old days, which left sheep vulnerable, he said, and they needed something to blame for their neglect. Wolves hadn't been reintroduced back then and grizzlies were few and far between.

"Talk about apex predators," the Montanan told me. "There's your apex predator: Old Griz. The Indians feared him like a devil and Lewis and Clark found out why when they came through."

It was interesting he brought up grizzlies, given the science-fiction story I was working on. He said the men of the Lewis and Clark expedition found out single-shot muzzleloaders weren't a lot more effective than bows and arrows. If the Big Sky Country was to be settled, Old Griz hadn't got the memo. He was absolutely fearless and damn-near unstoppable until firearms technology adjusted for his mass and vitality and incredibly brave bear hounds ran him to ground for guys with repeating rifles. Even then he did his share of killing men and dogs.

The Montanan had never heard of Daniel Boone's Yahoo, and tended to dismiss it. "If Boone ever got far enough west to cross paths with Old Griz, *then* he would have a yarn to spin," he said. "Lewis and Clark only mentioned Bigfoot once, and it wasn't about a Sasquatch. It was the name of a chief of the Osage Indians."

Which made an interesting anecdote that I folded into a story about sheepmen claiming Sasquatch was eating their sheep, together with an official if laughing denial by a game department official. I wondered what Joe

276

Consonants would think about sheep-eating skooks.

Saturday finally came. I didn't roll out at dawn and I didn't take Harry when I drove up to Joe's cave. He wasn't home but there was a scrawled note on the door: *"Gone to the Shovel."* He was eating biscuits and gravy when I got there. The waitress brought me a mug of coffee. When she was gone I asked if he'd had any luck.

"Ain't laid eyes on him yet," he said somberly. "But I got a line on where he's bound to be."

"From Aaron?"

"Yep. You got your walkin' boots on? An' your big pistol? I kindly 'spected you 'bout dawn."

"The cops are looking for him pretty hard down below," I said. "My wife is keeping the boy close today. And she's got a loaded shotgun and knows how to use it."

He swallowed a big mouthful. "Will she?"

"If he comes back? My bet is yes. Once is an accident, twice is enemy action. Even to her."

He pushed his plate back. "You ready to go?"

"I didn't bring Harry."

"Don't think we'll need him to track this time. Finish your coffee and we'll go."

In an hour we were high above the Carbon River at the mouth of a steep canyon that climbed even higher. The clouds had parted and there was mild sunshine sparkling on the higher snowfields; the lower patches were melting. Joe led out up the canyon. Even though he set a deliberate pace, I was running sweat and breathing hard inside a quarter mile. Not Joe; but he took a look at me and called a break.

"Ridin' a desk all week ain't no kind of trainin' for

this," he said kindly.

I sucked water out of my canteen and waited for my pulse to slow. "Tell me about it," I said finally. "I try to spend three lunch hours a week walking all over those Seattle hills downtown."

"Good for your legs."

"Yeah, but it's all pavement. This isn't."

He grinned. "You're doin' okay. We'll top out directly."

All told it was more like another hour before we reached the head of the canyon and followed old game trails zigzagging to the top. Joe flopped down cross-legged and wiped sweat off his head. I collapsed on a weathered deadfall.

"How much farther?"

"We're there." He waved an arm. "Look around."

We were on a ridge that ran between the canyon we had just quitted and two others, one a shallow open bowl in the mountains and the other steep and tree-choked.

"Is that a pond down there?" I put my binoculars on the bowl." It wasn't nearly as big as the one the loggers from Carbonado had shown me last elk season. "Looks like a beaver pond."

"It is. You look close you'll see the dam off to the left under them alders."

"Hell, there's a beaver! Gnawing on one of the alders." I passed the binoculars to Joe.

"Prime specimen," he said. "Nothin' much disturbs 'em up in here. Too far from any road."

"So why did you bring me up here?"

"There's an active skook cave in that brushy draw." He handed back the glasses and stared at the sky. "They're there."

I felt my pulse lurch again. "You saw them?"

"I don't need to, remember?"

"Should we be talking?"

"Too far away for them to hear, and the wind's wrong. Aaron thought they might be up here."

"How would Aaron know?"

"'Cause Adam went to see did Aaron have any medicine his baby could take. But it was too late. Another tragedy witnessed only by these mountains."

I thought about my son in the Enumclaw hospital, grabbed onto my empathy with both hands, and stuffed it out of sight. "So he decided to come to steal my son."

Joe shook his head. "I'm kindly sorry your wife dragged you back to the Plateau with her. Her dad was a good woodsman and her mom was a fine lady and I'm sure so is her daughter. An' now her son's been marked, sure as I was."

"I bet you never had a retard try to steal you," I said.

"That's a hard word, retard. But your heart is hardened against him. I can't blame you."

I had nothing to say to that. "Even if we could grab him up here, that's a hell of a drag to haul him out. He's too strong to march at gunpoint if he doesn't want to go."

"It is a piece. But don't get your cart afore your horse. First we gotta see if he's still with 'em."

"How do we do that?"

He dug a strip of jerky out of his possibles bag. "We wait."

Chapter Forty-Five

Clouds began to drift back over as the day went along. The wind from the beaver pond picked up. It had a bite in it, and I put my hat back on and buttoned my mackinaw. Joe found a natural windbreak of piss firs a couple of yards below the ridge crest, unsheathed his big knife and went back over the ridge. I could barely hear him above the wind, whacking branches back there.

He came back with an armful of aromatic Doug fir for insulated seating and hewed away ground-sweeping branches from two trees, so we could lean against the trunks completely out of the wind. Then he jammed severed branches in front of each position for a rudimentary blind. When he was done we had a comfortable spot below the skyline with a clear view of the brushy draw and the pond, where he said they came to drink.

"Could be a long wait," he said. "No need to court discomfort."

"How far you figure that pond is from here?"

"Maybe three hundred yards. A long reach for my ole rifle, or your pistol. But we ain't here to shoot."

"I was thinking it's a long way to try to sneak without being spotted, if Adam is there."

"First we need to find that out. Let 'em go about their business. Then I can cut his track and take us to him."

We settled in. The stand of piss firs blocked the wind

and the springy seating kept cold from seeping up our backsides. The shifting light caused by the moving clouds took on a hypnotic quality. I felt myself dozing. I dug out my Stanley, poured its cap full of steaming coffee, handed it to Joe, then filled an old plastic Thermos top for me.

"Tell me a story, Joe. I'm nodding off here."

He chuckled softly. "Ain't no snoozin' good as high-country snoozin' when you've climbed hard. It's the clean air. We got time to burn if you want a nap."

"I'd rather stay awake. You never told me the whole story about when skooks took you. Tell that one."

"I s'pose this country brings that into your mind." He kind of shrugged. "What part you want to hear?"

"How you and your buddy got lost. Start there."

He sighed. "One a' these quick-moving fall storms came in. Not cold enough for snow but rainin' buckets. We forted up under piss firs like these 'uns, shiverin' and soaked." He was speaking in a soft monotone, gazing toward the beaver pond. "It seemed to get dark awful fast. When the rain eased, we was completely lost. We heard a mine whistle, but it echoed. Couldn't tell where it came from." His gaze stayed far away. "We panicked and ran. Oh, did we run. Woods panic takes you that way. I told you we got separated."

"And the skooks found you," I said.

"Found *me*," he emphasized.

"You thought skooks scared Hoyt to death. Later you set out for revenge."

He nodded. "But that gets ahead of this story. I ran till I collapsed. Prob'ly the same thing Hoyt did. Couldn't breathe..." His voice tailed off. "Next thing I knew, I was snatched up. I smelled that smell."

"Skook smell."

"I like to puked. Seems strange now, it's so familiar." He rubbed a big paw over his face. "This big'un lugged me off like walkin' down Broadway on Sunday afternoon. There was more'n one. I could hear 'em muttering."

"Norgus porkus," I said.

"Can't say I heard anything like that. I took it for caveman jabber. That's pretty much what skooks are, troglodytes. Means lives in a cave."

"Yeah, I know. Like you."

He offered a small smile. "Mine's the Hearst Castle, compared. Their cave was darker than the darkest damn mine, cold, wet, damp. But the big'un put out a lot of body heat. I stopped shiverin'. I must of been hallucinatin' because it was like my daddy had me. My daddy was a big, strong man. Didn't smell that purty neither, what with rotgut whisky and snoose and bad teeth and not bathin' reg'lar."

"These skooks took you to a cave up here?"

"Yep. They had boughs and branches and stuff piled in there for beddin' like they all do. I could smell fir even through that stink. I couldn't see squat. Wasn't tryin', truth be told. I went somewheres else inside my head..."

He paused. I wondered what memories he was reliving behind that faraway look. His face was strained.

"What happened next," he said slowly, "is that I must of slept. Passed out, more like. Dehydrated, half-froze, hungry, my nose runnin' snot. I was crammed between two of them things but in my head I wasn't there. If I stayed under I could stay someplace else, way I figger.

That's when that other 'un nursed me."

We sat silently for a while, each with our own memories.

"To this day I think I could hear mine whistles, and a locomotive goin' into Melmont," Joe said finally. "Normal things. I dreamed my daddy callin' me." He stopped again. I waited. Finally, "Dreamed I heard his hounds. He had a couple of redbones to run cougars with. Gorge folks feared cougars most when their kids got lost in the woods. A big cat will take a child and eat him, don't b'lieve he won't."

"And that female skook marked you forevermore," I said. "Which is how you know they're up in that brushy canyon right now."

He glanced at me. "You believe me now. Hear it in your voice."

"Put it this way," I said. "I'm here."

"A-huh. Believin' don't come easy. I know."

"You said this Satiacum rescued you." I used the binoculars again; the beavers were still undisturbed.

"See anything?" Joe said.

"Just the beavers."

"Yeah, ol' Ronnie could track a ghost across a parkin' lot. I wasn't just dreamin' my daddy's hounds, see. They started lookin' for us at first light. The dogs found our mushroom sacks an' Ronnie cut my sign, found where the skooks got me. He told my daddy to leash the dogs and follow slow."

"I don't get it."

"He knew which way the skooks would bolt when they heard hounds. He didn't want to push 'em. They did hear the hounds and snatched me outta that cave. Not hurryin', just movin'. Satiacum cut cross-country on his best mountain horse, a big Appy. The ol' hammer an' anvil. My dad was the hammer, Ronnie was the anvil. When he shot that 'un carryin' me, t'others scattered." He absently stroked the weathered butt of the old rifle his mentor used to free him. "He scooped me in the saddle an' took me back to my daddy. The rest you know."

For the last couple minutes I had been vaguely aware of a faint distant sound. When Joe stopped talking I could hear it better: a thin far-off mosquito-like buzz.

"Must be roads beyond those hills," I said. "I think I hear a chainsaw."

"Closest roads over there are a mile at least."

The sound faded almost beneath hearing, then came a little stronger on a wind gust. "Hell, it's moving," I said. "It's not a chainsaw, it's a dirt-bike." The sound faded again. "Going down into a draw and then topping a hill."

"Two-stroke, yep. You got pretty good ears."

On cue, the faint two-stroke whine came back. Off-road motorcycles could go a lot of places; I'd seen a couple of those wrecking-yard bikers use a strange New Hampshire model called a Rokon to climb like a mule in impossible terrain. If the biker out there had one of those, he could come all the way into the beaver-pond valley and blow our stakeout sky-high.

Chapter Forty-Six

Joe shifted around, digging in his possibles bag, and came up with one of his homemade pipes and an old sock he used for a tobacco pouch.

"I know the wind's wrong," I said. "But should we be lighting up? Maybe that bike will go somewhere else."

He thumbed *kinnikinik* into the apple-wood bowl. "Skooks know my personal blend," he said "It was Ronnie's afore me. But you're right about that vanilla shit you favor." He offered me the sock and struck a kitchen match on his thumbnail. The windbreak was so effective the flame hardly flickered.

"Might as well." I filled my pipe with his mixture. "If that bike keeps coming all the way to that beaver pond we're screwed anyway."

"Poor ol' Adam," he said. "He usually stayed deep hid like the skooks he ran with. A cryin' shame this tragedy unbalanced him."

My old Zippo got the *kinnikinick* going. The dry flavor reminded me of English non-aromatics; something I noted only in passing, distracted by the distant buzzing.

"The police chief said he stole clothes and food in town," I said. "And he already *was* unbalanced if he was at that school. Did the skooks bring him to you like they did Aaron?"

Joe sighed heavily. "Took him to Aaron. But he wouldn't stay. Pore chile, all trapped up in that big strappin' body, ragin' with grownup hormones, an' don't know what to do with it. Not a talker, Adam. Even less so than Aaron."

"So he stole clothes and food in town on his own."

"Aaron woulda fed him and kept him in clothes." Joe sounded sad. "He did come in when it got so cold only a skook could sleep rough. Understood anyways that Aaron would feed him and let him bed down by the stove. But the other kids didn't like him. He smelled too much like a skook."

"Well you say he runs with them." The distant motorbike crept closer. Joe seemed to pay it no mind. "And screwed a skook female. And you were okay with that."

Joe looked at me sidewise. "Told you once I don't meddle in neighbors' sex habits. No way to guess they'd actually bring a young'un to term. Or how he'd react when it died."

"He reacted like a damn skook!"

I was going to say more, but suddenly I wasn't hearing the motorbike anymore. I waited for it to top out over another ridge. But the sound stayed gone this time. Joe smoked calmly and watched the beaver pond. Five minutes passed. The engine-sound did not resume.

"Looks like that bike stopped," I said.

Joe nodded. "Aaron wouldn't have 'em bring him all the way in."

"Aaron!"

"Yep. Lemme borrow them field glasses again."

I handed the binoculars across. "What makes you think that's Aaron out there?"

Joe was studying the far end of the valley. "I kindly forgot to mention Aaron had one o' them guys from the wrecking yard bring him up here to see could he do anything for Adam's young'un. That's how he knew where they laid up."

"Yeah, you did kind of forget that," I said grimly. "Like so many other things. Did you know Aaron was coming here today?"

He shook his head without lowering the binoculars.

"Then how do you know it's him? Why not a bowhunter looking for new territory?

"Bound to be Aaron. I told him we were comin', to try to bring Adam in. He wasn't happy about it."

I stuffed my pipe in my mackinaw pocket and unbuttoned two buttons for easier access to my pistol. "I like Aaron. But he better not try to stop me."

Joe handed me back the glasses. "No sign o' him yet. Aaron can't cover this rough ground very easy. It ain't that he would try to stop you. It just bothers him, the idea of Adam bein' stuffed back in that school an' restrained all the time."

"You mean locked up so he can't get back out."

"An' cuffs on his bed. Or a strait jacket."

"They *do* that?" Despite my fury at Adam, the image was unsettling.

"You know how strong he is," Joe said matter-of-factly. "Them school workers ain't strong as you or me."

I've always had good distance vision—to the point where soon I was going to need reading glasses to handle a typewriter. Now, far up the valley beyond the beaver pond, I caught a flicker of movement as something sky-lined itself. When I put the binoculars on it, it was Aaron.

"Well, you were right," I said. "There he is."

We took turns watching Aaron's painful progress down the valley. The binoculars brought the painful contortions of his pale face into clear focus. He was talking to himself. He fell twice, clumsily, and had a hard time regaining his feet. I could see he had a backpack and one of his old .22 rifles slung over his back on something that looked like clothesline. Despite what Joe said I wondered if the rifle meant he intended to interfere with Adam's capture, but I didn't say anything; I was just going to let this play out.

He got to more even ground, but was moving even slower, his head drooping to one side, shoulders hunched, limping. He stopped frequently to blow, sucking in deep ragged breaths. He was in even worse physical shape than I was. His lips kept moving.

"He's really talking to himself," I said finally.

"Countin' his paces, I expect," Joe said. "Cain't see the beaver pond from where he is now. Don't want to walk right past it."

""How's he going to get home?"

"When he's ready he'll call his ride on that three-channel CB he souped up, an' start walkin' back. The guy on the bike will come on in an' get him so he don't have to walk all the way back."

"I'm surprised those wrecking-yard tough guys would be so helpful to a guy like Aaron."

"They make good money on his fish," Joe said. "Then too, they know I take it kindly for them to look after him."

"Still, I'm surprised they don't try to follow and see

what's going on up here."

He chuckled without humor. "One did. Had a terrible accident. His bike got smashed up bad by some big ol' rocks. None o' his pals b'lieved he was chased all the way to pavement by skooks. Said they didn't, anyway. Had hell retrievin' what was left of that bike. So they do his way now."

"How the hell did Aaron get home when the bike was wrecked?"

"I borryed a horse and came got him."

"Of course you did. And read the old-time religion to those tough bikers. And they listened."

"He needs the help, see. Aaron's heart is stronger than his legs."

"I hope you're right. He looks right now like a heart attack waiting to happen."

"He'll have time to rest up when he gets to the beaver pond. The skooks will check his back trail before they approach."

"They won't check up here?" I touched the grips of my gun for reassurance.

"Not up here," Joe said with absolute conviction. "That's why we came in this way."

Chapter Forty-Seven

Aaron was obviously making enough noise to alert the beavers, but they didn't appear alarmed. They almost casually drifted into the water and slipped from sight, leaving only ripples to mark their going. Aaron shed his backpack and rifle, flopped facedown on the bank and splashed water all over his head. Then he rolled laboriously to a sitting position and unlaced his boots. With a lot of pantomimed grunting and tugging, he got his boots and socks off. He rolled up his britches before immersing his feet.

"He's going to catch pneumonia." I handed Joe the binoculars.

"He won't. Nothin' refreshes after a hard walk like soaking your feet. Once he's cooled off, he'll put his socks and boots back on an' feel a hundred percent better. Then he'll build a warmin' fire. Said the skooks like it."

"Like that bunch in British Columbia you told me about," I said. "Maybe they had an Aaron too."

"More'n I know. But I don't need to know everything in this world."

Aaron was drying his feet with his socks. He pulled another pair out of his backpack and sat on a deadfall to don them. After he had his boots back on, he spread the wet socks on the log, took what looked like a walkie-talkie out of his knapsack, extended the antenna and spoke briefly. Far away, the two-stroke engine cranked, revved twice and went away.

"There goes his ride."

"Aaron must be plannin' to be a while," Joe said. "Prob'bly told that fella to come back at daybreak."

The motor sound faded to nothing. The minutes ticked by. The overcast was solid now, and leaden. The wind blew colder. I thought I could smell snow in the wind. Up the valley Aaron dragged branches out of the alder thicket, produced a hatchet from his pack, chopped them smaller, and built a wood pyramid with handfuls of tinder in the middle before touching it off. He soon had a cheery blaze going and sat spread-legged against the old deadfall and worked a canteen thirstily. Little by little, wisps of sweet dry alder scent reached my nostrils on the wind.

"He found some good dry wood," I said.

"Prob'bly branches the beavers gnawed off," Joe said.

"I smell snow."

"A-huh. Liable to hit us about dark."

"It's already pretty damn dark. Getting down from here will be a trick."

"I brung a little flashlight just in case."

"Yeah? I have a headlamp I use duck-hunting to keep my hands free. It still will be a trick, if we get Adam. You should have brought that horse."

"We can come back, if he's here."

"Aaron probably came to warn him."

"We'll just have to wait and see."

After that we stopped talking. Joe nursed his pipe. I finished the last of the coffee; no sense carrying the weight back when I could urinate it on the way. The wind came and went in increasing gusts. Dark encroached by increments. It was approaching full twilight when Joe spoke again.

"There's the first 'un." I'd been pretty steady on the binoculars, but never saw it come. One minute Aaron was alone. The next, a big skook stood across the fire from him; a dark vaguely man-shaped bulk just within reach of the firelight. My pulse went into overdrive. This was my first sighting since the night in the Gorge when my world went crazy. My palms fairly itched for my Remington; at three hundred yards I couldn't miss.

"Steady," said Joe. "Killin' heat is leakin' off you."

The thing turned its head, almost as if it heard him. The firelight caught redly in its eyes, just like the eyes of the one that stole my son. I could barely breathe. Another dark form materialized. Aaron scrambled to his feet and started waving his hands around.

"What the hell's he doing?" I said.

"Signin'," Joe said succinctly.

I handed him the binoculars. "Can you *read* that crap? Since you speak Chinook so fluently."

"Aaron says fish are in. Says pemmican is ready for pickup."

The first skook waved its big hands back at Aaron. The second stood unmoving, arms dangling.

"The male's answerin'," Joe said.

"You *can* read it."

"It ain't exactly Latin. Male says they'll be down for their supplies."

"Aaron does this every year?"

"More'n I know. Don't need to know."

"Yeah, yeah, heard you the first time. What's he saying

now?"

"Askin' after Adam."

"By name!"

"Not perzactly. Close as I can read, it's the hairless' un."

"Adam isn't hairless by a long shot!"

"All in your point of view, I reckon." He handed me back the binoculars. "Watch close now."

A third, smaller-framed skook drifted into the firelight periphery. A female. The firelight glistened on its belly fur; something wet. It turned and looked into the shadows.

Adam came into view with a rush. His torso was bare; he had discarded the shreds of T-shirt I half-ripped from his body. He crouched at the fire and shoved his big hands almost in it. He was shivering furiously. In the binoculars he looked plenty hairy to me. As I watched, his shudders abated. His blank stare ... relaxed. He rubbed his bare arms and shoulders as if bathing in the warmth. Aaron fiddled with his backpack, pulled out a long-sleeved flannel shirt and handed it across the flames. Adam slipped into it without lifting his gaze and left it hanging open. It brushed the ground.

Aaron rounded the fire and said something. Adam stood up, head still down. Aaron carefully buttoned the shirt and reached up to pat the huge boy on the shoulder. I wondered irrelevantly where Aaron found a 4XL logger's shirt. The small female with wet fur came closer. She loomed over Aaron, a head taller than Adam, which meant she had to be damn near seven feet tall. The other two were even bigger. Aaron looked like a child among monsters but seemed perfectly at ease; he went back into his backpack for something to pass around to all hands. Whatever it was, it was edible; they all took a bite and stood chewing and staring at the fire.

"Aaron's feeding them." I handed the glasses back to Joe. "He brought Adam a shirt."

"A-huh, one o' mine." Irrelevant question answered. "He musta been awful cold, how fast he got to that fire." He had the binoculars up. "Smoked salmon, at a bet—the food I mean." He made a small, sad sound. "You noticed the young female still heavy-lactatin'?"

"I saw her stomach fur was wet."

"That 'un would be Adam's mate."

My emotions were in turmoil, triggered by Aaron's fatherly tenderness toward the huge hairy kid that tried to steal my son. And now, according to Joe, the tragic reason—for them—that Adam tried to steal my son stood beside Adam in the firelight. I might as well have been on that alien planet I was inventing, spying on an alien species. But there was no clever science-fiction air car parked over the ridge to lift me back to a safe and sane spaceport city. This was still the Cascade Mountains. But the twentieth century and its logic, let alone sanity, seemed far away.

Humans had been here as long as skooks, even if their settlements were farther apart than Texas according to Bill Simp; which left hundreds of square miles to the skooks. I was deep into their world now, accompanied by an improbable giant hermit who talked about ancient pacts between human and skook; and read alien sign language between two other improbable humans and skooks as easily as old newspaper headlines.

I wondered if skooks knew when Joe was around, since he professed to always know when they were. Awful late to wonder that, perched up here with it getting dark. But no; my elephant bell worked because they only came out of the foothills when my son's scent drew them. That part at least was logical; I was just spooked by circumstances. *And no damn wonder.* Because if they did sense us, and come after me, making it down the canyon behind us in the dark, even with my headlamp and big pistol, would be damn near impossible.

It was nearly full dark. The fire limned the tableau of figures, still motionless but for chewing and an occasional flicker of fingers. Joe still had the glasses to his eyes. But he had stopped translating. Now he muttered a weary curse after the last flickering finger-exchange.

"'Fraid o' somethin' like that." He climbed to his feet with a groan. "Stiffenin' up. Gettin' old." First time I'd ever seen him move like an old man.

"We going somewhere?"

"Not you," he said. "I need to go down there. If they wind you, they'll just scatter."

"You going to leave me stranded up here?"

"You could get back if you need to. But I'll come back."

Before I could argue, he drifted out of sight down the slope toward the distant fire. I noticed a slight haze across the firelight. A couple minutes later, the first invisible flakes of snow from the on-coming storm, cold and damp, brushed my cheeks.

I never felt more alone in my life.

Chapter Forty-Eight

Your eyes adjust when you're sitting outdoors as night falls. Even with the storm blowing in, it didn't seem pitch dark. But the snow thickened until the distant fire was only an orange blur. I put my headlamp in my left-hand mackinaw pocket for a quick draw if necessary and suspended my pistol by its grip between the big front buttons. With my hat pulled down, hands in pockets and my neck tucked deep in the wool coat collar, the cold was bearable. My legs were a little cold, but so far the felt-lined Sorels protected my feet.

The skook scream, when it came, froze me from the inside out.

Even muffled by the snowfall, it seemed right on top of me.

I thumbed on my lamp and snatched my pistol in less time than it takes to tell it. But something made me hesitate before I pulled the light out of my pocket. Not wanting to burn out my night vision, not wanting to light up my position—something.

The thing's challenge went on and on, louder than the wind, longer than seemed possible for anything without a gigantic set of lungs. Long enough for me to register that it wasn't really on top of me, but down-valley, borne on the wind. I kept my lamp in my pocket as my brain sorted and discarded possibilities at warp speed, and settled on one: Joe had been going straight upwind when he approached the fire. They couldn't have winded him, so the first twig he snapped—and he seldom snapped any—would have startled and spooked them into that scream. Like a dog's furious barking when caught off guard.

The scream cut off abruptly. It didn't come again. I had to assume they recognized Joe. Gradually my heart settled out of my throat and my testicles settled back from somewhere behind my esophagus. I pulled my binoculars from the protecting flap of my pack and peered through the snowfall. It was like trying to watch an old black-and-white TV with a faulty tube; for all my remote childhood, that was the only "snow" I'd ever seen.

Joe had come into the firelight. I couldn't see the skooks. Then the snow thinned momentarily and I saw the biggest skook, almost beyond the reach of the fire, making those finger gestures at Joe. He answered in kind. Then Aaron started in. Adam was crouched by the fire, hands out to the warmth, lost in his own world. I wondered if the other skooks were circling to check Joe's back trail. I put down the glasses and strained my ears for nearby sounds—pointless with the wind muttering in the trees. Should I start back down the canyon and risk an ambush? Or sit tight and risk them stumbling over me? On balance, staying seemed smarter. I had my back to a sturdy tree trunk that would deflect thrown rocks. A dense stand of piss firs all around and a steep slope behind. If they tried to come at me, they'd have to fight through the trees and that should give me time to shoot. Just enough time. I hoped. I laid the Casull on my lap and went back to the binoculars.

The signing down there seemed to be growing

agitated—if I could infer anything at all from alien sign language in a snowstorm. I felt a mad bubble of laughter try to work its way to audibility. I could hear Rod Serling's somber voice in some part of my brain: *Portrait of a twentieth-century male who spends his life in cities, working in tight white collar and a tie, marooned high in the wild Cascades, in a snow storm, trying to read cryptid sign language at a campfire built by an albino fugitive from a state school for retarded children.* How do you find yourself in predicaments like this, I asked myself. But had no answer. Of all the predicaments I ever got into, this one stood alone and unequalled.

When the snow thickened until the campfire scene was lost to view, the surrounding darkness seemed blacker. I must have ruined some of my night vision staring at the fire through the binoculars. I was absurdly grateful for that fire, as if that single spot of brightness was a lifeline. If it went dark I would truly be blind and alone, with no landmarks to guide me but the slope of land at my back. That canyon would look completely different in the bouncing beam of my headlamp; if I fell and sprained something or broke an ankle that would be the end of the line unless Joe found me.

Trying to time the waves of snow, I put the binoculars back up and could see again, fuzzily. The lactating female was back at the fire, standing over Adam. He stood up and faced her. She reached out and touched his face. He reached up and touched her face. Then she stepped back and signed. I knew I was losing it because I thought she looked down at him with an expression weighted by sadness. That had to be Joe's doing, making me see things

I wouldn't think to look for. Adam signed back, and raised his hand toward her. She looked down at the hand and up at him and I swear to god that alien face looked about to shed tears. Even a gorilla can look sad, and she was no gorilla. Adam made a purely human gesture of entreaty. She signed once more, faded into the shadows and was gone.

Adam turned toward Aaron and said something. I couldn't make out any expression on his face, but his big shoulders were slumped as in defeat. Aaron stepped up to him, put both hands up on those big shoulders and spoke earnestly up into the hairy face. The snow drew a curtain again. When it lifted they were still like that. But Joe had joined them and placed one of his big paws over one of Aaron's on the boy's shoulder. Aaron screwed his face up tight. I didn't have enough definition to be sure, but from the way his shoulders shook, he *was* crying. He said something aside to Joe. I guess Joe answered; I couldn't see his face.

Aaron dropped his hands and lowered his head, nodding. I saw Adam's frame stiffen. He threw Joe's hand off violently and turned away. The big skook stepped in front of him. The snowfall blotted things out again. I waited. When I could see again, Adam's neck was bowed and he stood spraddle-legged, fury eloquent in his posture. The skook signed to him. His hands stayed stubbornly at his sides, knotted into ham-like fists. The skook signed again; faster, shorter.

Adam hauled off and hit the thing square in the muzzle.

I flinched at the furious strength of that blow, a

straight overhand right with all his shoulder behind it and his thick legs driving. Somebody somewhere—maybe that damned school weight room—had taught him how to punch. If he'd tried that on me and I hadn't been able to slip it, I would have been down and maybe out, and he would have had my son.

The skook's head snapped back—maybe five inches. That was all. The massive frame didn't budge. Faster than thought it closed the gap between them, wrapped Adam in those huge arms and—lifted him clear off the ground. With his arms pinned, Adam writhed and struggled, kicking out with big bare feet at his captor. He might as well have been a child in the grip of King Kong. Then the snow blurred everything to invisibility but fire-glow. I cursed and stared; it felt as if my eyeballs were bulging into the glasses to force vision to come back.

The snow took its own sweet time about giving me another glimpse. A subjective hour. Probably closer to five minutes—an eternity in those circumstances. When I could see again, my brain didn't immediately register what my eyes told it. Then it did: Joe had Adam by the head and neck, and the skook had his feet; Adam's body stretched limply between them, no longer struggling. Aaron stood to the side, his mouth a dark O in his albino features. Joe and the skook turned toward the beaver pond. Before I could comprehend their intent, they swung him once and threw him in. I saw water splash up. The skook turned away immediately. But Joe stood at the pond, head bowed. I waited for Adam to crawl out, wet and subdued from being handled so harshly. But he didn't crawl out. I waited. He still didn't crawl out. Then the snow blocked all view again.

By the time I caught another gap in the snowfall, there were no skooks to be seen. And still no Adam. Aaron was slumped against his deadfall, staring into his fire. Joe hunkered across from him. Neither moved before the snow came back. I didn't know what to think. I had been an unwilling witness to whatever happened, but a poor witness due to the snow. I had half-expected to see a cowed and soaked Adam huddled by the fire, waiting for Joe to bring him out. But I hadn't seen that, or anything like it. If Adam had gone back with the skooks, he was going to be even harder to find after that kind of harsh handling. The hunt would have to start all over.

My old Filson and wool pants were so coated with snow by now I would have resembled a sitting snowman to any observer. Only the Casull was clear; I kept wiping snow off with the end of my scarf. The cold was leeching into my bones. I needed to get up, walk around and get my blood stirring. Given the thickness of snowfall and steady direction of the wind I said to hell with freezing to death and got up creakily, stomping my feet and beating my arms against my sides to restore circulation. I felt my way up to approximately level ground on the ridge and jogged in place until I broke a sweat under my heavy woolens. I had failed to note the time when Joe started down there. It felt a lot later than it was now: not even eight p.m. according to the glowing green numerals on my wristwatch.

Time had distorted since Joe headed for Aaron's fire. My last sight of Joe, he had looked immobile and settled, hunkering down there. Maybe his old bones were barking. I wondered if he planned to wait the night out by the fire with Aaron until his ride came back at daylight. If so, where did that leave me? I could try to find my way back down in the dark, probably over two hours on very chancy terrain. I could try to work my way down to Aaron's fire, where at least there would be warmth and another gun if skooks still were on the prowl. Or I could get out my hatchet and try to find enough dry wood with my headlamp to build my own warming fire and wait for developments.

I chose the third alternative, forgot about stealth, mounted my headlamp on my hat and scouted around with my hatchet in one hand and pistol in the other. I crammed the hatchet in my belt when I found some firewood, and dragged it back to my hide. Not being a mountain man, I had commercial fire starters in my pack guaranteed to start a fire in a blizzard. They worked. I built it up with all the dry stuff I found, and added some branches lopped off the underside of the piss firs when it was hot enough to burn them. With a roaring fire, I felt a hundred percent better; fire is man's most ancient ally. I was back against my tree out of the wind, with the fire's heat drying my face and melting the snow off my clothing, when I heard Joe's bass rumble above the wind.

"I'm comin' up. Don't shoot."

"Come ahead."

He came into the firelight looking as if he had aged twenty years since he left. Which would put him close to the century mark. He hunkered and warmed his hands, not looking at me.

"Aaron's not with you?"

"Nope. He's stayin' the night with Adam.

"The last break in the snow, I didn't see Adam. Just you and Aaron. The skooks were gone too."

"A-huh." He studied the flames like a man reading his fortune.

"Joe, what happened down there?"

"Adam won't trouble you and your'n again."

"What, because you dunked him in cold water?"

"Saw that, did you?" Joe wagged his big head. "Tol' you, sometimes a watcher has to do hard things to keep the pact. It comes harder the older I git. I hope I can last until your boy is ready."

That again. I let it go by. "Joe, what hard thing are you talking about?"

"Saw 'em signin'. Saw what they was thinkin' to do about him. So I had to step in. Adam couldn't be let to run loose after what he done. An' was fixed on tryin' again."

"He was, huh?" Which triggered enough hot regret I'd let Joe talk me out of bringing my rifle to forget about trying to stay warm. The bright plaid logger's shirt would have made an easy target, and to hell with the consequences. "So what changed what serves him for a mind?"

Joe glanced at me briefly. "Death in your voice agin. Th' big'un tried to tell him you are a lethal man. An' you might blame tryin' to grab your boy again on skooks. They fear you. It would be his death." He stared into the fire again. "Or yours. And you need to raise your son. Or the last link between our'n and their'n will be lost. Same thing Satiacum feared when I started killin' skooks."

When Joe got hold of a concept he hung onto it. I let his second reference to my son as future skook watcher go by without comment.

Joe washed his big hands in the heat and then stared at them like he'd never seen them before. "Not right for Aaron to have to do what they decided. He kind of loved that boy. But Aaron knew lockin' him up again was just a different dyin', only longer. I did offer to bring him out. But the decision was otherwise."

Looking at those huge strong hands, I felt an ugly little shiver that had nothing to do with the weather. "Joe, you told me that would be murder."

"Reckon it's how you do it." He was still looking at his big paws. "Anyone was to find the boy, they'd conclude he broke his neck when he fell in that pond."

Which explained why Adam didn't crawl out of the beaver pond. "Just another school runaway that died trying to live rough," I said. "Case closed."

"A-huh." He heaved a big sigh. "Leastways now your boy is safe. An' you won't have to be on high alert all the time. Aaron was willin', but it was my job. My job to protect the skooks' secrets." He stared up into the snow, unblinking. "On my conscience be it. Adam is free now. Maybe in his next life he won't be born flawed."

"You believe in reincarnation?"

He shrugged. "More'n I know, though those Nepalese fellers talked a strong case. Lots of Eastern religions do believe: Shintoism, Jainism, Buddhism. They make good arguments for it. If they're right I've got a load of karma to deal with my next time aroun'."

"You said Aaron was staying with Adam tonight. You meant with his body."

"A-huh. Close as he can get, until Adam's spirit is free

an' flown. Like a one-man wake, sorta." He stood up with an old man's groan. "When you're warm enough to travel, let's git you outta these mountains before you catch your death o' cold."

Chapter Forty-Nine

For the rest of my life, I've had nightmares about the descent through that black canyon in the snow. Shadows spinning and jumping like live things in the glare-back from my headlamp and Joe's little flashlight. The wind roaring in the Douglas firs so hard it blew some trees down, loud crashes out in the woods that had my nerves jumping and my fingers clawing under my open mackinaw for the .454. I'd had to holster it to have both hands free to keep from falling. I fell anyway, two or three times. I managed to avoid breaking or spraining anything, but had some dandy bruises later. Joe almost fell once, going to one knee and catching himself. He'd lost all that old fluidity of movement, and trudged like an old, tired man.

Sometimes in my nightmares, Adam comes back into my driveway and knocks my teeth loose with that ferocious overhand right. Sometimes he steals my car and escapes. For some reason I can't explain the car he steals is one that we bought later, after we had a daughter: an old silver 1966 Cadillac I used for my Seattle commute. It was a better snow car than my truck with a full gas tank over the rear axle and studded tires. In one dream, Adam has my son and I am chasing him up snow-choked Forest Service roads in the timber. But he's driving the Cadillac, and my truck keeps spinning its tires, losing traction and almost losing the road. Sometimes it does lose the road and crash down until thick brush stops it, and I find myself fighting through the thickets. It's dark and the snow is falling heavily and my headlamp creates those marching shadows and I'm going downhill behind Joe, even though Adam was driving higher.

Sometimes one of the shadows becomes a red-eyed skook, leaping at me out of the dark. The .454 blasts the night apart, two quick booms, and the skook goes down. When I get to it, it always is a heavily lactating female, reaching feebly up to me as the light fades from its stricken eyes...

I wake up in my quiet bedroom, my wife sleeping soundly beside me, and listen for the sound of our children in their rooms. My hand drops to the floor beside me to find the Casull. It was only a nightmare—I know this—but I ease out of bed and my bare feet touch Harry's warm fur. He's been sleeping as soundly as my wife but he's instantly awake. In the glow of the nightlight I see the frosting of age has advanced on his muzzle. His ears are cocked, watching me. I take the pistol and pad barefoot down the hall, listening subconsciously for the sound of the elephant bell. The night is quiet, no wind.

Each of the kids is sound asleep in their rooms, my son in his new bed to accommodate his lengthening legs. In my office I flip on the outside floods and a doe browsing in the pasture freezes, eyes gleaming in the light. The coffee pot is always on. I find my way through the dark kitchen by its red light and pour a cup, then go back and sit in my office chair overlooking the pasture. The doe is gone. I drink my coffee slowly and consider and reject having one of my Nicaraguan maduros. I need to get back to sleep because tomorrow is a work day…

I didn't have nightmares every night. But enough nights as the months and years went by. Not once in all that time, as far as I could tell, were we visited by skooks. I never went back to spearfish with Aaron's kid, or to get fresh salmon and steelhead from Aaron. When I hung around the wrecking yard, every time one of those bikers fired up a dirt bike I had flashbacks of Aaron struggling toward the beaver pond, his dead-white face slick with sweat. I never asked if one of them used the Rokon the next morning to climb all the way to the pond where Adam was entombed to bring Aaron home. I knew the cold water would hold his body down longer than in lowland waters from time on various police beats, but kept an eye out for any discoveries of a body in the high country. That news never came.

The years went by with no further alarms and excursions. Gerald Ford finished out Nixon's term and was defeated by Jimmy Carter. To me at least, Carter's administration was notable mainly for stagflation and the Iran hostage crisis. Advertising revenue for my publisher dried up until a new general manager ordered cutbacks and I was back to working part-time, but as an independent contractor, the tax advantages of which kept me almost level financially. But I took a civil-service test when the Game Department had a Public Information Officer opening and scored highest when they counted my veteran's preference. I gave up my independent contractor status for guaranteed salary and state insurance benefits. My commute to Olympia from the Plateau was almost exactly the same distance as to Seattle—within five miles give or take. My wife's boss blamed Carter for all his difficulties when the market for New Zealand jets tanked, and started talking about shutting down. She didn't wait, took a civil service test of her own and ended up as executive secretary for an agricultural extension service.

Harry died peacefully in his sleep one night, under his favorite apple tree in the backyard, when he was twelve. When my wife spoke to him out the bathroom window that morning and he didn't respond, she came back into the bedroom crying as if her heart were broken. When I got out there to check on him, slime trails of inquisitive slugs defaced his glossy coat. It felt as if part of me had been amputated and would never grow back. We buried him with a decoy bag for a shroud behind the fireplace with Paka. I was numb for days; your heart can get so tangled up in a dog things rip when he's gone. I hunted alone that year for the first time since his puppy season. I lost a couple of ducks but couldn't face the idea of a new dog yet; no dog born could step into Harry's place.

There was a clerk in my Olympia office who kept a calendar on the embassy hostages in Iran. Each day he added another sheet, with a new number for the days in captivity. He cursed Carter for his weakness. Ronald Reagan rode into Washington over Carter's crushed reelection hopes, and the Iranians almost instantly released the hostages. There was a new sheriff in town. He won his second election by a landslide and named the Soviet Union the "evil empire" and went eyeball-to-eyeball, trashing the previous years of detent. During those years my son grew into a tall and rangy teenager with sniper-quality vision; he shot my .22s with uncanny precision from his earliest training. My daughter grew into a lovely young pre-teen who read every book she could get her hands on and admired Jacques Cousteau.

To my disappointment, my son never took to duck hunting the way I hoped. He'd go with me, but bored easily. Before Harry died, the only part he really enjoyed was working with Harry on downed birds. For some reason, despite his eerie accuracy with a rifle, he had a hard time with a shotgun on flying birds, and it infuriated him. All his friends in school were big-game hunters with their dads, and that's what he relished.

When I complained that I didn't know enough about deer and elk hunting to teach him, my wife put me in touch with the boyfriend of one of her sisters, who was a dedicated member of what I came to call the Goulash Mafia. They had a specific way of team-hunting that always seemed to result in game hanging up. The routine was almost unvarying. I would arrive at the boyfriend's house in Enumclaw at five a.m. My sister-in-law would get up and put on cowboy coffee in an old fashioned pot to get things stirring, because the Goulash Mafia believed in partying hard the night before hunting and would be sleeping hard. They'd wander into the kitchen blinking and coughing, slurp down coffee, gulp down breakfast, and suddenly be bright-eyed and ready. They all were loggers but for Herb something, a Seattle accordion player and band leader whose schmaltzy polkas were the hot ticket with the Middle European community. Herb would lead out in his huge Chinook motor home. Then the boyfriend and I in his little Bronco, and the boyfriend's cousin, a dour old Slovenian in his half-cab Bronco with his partner known only as The Dutchman. We would park the Chinook at Bridge Camp and Herb would crawl in the back seat with us.

One trip among many stands in memory. We were turning up a canyon when Herb started banging on the back of my seat and yelling: "Elk! Let me out! Yellow ahsses, yellow ahsses, elk!" We rolled out and I had a round chambered in my Remington magnum while everybody else was fumbling with binoculars. One big animal across the canyon that all agreed was a cow went up a draw out of sight in the black timber. Another stood with its head concealed in Christmas-tree-size firs. I got a solid rest, put the crosshairs on its shoulder and kept saying tell me something, tell me something. But no one would, though all agreed later that hiding its head was the behavior of a bull. Then some damn idiot drove up and bailed out yelling at the top of his lungs: "Hey! Elk! Hey! There's elk over there! Hey!" The big critter assled deeper into the firs and was gone.

We went back and spread a picket line along the road. Tony the boyfriend went above, parked, and came down through the timber to push him out. Fog closed in. From my stand I couldn't see fifty yards. When we gathered later, Tony had pushed it out, a two-point bull seen too briefly by Johnny or the Dutchman to shoot and it circled above Tony, lost in the timber. I cussed all day because I should have taken the shot. We drove out several sections and every time we paused to glass, we had what Herb called, in his accent, a "connforonce." He though connforonces were hysterically funny, and demonstrated: "What do you think, Johnny? I don't know, Tony, whatta *you* think? I don't know. Dutch? "And so forth.

And that's pretty much the way my hunting went with the Goulash Mafia. We never tagged an animal while I hunted with them; they always seemed to score on days I was at work. After the novelty of hunting with them, including a tumbler of strong dark Austrian rum from Herb's Chinook at the end of the day, I grew bored with the whole exercise. I ate the amazing venison sausage Tony prepared and thick actual goulash from Herb's Chinook kitchen, and enjoyed their endless tales of the old country and hunts over there and here. But I guess I was born a duck hunter, and I stopped going with them. They considered me part of the group now, and were more than ready to take my son under their collective wing to teach him the ropes. My son was fourteen the year I turned into my driveway coming home from Olympia and saw Tony standing in my open garage, and then my son.

The last thing I noticed was a buck, swinging from the rafters with its hide half-off. My son's grin was electric as he tried to play cool, but Tony the veteran woodsman made no such pretense, waving his bloody skinning knife in all directions as he described the kill. Four hundred yards at a buck lying up behind a deadfall; one shot and it just toppled over, dead when they got there. Tony had banged up a knee that year in logging operations and couldn't help drag it out. He was almost beside himself describing the strength of my son in retrieving his first buck: like a young Paul Bunyan he said; he would make a fine logger. God, I hoped not; logging is damned dangerous work—his maternal grandfather died under a tree-fall—and I hadn't done the things I had to do to keep him safe, only to lose him to the damned woods. I wanted him to stay out of the woods unless accompanied by men with high-caliber rifles.

In those years I didn't visit Joe Consonants all that much. I would stop and talk to him if I ran across him sitting in one of his tourist-spotter rocking chairs, and he'd razz me for going to work for the Game Department. Sometimes we'd drive to the Shovel for coffee. Only occasionally did I join him by his stove to talk. His life force seemed much diminished, and his memory seemed to turn constantly back to his time among Nepalese holy men. He spoke more about reincarnation and said the closer he got to the end the more he thought about it. I told him there was a Buddhist temple in Seattle if he wanted to seek enlightenment. He snorted with his old vigor and said enlightenment is within yourself—or nowhere at all. He could still surprise me, because he kept his ear to the ground and knew all about my son's emergence as a deadly long-range rifle shot and strong man.

"Even them hard-core elk hunters respect that boy," he said. "Walks over mountains like on a Sunday stroll. Done walked the legs off some o' them guys thought they was bull o' the woods. You done a good job o' raisin' him right. Sets my mind to ease on that score. An' polite to a fault, respectful of old age."

"And how would you know that?" I asked him.

"I know you never brung him to see me," he said. "An' I understand and hold no hard feelin' because o' it. But somebody ranges far as him is bound to run up on me in the mountains, 'cause I still range a ways, if not far as always. Lone men on the trail tend to stop awhile together for a palaver. Been ever so. He is one fine young man."

Well, I couldn't keep a teenager with a growing reputation as a mountaineer wrapped up in swaddling clothes. But I didn't have to like it.

"I hope you didn't fill his head with all those wild tales," I said.

He smiled sadly. "He knows somethin' is out there."

"What do you mean?"

"Told me a huntin' yarn 'bout followin' up a wounded deer in the big timber at night without his rifle. Felt somethin' followin' him. Just *felt* it, understand, but trusted his instincts. Put his back to a big tree an' hauled out that there big pistol of yours. Ready to fight. He said he ain't strong enough yet to use the big loads, but five rounds o' .45 Long Colt oughta get the job done. Waited till whatever it was decided to go elsewhere. Just kinda knew—didn't hear or see anything."

I didn't know what to say. It was like my nightmares crawling into the daytime.

"They ain't gonna hurt him," Joe said quietly. "Told you that long ago. Just lookin' him over. Good thing, too. Not sure a teenager with a .45 would give 'em pause if they meant ill."

"You've never seen him shoot," I said.

"You're right to be proud. I suspicion they know I ain't long for this world, is why they're lookin' him over. It'll be the learnin' when not to shoot he may have to work on. Same as me."

Chapter Fifty

I went back to Lower Fairfax in the Gorge with my son the spring day Mildred Fenton chose to scatter old Ralph's ashes in the Carbon River. He had no known relatives and I don't know how a soldier's-home nurse got authorization to do that, and didn't ask. She said Ralph had been happiest at her place in Upper Melmont and I expect she was right. She chose Lower Fairfax for easier access to the river; I had a flashback when I saw Petoskey's vacation cabin, but suppressed it. Mildred was waiting and gave my son a tight hug and kissed him, and he turned red around the ears. She smiled up at him and said some of Ralph's happiest times had been spent playing "cheggers" with him.

"That's how you pronounced checkers when you were knee-high," she told him. "You were awfully young, so you probably don't remember."

"I remember Ralph," he said quietly. "He was sure big!"

"So how do you pronounce Neapolitan now?" she said slyly. If I didn't know better I would have sworn she was flirting. My son's grave, courteous demeanor seemed to bring that out in women of any age.

He grinned at her. "I like Neapolitan. Ralph did too."

"You remember that?" Her eyes brimmed.

He ducked his head. "Sure."

She heaved a tremulous sigh. "Well, no point in

waiting. I hoped Joe could..."

"Is that Joe?" my son interrupted. "Coming down through the trees?"

I looked around. I hadn't heard a thing. But there he was, sliding into view, silent as always. Barefooted, of course; it was spring. He was wearing his giant knife as always, but didn't have his rifle. He had a little hitch in his step that gave me an internal twist: Joe was getting on towards ninety and really was feeling his age.

"Mildred," he said somberly. "Thanks for letting me know."

"I was just about to get started," she said.

He nodded and said to me, "So this is your son. We've met."

My son stepped up and offered a handshake, man-to-man. "Been doing any hunting?"

"Why, young man, the season ain't on. An' your daddy works for the Game Department now."

My son grinned at him. "Since when did Joe Consonants worry about seasons or the Game Department? You're kind of a legend in these parts according to Bill Simp."

Joe's smile rearranged his bushy whiskers. "And you will be."

"Not likely," my son said, and laughed.

"Oh, yeah. Last an' best o' the mountain men, people like Bill Simp say. Prob'ly behind your back."

"He was such a good boy," Mildred chipped in. "He made a fast friend in Ralph."

My son's ears got red again; well, he was still a teenager after all.

"It was good of you to come to see the ol' cowboy off over the Great Divide," Joe said to my son. "What I read about the new generation don't give me much hope, but you're a fine exception."

I put my arm around my son's shoulders. "Now if his mom could just get him to clean his room..."

Joe let out his big haw-haw and Mildred laughed. My son smiled, relieved. The laughter died and the Lower Fairfax quiet came back.

"Well, Ralph," Mildred said to the urn on the tailgate of her truck. "Let's do this."

We followed her to the river. She knelt and released the ashes into the current. As they fanned downstream a bright spring Chinook, fresh from the sea, leaped right through them on its way upstream.

"Oh, my," Mildred said, choked up.

"There's religions would take that as a sign from the heavens," Joe rumbled softly. "Godspeed, Ralph."

We all just stood there with our own thoughts until my son cleared his throat. "My mom's people came from Vikings," he said. "Warriors go to Valhalla. I hope they left the light on for Ralph."

Joe regarded him with open respect. Mildred stood up crying and came as naturally into my son's arms as if she'd always known him. Well, from his perspective she nearly had. He held her quietly, saying nothing, sturdy as a young oak. When I looked at him I saw the man he was becoming and felt choked up myself. We waited, honoring her grief. When she composed herself, she did it with grace; no silly apologizing for her running mascara. She dug in her pants pocket and produced a slim worn box.

"Ralph would have wanted you to have this," she said to my son.

He held it and looked at her. "What is it?"

"His Silver Star."

In those post-Vietnam days of the eighties, I had no idea if he even knew what that meant. But my son was full of surprises. "So he belongs in Valhalla. He was a hero."

She sniffled. "He must have been, because it came with his effects when he came to us. The records were incomplete. But all he got for his bravery was too many years in the Soldier's Home."

I touched her shoulder. "He could have done way worse. You did everything you could to ease his life. Everybody who understands is proud of you."

She gave a kind of lopsided smile. "Even your wife?"

"Her especially. Ever since you introduced our son to Ralph. She just didn't know if she'd be welcome here."

"Old feuds," she said. "They seem silly now. I saw her with the Petoskeys at old Mr. Tuchi's funeral. We even spoke." She produced a handkerchief and scoured her face. "Let's drive up to my place. Joe, you ride with me. I've got coffee and some pastries."

"No Neapolitan?" My son smiled at her.

"Don't be silly. Of *course* I've got Neapolitan."

So we went to Mildred's and had coffee and pastries to celebrate Ralph's voyage home. My son had a bowl of Neapolitan and a Coke, and she showed him the checkers he had rolled across the table to Ralph. When my son openly admired Mildred's .348 Winchester on pegs by the door, she took it down and showed it to him. Joe smiled in his whiskers at his methodical and safe handling of the firearm, reminding me of the first time I saw him, at twilight in the rain, commenting on my own gun-handling. It seemed a lifetime ago.

When we got ready to leave, Joe shook hands with my son again and invited him up to his cave for a visit.

"Your daddy used to stop by often, but not so much anymore," he said. "We could swap huntin' lies and talk about legends."

I guess I glared at him, because he chuckled. "Runnin' with them Central Europeen loggers, he's already had an earful. Time he hears it from the horse's mouth. Come with him—I'll find us another chair."

I didn't yell at him or cuss him out; old Southern rules of being polite as a guest won out. I just shook my head and said, "We'll see." My son blinked. I recalled him as a young boy pouting and saying that phrase meant the same thing as no. We said our goodbyes and left.

On the way home, my son said, "He really lives in a cave, Dad. An old coalmine."

"I know," I said.

"Oh, right. He said you used to stop by. But you didn't seem to like him inviting me. I wouldn't mind hearing his version of some of Bill Simp's stories. Like did he really go to Nepal with an Army officer and shoot a Yeti?"

"You've heard that one have you?"

"Sure. It's part of his legend around here. And he met Mahatma Gandhi?"

"So he says. And studied Eastern religions with holy men over there."

"So what's the big deal, Dad? He is a kind of legend, but he won't last forever, and I'm kind of interested in all those old stories."

I sighed. "I'm just afraid he'll fill your head with all those crazy stories about skooks."

My son laughed right out loud. "You sound like a Gorge resident, 'skook.' I hear they don't like to use the word Sasquatch much for fear of being laughed at."

"Where did you hear that, Mildred? She's the one who told me that when you were two years old."

"All the old-time hunters know about it, Dad. Bill Simp, all the Goulash Mafia as you call them. They say the Gorge people are more skittish than most because the skooks live up here. But nobody likes to talk about their encounters with Bigfoot in these mountains. Same reason the Gorge residents say skook to keep outsiders from knowing what they're talking about. They resent being made fun of."

We were approaching the power-line road. I pulled off the pavement and looked at him. "You've covered a lot of these mountains hunting. Ever had an encounter of your own?"

His eyes twinkled. "Ever heard one of them scream?"

I dropped my eyes. "Have you?"

"Oh, yeah. The hair on my neck stood up. Funny thing is, I knew exactly what it was. Almost like I'd heard it before. I knew it was a Bigfoot."

"When did this happen?"

"Last year. I was hunting with Brett in the black timber. We heard something ripping and tearing things up in some thick brush. Brett thought it was a bear and tried to sneak it. But somehow I knew it wasn't a bear. I went in behind him to cover him. This thing made a heck of a leap over some devil's club—all we saw was a blur. A damn big blur. It stopped and screamed at us. Man, it was mad! That screech went on and on."

"What did you do?"

"We got our backs to some trees and took our safeties off. It was too close to fool with a safety if it came at us. It moved *fast*." He shrugged. "Guess it was scared of us as we were of it. It must have sneaked off. We waited, then eased out of there, watching our backs the whole way."

"For God's sake." I looked at him. "Joe told me he met you up in the mountains and you talked about something following you in the dark. You never mentioned that to me."

He shrugged. "No big deal. I went back the next day with Brett and found my deer. It was one of them following me that night, I'm pretty sure. It was like I could feel it. I didn't say that to Joe because I didn't know him from Adam."

A common-enough phrase, but I felt as if I'd been punched in the solar plexus. I flashed back to the snowing night Joe sent Adam over that Great Divide he mentioned today at the river.

"You okay, Dad?"

"I just don't like the idea of cryptids in proximity to my son."

"What's a cryptid, Dad?"

"A mythical creature," I said.

"That one made an awful lot of noise for a mythical creature," he said. "You think I'm telling you a tall tale?"

"I wish you were."

"You never answered me, you know. About if you ever

heard one scream."

I gazed out up the winding power-line road beneath the big steel Bonneville pylons carrying heavy transmission lines toward the White River. Somewhere up there skooks had crossed, moving down toward our house, following my son's scent when he was four. The year Nixon resigned in disgrace. In the time it took my boy to reach seventeen, three Presidents later, Nixon had reinvented himself as a respected elder statesman with a broad grasp of realpolitik. The Soviet Union, which had seemed so monolithic and invincible to Americans who seriously asked whether it was better to be Red or dead, was in retreat and showing serious cracks in the monolith. So many things had changed out in the world. But the Gorge kept its secrets. And I had the engrained habit of keeping those secrets.

"Dad?" He sounded concerned. "You're not old enough to be having a senior moment. Are you okay?"

"Five times," I said. "I heard skooks scream five times." Twice when that female came to steal him, twice when he was four and their attempt to see him was thwarted, and once when Joe surprised them at Aaron's campfire. But I didn't say that then. I was remembering how Joe led me step by step into his unbelievable world. Now it seemed I was going to follow his lead.

"Jeez, Dad! You talk about *me* not telling things. You never once told me any of this. Five times? There's got to be some stories in that."

I heaved a sigh; it felt like a huge weight was gradually lifting off my shoulders. "There's things I know about skooks and the Gorge," I said. "Not by choice." In the back of my mind I heard Joe's rumble saying almost the same thing to me. "Things I never wanted to know that I was forced to learn."

"You know a lot about skooks, Dad?" He smiled. "Those mythical creatures?"

"More than I ever wanted to know. And it's time you learned."

He started to laugh at his foolish Dad, but stopped. "Are you *serious*?"

I looked at him, rangy and fit, sitting at ease like some young prince unaware of his heritage. Perfectly confident in his own abilities. Waiting to find a sword to pull from the stone. I suppose that image crossed my mind because Big Joe lived in a cave. An old coalmine, though, not the mythic crystal cave of Merlin. I recognized my wildly oscillating thoughts as avoidance. Though admitting to my son had felt like laying down a heavy burden, the habit of secrecy was strong in me still.

"Tell you what," I said. "Joe invited you up to talk to him. That's where we should talk about all this, with Joe. It will be a circle coming full, because that cave is where I learned about skooks. I'll even bring my own chair."

Thank you for reading.

Please review this book. Reviews help others find me and inspires me to keep writing!

If you would like to be put on our email list to receive updates on new releases, contests, and promotions, please go to AbsolutelyAmazingEbooks.com and sign up.

About the Author

William R. Burkett, Jr. published his first novel at 18. He was a strapping youth who lived with his grandparents at Neptune Beach, Florida. His first job was as a copy boy for the *Florida Times-Union* and *Jacksonville Journal*, but that soon gave way to a position as feature writer. After a tour of duty as an M.P. in Germany, he resumed his journalistic career. Working in both the States and the Bahamas, he pursued a particular muse - duck hunting. That led to writing for hunting magazines and doing PR for the Washington State Highway Patrol and settlement in the Pacific Northwest where the ducks were plentiful and the fishing was good. And legends of "wild men" abound.

ABSOLUTELY AMAZING eBOOKS

AbsolutelyAmazingEbooks.com
or AA-eBooks.com

CPSIA information can be obtained
at www.ICGtesting.com
Printed in the USA
LVHW081156060322
712757LV00022B/581